MR IVES'
CHRISTMAS

OSCAR HIJUELOS

MR IVES' CHRISTMAS

BLOOMSBURY

First published in Great Britain 1995
This paperback edition 1996
Copyright © 1995 by Oscar Hijuelos

The moral right of the author has been asserted

Bloomsbury Publishing Plc, 2 Soho Square, London W1V 6HB

A CIP catalogue record for this book is available from
the British Library

ISBN 0 7475 2605 2

1 3 5 7 9 10 8 6 4 2

Printed in Great Britain by Cox & Wyman Ltd

It is difficult to be religious, impossible to be merry, at every moment of life, and festivals are as sunlit peaks, testifying above dark valleys, to the eternal radiance.

—Clement A. Miles

The author expresses his gratitude to the following persons:
Harriet Wasserman; Robert S. Jones, my editor; Lori Carlson;
and Philip Graham.

Long Ago at Christmas

LONG AGO AT CHRISTMAS

Years ago, in the 1950s, as a young man working for a Madison Avenue advertising agency, Ives always looked forward to the holiday season and would head out during his lunch hours, visiting churches, to think and meditate, and, if he was lucky, to hear the choirs as they practiced their hymns and sacred songs. Often enough, he walked along the burgeoning sidewalks, crowded with shoppers and tourists, and made his way to Saint Patrick's Cathedral, where he'd become lost in a kind of euphoric longing—why he did not know. And in a moment, he would find himself, as a child, attending Mass with his adoptive family again, so many memories coming back to him: of standing beside his father during the services and noticing, as he looked up at his father's kindly face, just how moved he seemed to be by the prayers, and the Latin incantations, and the reverential chants; so moved, especially during the raising of the host, that he almost seemed on the verge of tears.

Each time he entered a sanctuary, Ives himself nearly wept, especially at Christmas, when the image of one particular church on Seventh Avenue in Brooklyn, whose choir was very good and the worshipers devout, came back to him, its interior smelling mightily of evergreen boughs, candle wax, and pots of red and white blossoms set against the columns. Dignified Irishmen, with greatly slicked heads of hair, dockworkers for the most part, turned up in ties and jackets, their wives and children by their sides. And there were bootleggers and policemen and carpenters and street sweepers in attendance as well. And a blind man whom Ives sometimes helped down the marble stairs; a few Negroes, as they were called in those days, all, Ives was convinced, believing in the majesty of the child. The old Italian ladies, their heads wrapped in black scarves and their violet lips kissing their scapular medals, and crucifixes and rosaries, kneeling, nearly weeping before the altar and the statues of Christ and His mother; and at Christmas, the beginning of *His* story, sweetly invoked by the rustic and somehow ancient-looking crèche.

The fact was that Ives, uncertain of many things, could at that time of year sit rather effortlessly within the incense- and candle-wax-scented confines of a church, like Saint Patrick's, thinking about the images, ever present and timeless, that seemed to speak especially to him. Not about the cheery wreaths, the boughs of pine branches, the decorative ivy and flowers set out here and there, but rather about the Christ child, whose meaning evoked for him a feeling for "the beginning of things," a feeling that time and all its sufferings had fallen away.

Of course, while contemplating the idea of the baby Jesus, perhaps the most wanted child in the history of the world, Ives would feel a little sad, remembering that years ago someone had left him, an unwanted child, in a foundling home. (To that day, to all the days into the future, there remained within him the shadowy memory of the dark-halled building in which he lived for nearly two years, a place as cavernous and haunted as a cathedral.) A kind of fantasy would overtake him, a glorious vision of angels and kings and shepherds worshiping a baby: nothing could please him more, nothing could leave him feeling a deeper despair.

Enflamed by the sacred music and soft chanting, his heart lifted out of his body and winged its way through the heavens of the church. Supernatural presences, invisible to the world, seemed thick in that place, as if between the image of Christ who is newly born and the image of the Christ who would die on the cross and, resurrected, return as the light of this world, there flowed a powerful, mystical energy. And his sense of that energy would leave Ives, his head momentarily empty of washing machine and automobile advertisements, convinced that, for all his shortcomings as a man, he once had a small, if imperfect, spiritual gift.

That, long ago, at Christmas.

More sentimental than he would let on to others, Ives, in his later years, was the kind of fellow who saved just about everything, a practice that had something to do with his foundling beginning. In his study, he had file cabinets filled with letters, postcards, and Christmas greetings. He kept funeral cards, Jesus Christ with His burning heart welcoming the sanctified into heaven, the glorious place. He had autographed drawings from Winsor McKay, Walter Lantz, Otto Messmer, Lee Falk, Dick Caulkins, and dozens of other cartoon artists. And piles of cards and correspondence from commercial artists like himself, many of them friends with whom he had collaborated over the years. A curiosity: somehow and somewhere, he had acquired an autographed publicity shot of the actor Ray Milland. And there was also his collection of, affectionately kept, handwritten notes from fellow artists much more famous than himself. His favorite, because it took him back to a happier time during his childhood, was the note Walt Disney had sent him back in 1935, when, at the age of thirteen, he submitted some funny-animal drawings and gag ideas on the chance that he could go to work for the Disney studio, then making a new kind of animated, feature-length film called *Snow White and the Seven Dwarfs*. A form letter turned him down, but a few lines had been added, which said, "Keep in touch and keep it up, your work is swell! Walt Disney." Ives showed the note to all his friends and passersby, as they walked by his stoop, the mild praise had him floating for weeks.

(He even had a crinkly-edged black-and-white photograph taken of him back then—Ives in a tie and jacket posed on the steps of his building in Brooklyn, just after he'd come back from Mass, with the letter held up before him, for all to see. His expression was happy. Ives with his long dagger nose, dark eyes, and wavy hair did not look like someone named Ives but rather a Spinelli or a Martinez or a Jacobs, though that had not mattered to the man who had adopted him. The picture was taken by his older adoptive brother, Johnny, in his pinstriped suit, a toothpick in his mouth, his handsome face gnarled from concentration as he took the shot, his pretty flapper-looking date by his side. "Smile, Eddie," and *click* . . . He sat there, his shoes and hair shiny, a missal on his lap, his coat by his side, a goofy grin on his face, nothing of his sad feelings about life showing in that moment. A friend, Butch, a tough alley cat of a street kid, stood off to the right and stared into the camera, a menacing smirk across his freckled mug. Then the doorway, the hall, a second door and, if you squinted, Ives' adoptive sister, Katherine, about his age and pretty but thin and lost and not the brightest kid in the world. In a straw hat with flowers in its brim and opened coat with three of its buttons torn off, she seemed to be looking sadly out through the shadows.)

He had portfolios with hundreds of drawings in them, none of which he ever looked at anymore. And comic-strip ideas that had never quite cut it, for all the times he had tried: "Cosmo the Ghost," "Nicky Steele, Private Eye," "Lord Lightning" were the titles he remembered. He kept oil paintings and watercolors that he had done over the years, and many early nudes of his wife, and studies, done casually and nearly effortlessly, of his two children, during certain moments of rest or play or prayer when they were small.

He had a favorite possession: an authentic etching by Albrecht Dürer, bought at the height of the depression from a down-and-out art dealer in Greenwich Village, a man with a mad Russian face and trembling hands, as kindly as his adoptive father, who'd sold him the work for ten dollars. He had a pencil sketch by George Bridgeman, with whom he had once studied, another by Burne Hogarth. He had a lacquered, souvenir-shop, postcard-sized reproduction of Raphael's "La Madonna del Granduca," a heartbreakingly beautiful portrait, done in the tondo or circular format, of a young Florentine noblewoman in white, a Christmas gift from his daughter, Caroline. She'd bought it for him when she was a teenager and knew him well enough to remember that, in his opinion, it was the finest portrait, ever, by any artist. He loved it because it was an exquisite work by a true genius, and because the first time he'd laid eyes upon it, hanging on a cluttered wall in a second-floor gallery in the Pitti Palace in Florence, it was 1960, and they were on their first European vacation as a family and his son, Robert, was still alive.

What else did he have? The better question, what didn't he keep? In boxes that sat in the attic study of their little country house there remained a half-dozen two-tone erasers, some worn more than others, from the days when he was an in-betweener for the Steichman Brothers animation studio of New York. And there were some old No. 2 pencils, still in their boxes, from that period, and in a manila envelope, wrapped in a thick rubber band, several dozen 1939 wallet calendars that he'd knocked out for a plumber's outfit, which gave them away by the entrance to the World's Fair. In his closet, he had pads and sketchbooks and samples of artwork from the time he was a teenager: a few of the hand-drawn Christmas cards that he peddled from door to door and sold for a nickel apiece, and everything else from match-book covers to beer coasters, girly posters, horror comics, religious drawings, and book illustrations and mounds and mounds of mechanicals and studies for print ads, some of which had been highly regarded in their time by fellow professionals. He had a dozen old course certificates from the Advertising Club of New York. And dozens of promotional pens and paperweights put out by his agency on behalf of tobacco companies, foundation-garment manufacturers, and just about anything else from gentle laxatives to pipe cleaners. And reams of old stationery from the place where he'd worked for thirty years, with the coolly scripted company logo saying: THE MANNIS AGENCY, 10 EAST 40TH STREET, NEW YORK 16, N.Y. NEW YORK, SAN FRANCISCO, LONDON, MEXICO CITY.

But most sorrowfully, there were a few items kept hidden in a closet that related to his son—a white leatherbound New Testament, a baptismal card, a pile of paperbacks, and a new watch, never used, that had been purchased as his Christmas present at Macy's the afternoon before his death.

That sad event took place one evening, a few days before Christmas 1967, some six months before Robert was to enter the Franciscan order as a young seminarian; just a few minutes after attending a late-afternoon choir practice at the Church of the Holy Ascension, his life had ended. He was seventeen at the time of his death, and not an hour passed when Ives did not calculate his son's age were he still alive. Now he would have been in his early forties and working as a pastor somewhere, maybe as a priest for the Church of Saint Francis downtown, or teaching seminarians upstate near Albany. Ives liked to think that they would have remained close over the years. In one of the dreams that he had long stopped having, he'd find himself sitting in a church and watching his son raise the Host at the altar. Then the time would come, and he'd kneel by the communion railing, his wife by his side, and, with his eyes closed, his head lifted toward his son, he would wait to hear the words "Body of Christ" and for his priestly hands to slip the consecrated wafer upon his tongue. . . .

In his retirement and much slowed down, Ives still had days when he blamed his son's death on God's "will." God had timed things so that his murderer, his face scowling, came walking down the street just as his son and a friend were standing around talking. *Pop, pop, pop,* three shots in the belly because his son had simply turned his head to watch his murderer's exaggerated and comic gait as he went by. A fourteen-year-old kid, who'd reeled around asking, "What chew looking at?" his gun out before an answer. A kid, now a man, whom Ives should have forgiven, but couldn't, even when he tried to—Lord, that was impossible—so filled was his heart with a bitterness and confusion of spirit that had never gone completely away.

"YOU HAVE TO PUT IT BEHIND YOURSELF"

Since his retirement from the agency in 1982, Ives and his wife divided their time between Manhattan and their small getaway home near Hudson, New York. There wasn't much around their tract of land other than a pretty view, magnificent and blooming with flowers and trees in the spring and summer, frigid and desolate in the colder months, which drove his lively wife, Annie, crazy. They had some moody younger neighbors about a quarter mile up the road, and there were a few deserted summer houses further on, so that on some days they hardly saw anyone, an isolation that made his wife eager for their flat in the city, on Ninety-third Street off Columbus.

They moved downtown from Claremont Avenue some ten years before, in '84, after their apartment had been burglarized and because Annie had thought the change would do her husband some good. His stubborn inability to stop mourning their son, to keep his sorrow hidden from others but to let it flourish around her, had tempted Annie to leave him several times over the years. But she loved him too much. Again and again, she told him, "You have to put it behind you, my love," but as the years passed, nearly thirty of them, with their thousands of days and hundreds of thousands of hours, he still could not get a certain image out of his head: his righteous and good son, stretched out on the sidewalk, eyes glazed and looking upward, suddenly aware and saddened that his physical life was ending, that image coming to Ives again and again.

Trying to make sense of what had happened, he awaited a revelation but over the years had been let down often enough so that, after so many years, Mr. Ives, formerly of Brooklyn, New York, and Madison Avenue, had gradually turned into stone: a civil, good-hearted man, but one made of stone all the same.

There had been his bad dreams and his bad skin, tormenting maladies that had come about after the death of his son and had gotten gradually worse, not better, with time, Ives keeping Annie up on many a night with his twisting about and endless scratching. There had been his daylong silences and his overwhelming solemnity toward the most ordinary things, like going to a movie, and the way he would sometimes stand by the window at night for hours, as if waiting for someone. Though she loved him, all this sometimes made her feel a little boxed in, and she would fall into her own state of gloom. That's when she would ship him off to Hudson, so that she could work in the city on her various educational projects in peace.

Every so often he would catch an Amtrak train north and spend a week at a time in that house, drawing, reading, and taking care of his mutty hounds, Rex and Alice. And while doing so, he would think of just how much his son had loved his life and had loved God, and Ives would doubt that God existed.

Then the holidays would come and the past would hit Ives like a chill wind. Memories of his son plaguing him, there came many a day, around Christmas, when Ives would plaintively wait for a sign that his son, who'd deserved so much more than what he had been given, was somewhere safe and beloved by God. Each day he awaited a slick of light to enter the darkness. And when life went on as usual, without any revelation, he'd await his own death and the new life or— as he often suspected—the new oblivion to begin.

HE USED TO LIKE SPEAKING SPANISH

In the years just after his son's death, when he'd become a somber man, Mr. Ives would walk over from Claremont Avenue, in upper Manhattan, toward the subway on 125th

Street on Broadway, on his way to work, with a black portfolio or a briefcase in hand, unable to look at anyone, his head down, a hand in his coat pocket. And when he did make contact, his eyes were as wide open and filled with as much pain and disappointment as any eyes had ever been. Everyone who knew him in the neighborhood, for his righteousness and mellow demeanor—the way people had thought about his adoptive father in Brooklyn—felt saddened by that event, but the shooting had been a source of particular disgrace for the Spanish-speaking inhabitants of the neighborhood. As an important enough Madison Avenue executive who had helped many of the local Hispanic families with jobs and whose best friend was a Cuban man, named Luis Ramirez, Ives watched his love and admiration for the culture diminish; for a long time he would not forget—though he had tried— the fact that his son's murderer was Puerto Rican.

It wasn't easy or pleasurable for Ives to have such feelings: Ives himself, over the years, was sometimes taken to be a person of mixed blood, in looks if not manner, and therefore had been the victim of prejudice himself. Looking in the mirror, as if at a map, certain of his features revealed a bit of ethnic identity, startling him. His almond eyes and the darkness of his own countenance were such that different people often took Ives to be one of their own. With his unknown beginnings he might well have had Spanish blood; perhaps his mother was Puerto Rican, Cuban, or from the Dominican Republic. But even without knowing the truth, he had gravitated toward that culture simply out of curiosity and affection.

For years he would stop by Juanito's barbershop and speak a Spanish that, while imperfect, was affable and diverse; the Spanish of a man who had never formally studied but had related to and loved the language. For years he had read *El Diario* and the *Desportes* columns, just so he could participate in conversations about baseball and boxing; and he used to enjoy leaning back in the barber's chair and listening to the

Spanish-language radio and its sweet *canciones*. He used to go there every couple of weeks for a trim, and always waved and flashed a smile at his friends, as he walked by. But one day he had not bothered to even look over and refrained from going in, his contemplative face and sad expression something they now viewed from afar, through a stencilled sunlit window.

The Foundling Home

Even in his youth, he had a pensive disposition. But he was not especially bright (or at least he never thought so), and though he was not a wildly funny young man, he loved people and things that were amusing: humorous illustrations from old books, illustrators like Soglow of "Little King" fame and George "Krazy Kat" Herriman, satirical cartoons, newspaper comics, screwball comedies, animated cartoons, and, going back, certain silent-screen comedians like Laurel and Hardy, Chaplin, and Harold Lloyd (the latter to whom he thought he bore some kind of resemblance). Having to wear glasses as a teenager, Ives chose round tortoiseshell frames like Mr. Lloyd's and wore a black-ribboned straw boater, which gave him a jaunty air.

Outwardly lighthearted and ever courteous, Ives had lived with a notion that he was worthless. The first three years of his life were largely a blank; his fourth and fifth years were spent in Saint Stephen's in Brooklyn. Not a day passed when certain thoughts about that place and the circumstances that led him there did not fail to depress him. As he walked down the avenue, or made his way along the busy halls of his agency to show sketches to his art director, certain remembrances weakened his knees and stopped him in his tracks. Ives would suddenly pause by a water cooler or mimeograph machine or by a pretty secretary's desk, to look off into the distance, his mind lost in some sad dream. To those coworkers who found him staring out the window, with its grand view of the avenue stretching northward toward Fifty-seventh Street, he'd seemed to be musing about life or the weather—how dainty the clouds looked on certain days—or about the spectacular beauty of the Art Deco edifices, office towers with their ziggurat tops and black marble-slab walls. Yet what he really saw instead, in some dark place, was another view from another window: a dingy tenement somewhere in Brooklyn in the early 1920s. In his thoughts, it was always night with snow on the ground, and he was cold and lost and peering out desperately, furtively toward the other windows and rooftops and wishing he could run away. A memory, passing in a flash, of his mother, a pretty woman with olive skin, dark hair, and frightened eyes, huddling in a corner and calling to him in a language that he could not identify or remember; and of a man, immense and beastly, shouting and breaking things; and his mother breaking up inside herself and weeping; and a hard slap to his face and a strap of a belt against his legs and the room turning.

He believed that his father had been a man of foreign extraction who'd had something to do with the sea—a fisherman or a sailor, who'd perhaps met his mother on a night's leave in Brooklyn, ravishing her on a pile of coiled ropes or burlap bags by the harbor or in some flea-bitten hotel. In all likelihood, his mother was typical of the kind of women who abandoned children: young, very poor, and scared for her life. She was probably a factory worker, or a prostitute, he sometimes thought, the latter notion both tormenting and fascinating him.

(One day, when he was in midtown on his way back from a job, he wandered into the Forty-second Street library. Although he wanted to find some art books, he somehow found himself sitting at a table reading an archaic book of statistics, put out by the New York City Department of Child Welfare, which had information about the number of orphans and abandoned children in New York in the 1920s, the period of Ives' tenure in his foundling home. The book contained many confusing charts and tables, statistics with miniature citations in their upper right-hand corner that he carefully studied and tried to comprehend. There were statistics about the occurrences of tuberculosis, pneumonia, rheumatic fever, blindness, and deafness "per ward" in a given calendar year—columns and columns of numbers that referred to the many unwanted children, but told nothing of their stories, Ives daydreaming about the very home where he had stayed as he read over the lists.)

The good nuns had found some of their children waiting hungry and exhausted on the steps of the home, before its thick double doors, and some were delivered like laundry by the city, whose own agencies and wards were always jammed to bursting; and some were carried in the arms of softhearted cops who'd discovered the runts, tots, and abandoned infants wrapped in rags or newspapers in dustbins or garbage cans or left on subway or trolley car seats; and some arrived in the arms of distraught mothers—poor flower girls, foolish actresses, dime store clerks—who for whatever their reasons, pleaded with the nuns to take their babies inside. Some arrived wearing dainty lace bonnets and underthings and embroidered blouses and gowns, as if they had been dressed as a last gesture of care, but most arrived filthy and weeping and starved to the bones, and some were covered with bruises. Some arrived with birth certificates or names written out on pieces of paper, and often misspelled, but written out all the same, and some, like Ives, came into that home without so much as a slip of paper to say where he might have come from, their veins filled with the blood of parents they would probably never see again, their brows wrinkled by confusion, and their expressions reflecting an innocent acceptance of destitution.

In the foundling home there were dark rooms, lonely hallways, and high windows that looked out onto sooty brick walls. There were nuns whose mysterious ways had sometimes frightened him. There were crowded rooms and crowded beds, and nights when he was afraid to shut his eyes. And there was a little chapel in which he learned to pray. In that room he would kneel before a statue of Jesus as a boy, and touch its marble face, as if it might suddenly come alive. And there was a room in which, if he'd soiled his bed at night, the nuns would lock him for hours at a time, alone. There were black-and-white tile floors in one of the rooms, cracked white tiles in another; a clock out of whose bottom crawled cockroaches the size of watermelon seeds, which hung on a wall above a statue of the Holy Mother. Each dormitory had high double doors with small rectangular wire-crossed windows, which were locked at night and impossible to open even if one pushed and pushed.

But he was lucky: several times a month, the nuns would dress the children up, girls in one dormitory, boys in the other, and march them out into a grand hall with lime-green-flecked walls where they would sit on benches awaiting the chance to meet with prospective adoptive parents. Graced with pleasant enough looks and a quiet, though vaguely shocked demeanor, and neatly attired in knee pants, clean shirt, and bow tie, he made a good impression. With eyes that invited pity and a sad smile, Ives was a fine example of "a poor poor thing." On one of those visitors' days, around Christmas, he found himself standing before a well-dressed, middle-aged genteman, whose own eyes were sad—the older Mr. Ives—who placed his warm hand on the boy's face and kneeling before the lad, took a long, long look, making his decision.

He'd remember that he had trembled; that he could barely look toward that kind face; that for all his timidity, he soon enough found himself living a new life.

That, around Christmas.

HIS ADOPTIVE FATHER

The older Mr. Ives, a widower who worked in the printing business, had never been able to provide him with more than the name of the foundling home. Although he gave his son the strong faith that he had through much of his youth, he could not give him a history. In fact, his father had been a foundling himself, his name, Ives, coming from a priest who had taken it from a Currier & Ives print popular in 1870, the year his adoptive father was born. (Framed Currier & Ives prints could be found everywhere in New York back then, on bar- and poolroom walls, in hotel lobbies, in bowling alleys, in restaurants, on Third Avenue trolleys.) In terms of appearance, the older Mr. Ives could have been French, as in Yves, or of

English or Scottish extraction. He had a gaunt, intelligent face, a furrowed brow, aquiline nose, and deep blue eyes, and dressed, despite his lack of formal education and working-class manner, like a gentleman, often wearing a long coat and top hat, and carrying an ivory-tipped cane. And although he could give his adoptive children a history of his life in the printing business, and the cause of his wife's death in childbirth ("a puerperal infection had taken her, God bless her soul . . ."), he had nothing by way of insight to offer his son, for whoever had brought Ives to Saint Stephen's had left him with neither a note nor a word to anyone, and he'd been admitted into the home on the evening of December 22, 1924, and adopted several years later, during the very same holiday season.

Mr. Ives Senior was able to give his third son clothes and books, two brothers and a sister, a little money, and a room in his large, somewhat rundown brownstone, three stories high, on Carroll Street. And a name: Edward. And encouragement when, in one of the miracles of his life, young Ives, at the age of seven or so, had started to draw, spending his leisure hours not out on the street playing with the local ruffians, who'd slide down coal chutes and throw bottles off rooftops at passing trucks, but resting on his belly on their front parlor floor, copying out drawings from newspapers and the illustrated books that found their way into the house. His father had liked such books very much, notably those from England with engravings by the likes of John Tenniel or those artists who illustrated the works of Charles Dickens, whose line drawings enchanted the young Ives. (There was a row of books, memoirs and sporting novels, illustrated by Phil, Cruickshank, Alken, Leech, Seymour, and Heath, among others.) He also taught his son how to pray, when to kneel and stand and bow his head and close his eyes during the consecration of the Host; taught him to take in the beautiful goodness that he was desperate to believe existed; to tremble before the "enormity of it all."

*   *   *

His father managed a printing plant on Chambers Street. It was a large operation that took up the ground floor of a building, its façade zigzaggy with fire escapes, its interior a thunderous, machine-filled room the size of an airplane hangar. He ran the plant for its rich Park Avenue owners, overseeing a crew of compositors, machine operators, make-readiers, engravers. There were a number of cubicles for proofreaders and rows of large and noisy many-geared presses smelling of ink, turpentine, and oils. Books, all manner of pamphlets, playbills, and print advertising art, were printed though not bound, but now and again some quite delicate engraving work would take place on the premises. In this atmosphere, the young Ives had passed many a day, as a general assistant, as a collater of pages, as a messenger scrambling about, watching the typesetters and lithographers at their trade. Even as a child he enjoyed the work, reveling in the tactile pleasures of the business, the smell of ink and lead and pulp and metallic filings, and took joy in the weight and detail of the loose letters in the printers' trays, which he'd played with like soldiers on the floor. He'd remember much about that place, remember faces as well: so many of the babushkaed, sad-eyed women who walked up and down the streets near the plant on their way to their jobs in dress mills, shoe, eyeglass, and watch factories, whose narrow entranceways always saddened him. And there were the men who stood by their soup and hot-chestnut wagons across the way, stomping on their feet in the cold, and the dirty urchins with blackened hands who came down the street begging every so often, especially during the worst years of the depression. On the corner, a certain bald Mr. Mullins, a man in his forties who had lost his sight during the First World War, to whom Ives' father gave twenty-five cents—enough for a warm meal—each day, until the winter months when Mullins would be paid to stand inside the front doorway of the plant, functioning as a kind of concierge, for a dollar.

Though he did not speak the language himself, his father had in his employ a dozen or so Spanish-speaking workers—some from Puerto Rico, some from Spain or Cuba. Most were machine workers, but because he published many magazines and books in Spanish (there were many Spanish-language publishing concerns in New York before the depression put most of them out of business), he had a Spaniard working as a compositor and a Cuban proofreader at the plant, and they had taken an interest in the young Ives. He would always remember a certain Mr. Dominguez, an elderly Cuban, who ran one of the press machines. From the time Ives was a little boy, Dominguez always regarded him with a kind of familiarity, and would often say, "You know, you're so much like a brother I once had, when he was your age." Or "If no one has told you before, I will now. You look like a Spaniard. Did you know that?"

And he'd tell him, in his homesickness, about a beautiful place he had come from, Cuba, his home. Across the sea to the south of Florida, *his* little island. He'd bring Ives some bakery pastries from a Spanish restaurant, run by a brother, and meat pies—cumin, garlic, and onions among the magic ingredients. He would send him out on errands and throw him a dime, when that was good money, and in general treated him well. He'd call Ives Eduardo, never Edward, and would sit at lunchtime writing out certain words in Spanish, alongside their English counterparts, on a pad of paper. In his foundling's loneliness Ives tended to associate such simple kindnesses not with foreign lands, nor with bent-over white-haired men with exhausted eyes and filthy lead-blackened fingers, but with a simple notion of calm and, perhaps, love.

Other memories? He'd liked the idea of being a Spaniard, even if it was a fantasy. Working alongside Dominguez, he got into the habit of learning, little by little, something of the language. He'd picked up some Italian as well and a few phrases in Yiddish, from some of the other workers. But he was most attentive with Dominguez, who was so touched by his interest that he gave Ives a few basic Spanish grammar books. Ives never perfected his Spanish, but continued to study it, on and off, when he could, over the years, getting to the point where he could visit Dominguez at his home in Staten Island, near the harbor, the sea always delighting him, and have rudimentary conversations with Dominguez' family, a raucously friendly consortium of plump and beautiful children and adults, who made barbecues yet dressed formally, in suits and dresses, simply because they were having guests. Then there had been the marriage of Dominguez' daughter to an Italian man. The Ives family had been invited, and they all went, turning up at a rented hall on Fourteenth Street for the reception, where a rumba orchestra, presided over by a short Rudy Vallee–looking man who sang through a megaphone, providing the music. That afternoon the *jefe*'s son, Eduardo Ives, was cheerfully harassed by dancing old women and young women in bright pink and yellow dresses with flowery skirts; they made him blush, during one song after the other. He was the kind of kid whose feet ached, but who did not complain, and sat ever so politely next to the old grandmothers, who told him stories about distant places he had never seen and which, even when he was so young, he daydreamed might well have been the land of his ancestors. He'd talk to priests, and struck people as a "good" and guileless boy.

And at these parties he would attempt his conversations in Spanish, and hit the piñatas with the other kids, and later go home to Brooklyn with his pockets stuffed with candies, his head filled with certain new words, which he wrote down in notebooks, as if those words somehow eased the loneliness he felt within.

HIS NATURAL MOTHER AND FATHER

For all his grief, he somehow kept a warm spot in his heart for the idea of the parents who had abandoned him, and although he loved his adoptive father and got along with his siblings, he had always wanted to meet them. Those cravings grew their strongest when he was a teenager and just starting to draw nudes at the Brooklyn Museum—the first sight of a grown woman's bristling pubic hair startling him. In those days, when he had started getting out more on his own, he got into the habit of traveling by himself around the city with a sketchbook, making quick studies of people's faces, as one would encounter them, on the streets or living in shanty-towns. Mornings would find him in the Fulton Fish Market or on a jaunt through the Brooklyn Navy Yard; out on the ferry to Staten Island or to Hoboken or Weehawken. Or over to Chinatown, or off to prowl about the seasonal art shows in Washington Square . . . or drifting through midtown Manhattan, gawking, impressed by the architecture. . . .

And everywhere he went Ives would move through bustling crowds and, catching sight of a man or woman who seemed vaguely familiar, wonder, with a strange hope raised, whether that man or woman might be a relation. Or he'd ride the cane-seated subways and notice someone staring at him, as if a process of recognition were taking place, a vague feeling of disappointment coming over him when the eyes turned quickly away.

As a teenager working at the printing plant in Lower Manhattan, he'd sometimes make the trip over from Park Slope on foot—since he loved to walk if the weather was good. His route took him up Flatbush Avenue, across the glorious Brooklyn Bridge, into the Lower East Side, where he sometimes saw aspects of his own appearance on the faces of the Hasidim. At the same time, it was not unusual for him to sit down in an Italian restaurant on Mulberry, where the senior Mr. Ives liked to eat, and have a waiter, unacquainted with him, ask for his order in the Sicilian dialect.

Once, when he was about sixteen, while delivering some printer's proofs to one of his father's clients in the Wall Street area, Ives began to follow a petite, harried-looking brunette in her late forties. It was about seven at night and dark, the streets deserted, and without knowing why, Ives adopted a protective attitude toward this woman, whom he had first seen standing on a corner, waiting for a light to change. Watching her, he had been struck by how much her dark and brooding face, pretty in a defeated kind of way, appealed to him, her emotional fragility being something he had experienced in himself.

He was about five feet ten and thin, but able to take care of himself, his older brother Harry having taught him to box. A quiet fellow, Ives had simply smiled at her as if to say, "Don't be worried, I'll walk with you and make sure that no one bothers you," but that only seemed to have made her feel anxious.

She walked on one side of the street—was it Church or Broad?—he on the other, a vague sense that he may or may not have known her having come over him. Without realizing it, though he was earnest and well-intentioned, he was frightening the woman half to death—she must have thought him a thief. In one instant, Ives, four blocks out of his way, and laden with heavy engravers' plates, had smiled and waved and with that, he crossed the street. But she ran into an alleyway, shouting in a shrill accent, "Help, police! Help! Help!"

Ives did not follow her but headed off in a bewildered state to drop the plates off in an office in a high-rise by the river. And walking, he later found himself sulking by the waterside, the widening blackness of the water, with its little jewel-like moons, ever so inviting.

CERTAINLY HE WOULD HAVE BEEN A PRINTER

Over the years, while working on and off in the plant, he learned much about the business and became something of an asset. Helpful to the workers, he never displayed the kind of torpor or disdain for "dirty" work, as did Harry, who'd show up on weekends with his college textbooks and girlfriends' telephone numbers, and spend his days with his feet up on his father's desk, studying or reading the newspapers or yapping on the horn. But Eddie or Eduardo, as certain of his father's workers called him, loved that atmosphere, so much so that he'd sometimes come in on his own time, just to watch the engravers, even then a dying breed, as they transferred illustrations onto acid-etched plates, the simple pleasure of watching something beautiful being made enchanting to him.

Certainly he would have been a printer if he hadn't been so interested in drawing. He took classes whenever he could and had the good fortune of studying with George Bridgeman for figure drawing and Max Bechman for painting at the Art Students League. Although he had never been the most talented of artists, as he'd tell his son, Robert, years later, he had a highly developed work ethic. A conscientious and self-effacing laborer, ever humble before his craft, he 'never thought he'd have any money and figured out, as a young man, that he would always live humbly, "without means," practicing his illustrative and painterly skills into his old age. And if he was lucky, getting along on numerous fleeting jobs, he might one day have a show of beautiful portraits—he very much liked the works of John Singer Sargent and in another life would have been content as the official portraitist of an exclusive men's club. Perhaps he would make enough money to see something more of the world than just the view from his window or where the trains and subways of the mass transit system would take him. Paris, Tahiti, Rome—names that he associated with artists and adventure. That was all he wanted.

He also wrestled with his conscience about another vocation: the priesthood, which, when he prayed and felt protected and loved in church, and witnessed many times the devoutness of his father, seemed like a most inviting calling. But coming from a void, he had always wanted to have his own family one day and, though he was tempted by the quietude of that life, he turned his back on that vocation. He wanted to study art in college instead and, truthfully, he did not consider himself strong enough to resist the company of a woman. Having looked at so many of their naked bodies, he had a natural curiosity and a sinful desire to experience such pleasures.

AS A TEENAGER JUST TRYING TO FIGURE OUT SOMETHING MORE ABOUT LIFE

Before the war, as a teenager just trying to figure out a little more about the world, when he was not working in the printing plant, he had also held other jobs. For a time he had been an usher in a big movie house on Ocean Avenue several days a week. It was a job he did not mind because he loved gangster stories and Westerns and animated cartoons with rubber-limbed animals. Movies about orphans, like *Little Lord Fauntleroy* and *Oliver Twist*, often made him get teary-eyed and sad. (Images of redemption and eternal salvation, such as Christ rising in a radiant cloud to heaven, in churches did the same.) And he enjoyed wearing a velvet-buttoned dark gray outfit and escorting the perfumed pretty girls down to their seats. He fell in love every week but was too shy to do anything about it. He also painted window displays and made special signs for local Brooklyn merchants, and worked in big stores like Macy's doing the same, for a friend named Mr. Frankie. He picked up a little extra money working as an occasional messenger boy for the local Western Union office on Atlantic Avenue, and sometimes worked as a temporary mail sorter in the post office at Christmas. Every so often he had gone to work for the Steichman brothers, whose animation studio was down on Lafayette Street; and, on occasion, he had been a pallbearer for the local funeral parlor, as well.

(For his part, Ives had most enjoyed his on-and-off job with the Steichmans. It was an obscure studio, the big animation houses being out in California—Disney, Lantz, Warner Bros.—and it produced mainly kiddie melodramas, its characters bugs and and tender animals with cute names like "Mike the Moth," "Zippy the Squirrel," or "Trinket the Tomcat," creations that never really made it with the public. Now and then he went to work for them, after school hours and on the weekends, mainly drawing backgrounds and inking minor characters. The other artists wre usually young Jewish art school graduates, though a few were Italians, and they were all underpaid and approached the job as a kind of education. The storyboards were the brainwork of the Steichman brothers, and their scenarios usually involved grisly monsters chasing after helpless little creatures—a formula they repeated again and again that had something to do with the fact that the brothers had strong memories of the pogroms in Russia. "You, Ives, wouldn't have any idea of what it was like," Julius Steichman would tell him. "You with your nice shoes and gabardine trousers wouldn't know about having your home burned down or what it would be like to see your dear uncle hanging from a tree.")

Then the war had come. Exempted from active service because of bad hearing in one ear, from a time he had nearly drowned while swimming at Coney Island late one summer, he did his bit as a civilian employee with a unit of the Army Information Service out in Secaucus, New Jersey, where he worked for three years during the war, churning out instructional comics with titles like "Health Tips for the Lonesome G.I." and "Hygiene at Sea," pamphlets, and posters about everything from malaria to VD, dental hygiene to the practical necessity of using a condom during the act of love. Every so often he was sent over to one of the military airfields, where he would spend many an hour in the open air painting inspirational insignia, cartoon characters, and movie stars on the fusilages of bombers and fighters—Betty Grable in a bathing suit one of his specialties. He even had a chance to work for six months in La Jolla, California, for Walter Lantz, creator of Woody Woodpecker, whose studio had been making animated shorts for the army. He had a cubicle in a long barrackslike building and spent day after day inking animation cells, work, in its tedium, so heartbreaking that by day's end he would walk back and forth along paths that overlooked the Pacific Ocean, daydreaming of some other life, perhaps as a sailor or a porpoise, whose arching backs he sometimes saw popping out of the ink-stained waters.

SOMETIMES WHILE RESTING IN THE DARK

Other things came to him with a fine immediacy. Sometimes while resting in the dark, traffic noise would take him back to his early days in Manhattan, after the war, when he lived in a walk-up on Fiftieth Street and Tenth Avenue, as a plodding, ever slow but first-rate free lancer, who fell in love with Annie MacGuire. He would see his old RCA radio, which he'd hauled up out of the street and fixed with some new tubes from the corner store; and next to that their rust-bladed electric fan, which used to make the living room, an oven in the summers, a little more bearable; and then his old drawing board, the old-fashioned kind with a heavy steel frame that he'd bought from another of his teachers, Max Rosen of the Art Students League, for five dollars—Max who'd thrown himself off the Williamsburg Bridge; then the artwork, a few mock-up ads for a new kind of hosiery, a "nudie" pinup, a page of free-lance comic-book art, for *Planet Comics* or *Mutt and Jeff* or *Felix the Cat*. An ashtray filled with cigarette butts; his stained corduroy vest, draped over the back of his chair; a visored cap, such as card dealers wear; a pair of his round tortoiseshell-frame glasses on the board itself. Then their little record player and the pile of recordings they kept, most out of their sleeves. The "classical" pieces were his, the jazzy stuff like Spike Jones and Duke Ellington hers, though there were a few cha-cha-cha records that he'd gotten from his friend Ramirez, the bartender whose acquaintance Ives had first made at the Biltmore Hotel's Men's Bar. The lamp with the torn shade. The goldfish bowl in which they kept pennies. The little Swiss cuckoo clock with a barometer that had a little sign saying RHEINGOLD BEER, in which they'd stash their savings, five- and ten-dollar bills. A Chinese screen, and then, later on, the crib in which his son, Robert, or Roberto as he'd call him, would sleep. Adorable and ever so tender, on his back, little feet up, his face would go into delighted contortions when Ives, the shyest and most reticent father in the world, would stand over him and touch his belly. His son's tender skin.

DECEMBER NIGHTS 1948

Thinking about Robert, Ives would always fondly remember those evenings he spent in 1948, at the Art Students League on West Fifty-seventh Street, where he took classes several nights a week. After a day freelancing, he'd walk in and sit in the back, his sketchbook, charcoals, and pencils set out before him. And often enough he'd notice that among the twenty or so students there sat the quiet Annie MacGuire, whose intensity and concentration had always impressed him. The few times he had spied her work he had been struck by the simplicity and elegance of her drawing—words which he would have used to describe her. He did not know much about her, other than what he'd once overheard her saying during one of the breaks, when the artists would congregate out in the hall chain-smoking. That she was an art and English teacher at a Catholic girls' school on the Upper East Side, her pay lousy. She liked books, he'd noticed, and was probably taking a night course in literature, because she always walked in with thick novels, PROPERTY OF HUNTER COLLEGE stamped on them. Novels by Fielding, Smollett, Trollope, and Dickens, the latter of which Ives knew best, mainly through their illustrations.

She was shapely, of average height, with a demure and reserved bearing, and when she'd walk into the studio, her portfolio in hand, she'd barely acknowledge the presence of others. Ives couldn't tell if she was a snob or simply private like himself. In any case, she rarely noticed how Ives often watched her. Half-ensconced behind an easel, pretty, with her Celtic, wholesome features and piercing eyes, her thick dark and curl-tipped hair cut to just below the ears, she seemed completely entranced by the quietude of drawing.

At first she wore rather ordinary conservative dresses— much of the time, a schoolteacher's understated outfit: a long blue cotton skirt, ruffle-collared blouse, and large bow at her neck. She favored dark stockings and thick, low-heeled shoes. A thin, nearly imperceptible gold crucifix hung down, glowing (in Ives' vision of her), just below her chin. Most of that time she upheld an image of wholesomeness, but then for several months began to turn up with a fairly good-looking but strange-behaving friend. A colleague from night school, who'd cultivated a bohemian air. While most of the artists usually began their charcoal or pencil drawings with the spinal column, this fellow started his drawings haphazardly. With a hand-rolled cigarette dangling from his mouth, he drew with various colored crayons in a frantic and noisy abstract style, his drawings and manner turning Ives' stomach. She got rid of him, thank God, Ives thought, but, to Ives' displeasure, soon started showing up with another fellow, a cheerful-looking and quite handsome actor with a cleft chin, sparkling blue eyes, and a beautifully winning smile, whose drawings were rigid, bottled-up things—nothing fluid about them. And they seemed very much a couple, to the point where on one occasion each had come to class wearing an identical aquamarine silk scarf. Then that was over. That's how it went. Sometimes she turned up, sometimes not, Ives and Annie passing certain evenings sitting on opposite sides of the room, sweetly isolated from the troubles of the city and keeping to themselves.

But then there had been the night when the scheduled model did not show up and Max Rosen roamed the halls looking for a replacement. He was about to cancel the session when Annie got up and walked over to him. They spoke for a few moments and then, as if it were the most natural thing in the world, she went behind a Chinese screen, which was off to the side of the models' platform, pinned back her thick brunette hair, slipped off her low-heeled shoes and nylons, removed her dress—blue with a skirt to the ankles, white mother-of-pearl buttons, a black cloth belt—and her undergarments. Shortly she stepped onto the platform, where, in the powerful beams of overhead lights, her quite naked body exposed for all to see, she embarked on a series of everlengthening poses. To put it mildly, Ives, who had been drawing naked female models from about the time he was twelve, was further stricken. There she stood, voluptuous and muscular, her body sturdy as a swimmer's—in fact she swam several miles a week at the Y—her pubic mound a burst of thick, yet curiously flattened hair that seemed to flail upward, as if while getting undressed she had taken a hairbrush from her purse to groom herself there. Her breasts were fuller and more firmly shaped than Ives could have envisioned, nipples surprisingly inverted, until a chill swept through the room during one of the longer poses, and they turned dark and engorged.

Now it happened that during a break in the session, when many of the students were out in the hall, Ives had come back from the men's room to find Annie, in a terry-cloth bathrobe, looking over one of the drawings he had lovingly made of her. Nodding with approval, she told him, "You've got something here. How long have you been at it?"

Ives told her, "For as long as I can remember. I guess I could draw before I could write my name."

She nodded, as if to say, "It was the same for me," and began to search through her robe pocket for something and then said: "You wouldn't have a cig, would you?"

Remembering that Rosen usually kept a pack of Camels or Luckies on his desk, Ives found himself rushing over to get her a cigarette, his hand trembling as he lit a match, her slender and artistic fingers holding him by the wrist, Annie inhaling. Then she looked off, as he sometimes did, at nothing in particular, and he felt a wave of shuddering sadness coming from her. No one else would have noticed it, but Ives did, and she seemed to know that he had. Shortly she came out of that state and asked him, "What's your name, anyway?"

"Edward Ives."

"Well, I'm Annie MacGuire."

She lingered for a bit, looking at some of his other drawings from earlier sessions, and while doing so, she kept her robe closed. Every so often when she would lean forward, the proximity of her plump breasts, the crucifix dangling between them, made him a little delirious. At that moment it occurred to Ives to ask her out. He'd wanted to say, "You ever go to the museums on the weekends?" Or "You ever take this one class they hold down at the Cooper on Saturdays?" Or "You like to go to the movies?" Or "Ever check out the tree over at Rockefeller Center?" but he couldn't bring himself to do it.

Just as he was finally on the verge of suggesting they have a coffee or some such thing, the other artists started to file back into the studio, and she told him: "Look, I've got to get ready here. See you, okay?"

Later, after the session had ended, he walked to his flat, carrying not just a memory of her beauty but some thirty drawings that he had made of her that night. He walked so quickly that passersby seemed like fleeting shadows, and when he got upstairs to his fifth-floor apartment, he soaked his feet in a white pan filled with Epsom salts and water, washed his face, and then, resting in his bed, looked over those drawings again. And it made Ives, an uncrazy man, feel crazy.

Walking home, he had even managed to pass a local church without crossing himself, and he had made his way along the largely deserted streets feeling tremendously lonely and thinking, with the sentiment of an abandoned child, how no woman would ever really want him. At the same time he found himself repeating in a staccato fashion, "You fool, you fool, you fool."

MODELS

Like many artists, Ives had come to appreciate the obese and the old, with their rolls and sags of flesh, as subjects more interesting to draw than, say, a beautiful young woman. Somehow a body in decline, with all its flaws, with a lifetime of experience in the traumatized surfaces of the skin, seemed endlessly appealing, its battered or self-indulgent soul evident. One December night, however, the model was a young woman of about twenty-five with waist-length red hair, a pronounced pubic bone, and an expanded belly. She was in her sixth month of pregnancy and carried a great weight, balanced sufferingly upon her thin legs, and the difficulty of her movements prompted one of the artists to give her a chair. She had not been the first pregnant woman the artists had drawn—Max said that he once hired a model whose water had broken in midpose—but this young woman, with the kind of nearly transparent skin through which one saw the suggestion of every vein, tendon, and bone, invoked pity. Although she was so very pregnant, with whorls and splints of flaring tissue along her ballooning stomach, she wore no wedding ring. That she sometimes let out the deepest sighs and yet could still smile at the artists, between poses, invited their curiosity and admiration.

There had been other models, oftentimes well-muscled young men, actors or struggling painters, moonlighting for the paltry pay or for the sake of self-exhibition; some delicately feminine, others manly in their self-assurance. Most were quite professional about the business of posing, though there was the occasional startling incident. (One night—and Annie had been there—during the course of a twenty-minute pose, Ives, like many of the males present, felt shocked and vaguely amused by the suddenly aroused and quite well-developed genitalia of one nervous male model, whose embarrassing but splendid physicality caused the majority of the ladies—giddy, blushing?—to leave the studio. The men remained wearily in their places, egos bruised, sketching on, smoking more cigarettes and smirking, until that moment when the young man, trying to maintain a pose like Mercury, head tipped back, eyes closed and crying, began to produce from his penis a substantial volume of a well-known primal resin, the color of moonlit pearl.)

But on the night that the pregnant woman was modeling, Max decided to cut the session well short of its usual two-hour duration, as no one wanted to work her too hard. Gathering about the paint-speckled table in the back, on which sat a small Christmas tree, the crew of merry hopefuls ate chocolates, potato chips, dips and cheese, and some homemade cake that one of the women had brought in, and drank cups of spiked punch and other kinds of booze.

Walking in earlier, Ives had been happy to see one of his good friends, Father Thomas Bernhardt, a Jesuit priest from Fordham, or Father Tom, as the artists sometimes called him. He came to class infrequently, having a long commute and many responsibilities. But when he did, he wore his civvies. How they had been shocked, Ives included, when Tom, whom Ives considered a kindred soul, turned up one night in his priest's habit and sat happily sketching an attractive and flirtatious young woman with a propensity for athletic poses.

Toasting the holiday with Father Tom, Ives kept looking over at Annie, who had arrived earlier with yet another male friend. While Father Tom, a man of exceeding good cheer and an intellectual who was not a snob, spoke of his prospects for the future—a sojourn perhaps at the Jesuit Institute or at the Gregoriana in Rome—Ives' mind drifted. He felt a kind of ache that he had never experienced before, having to do with Annie. It had tormented him for several months now. Begrudgingly, Ives had started to have certain amorous fantasies about her, though without any true hope of realizing them. Despite a few chance encounters with the opposite sex, Ives liked to believe that intimate relations really didn't matter to him, that in his indifference to certain earthly pleasures, he, like a saint, was not all of this world. At best he might cultivate a "friendship" with her. Nevertheless, Ives found his own convictions floundering in her presence.

Suddenly he was no longer speaking with Tom but with the pregnant model, who identified herself as "Mary from Greenwich Village," now in a maternity dress and sitting with her elbow propped on the table, sipping some deli soup that one of the boys had gotten her, smoking cigarettes, and, despite her pregnancy, nursing her second or third glass of punch.

The fellows all gathered around listening to jokes, Ives laughing at the punchlines but not always really hearing the jokes at all. Instead Ives daydreamed, watching Annie's every movement. She was leaning against the wall, talking to a tall and lanky fellow, a drink in hand, and unless Ives was completely wrong, from time to time she would turn to look at him. It bothered Ives to notice how Annie, with a most enthralled expression, would occasionally brush her hand endearingly across this lucky fellow's face—obviously they had something going, Ives thought gloomily. He drank one scotch and then another. And then because he was a little drunk and because this woman, the model, was very pregnant, Ives, toasting her, said, "Oh, Mary, can I tell you that tonight you're the most beautiful woman in the world."

Later, dreamily quiet, an air of sanctity about him, Ives stood in front of the little tree with Mary and a friend, Caggiano, imagining a great future love.

Afterward they headed over to Tenth Avenue, where they'd planned to continue their little party, and as they made their way out into the glory of midtown at Christmas, there was something ever so special about the fact that Christmas was not so far off and Mary was pregnant. There were many jokes about having to take her to the hospital or having to deliver the baby right there on the sidewalk, and they laughed. And yet in the little silences there was a sense that something beautiful was going on and the men formed a procession around her, as if they were all headed off to Bethlehem instead of to an actors' saloon, where they might get more drunk. Their engines all warmed up, they passed little flasks of booze among themselves, a troop of advertising chaps, aspiring painters, portfolios in hand, now singing and wavering on the sidewalk, through the crowds, and through the lovely snow that had started to fall, over toward Seventh Avenue.

For his part, Ives found himself walking along beside Tom and Max. ("I got the perfect drawin' board for you, Ives; it's one of those sturdy metal-frame old draftin' tables, promise you, you'll love it, and I'll sell it to you for five bucks, and maybe throw in a light box too, now you can't beat that, can you?") But by and by, he'd sort of drifted over toward Annie, and with his black portfolio, his overcoat and hat, chin pressed down into his scarf, as if to help keep out the cold, Ives was wondering, wondering just what he might wittily say to her.

There were Santa Clauses on the corners and blind men working the crowds, and drunken soldiers following a bagpiper down the street, making jokes about his kilt and fur pelisse. Down the street a crowd had gathered around the back of a flatbed truck from which a preacher stood shouting in a ferocious and regal voice at passersby, the man thumping a Bible against his chest: "Though it is the season, many a person will close his eyes for the final time in these days of joy and celebration, and be lifted to the gates of judgment where they will open their eyes upon the Glory and Mercy of God!"

Then, even as the preacher shouted, "Sinners, listen!" the artists, laughing, continued toward the bar.

On that lovely night, Ives and Annie and this other fellow, whose name was Carl, had crossed another street, when, as if to accentuate the preacher's ongoing sermon, still echoing in the distance, "The Door is constantly open for the salvation of the soul! But death will close it," they heard a tremendous

36

commotion of shattering materials, glass and wood and metal, high above them, a large window on the twentieth floor bursting free of the corner building. Everyone on the street and sidewalk looked up and then ran in all directions, scattering in fear. Across the way, Ives calmly noticed what, at first glance, seemed like a falling comforter, a heavy coat, a laundry bag weighted down with clothes, all wavery and turning in circles. Then he thought that the form was a bundle of wildly agitated rags, and soon enough realized that he was watching a woman slipping down through the gusting, snow-dense winds.

They couldn't hear her screams.

What had happened? Some twenty stories above them, in a fancy apartment, a young woman had been putting up a garland of ivy on the wall molding above one of her living-room windows when the ladder underneath her had slipped, the poor woman crashing through the glass: or in a moment of unhappy distraction, she had decided to let go of her worldly existence and jump, then changed her mind, her descent rapid and impossible to stop.

Soon enough, above the din of sleigh bells and music and traffic and murmuring voices, a *wooooomph* and a loud whack as if someone had attacked the snowy pavement with a base-ball bat. Not twenty feet in front of them, the young woman bluntly landed, her bones breaking, blood spreading out from her head and out the tips of her fingers, her hands curling up and opening in spasms, her chest, its rib cage hidden under a cashmere sweater, all caved in, heaving ever so slightly. And steam was rising out of the exposed surfaces of her skin despite her clothes (as if radiator pipes had shifted and come out, up through her broken skin).

A European tourist in a mink coat, who had been standing under a nearby awning, waiting for a taxi, had made the Sign of the Cross and cried out, *"Mein Gott!"* And soon enough, passersby had begun to gather, a cop and a doorman already pushing through the crowd to examine her. As he stood beside Annie, the first things that Ives noticed: the young woman seemed to have had her hair recently cut in the style that was then called the "Peter Pan," and she had not been wearing shoes: on her twisted feet, in fact, were a pair of bright red woolen stockings, perhaps from Scotland, that looked rather new or in any case quite comfortable.

They were steaming too.

"Annie, do you see that? She was planning a party or something, and looking forward to the season like everyone else, the poor girl."

And then an interesting thing happened. Even while Annie was holding on to her friend's arm, she took hold of Ives' hand and squeezed it, as if to imply, "I'm here for you," and did not let go.

From the building entranceway, a woman of middle age in a bathrobe and bedroom slippers, her heavily madeup eyes bewildered and runny with mascara and grief, repeating, "Please don't tell me . . ." and "Oh my God." Another much younger woman, in a party dress, the dead girl's sister perhaps, came out and, taking one look, reeled back, crying, into the arms of a well-dressed young man who'd been waiting just behind her. Then a second doorman came out with a blanket and placed it over the girl who had fallen, delicate crystals of snow covering her as well. She must have died in that moment, because, his skin prickling over, Ives felt a wave of powerful melancholy passing through him, and that sensation must have also affected Annie.

Leaning close to Ives, she whispered, "Jesus, I just had the strangest sensation, did you?"

Ambulances and more cops and the crowd, bigger than before, jostling about. A kid, with a cunning expression, pulling upon Ives' coat sleeve and offering him, even as the young girl lay there, "Mister, you want to buy a rose for the pretty lady?"

"No," Ives told him, the kid getting another idea, saying, "Buy the rose and leave it for the dead lady," but that did not work and he moved scornfully on.

Later someone said, "Let's get out of here," and they did, continuing westward, Annie and Ives walking in silence, her companion, Carl, repeating, as if they'd just seen a quite convincing disappearing act at a carnival, "That was really horrible, wasn't it?" but almost joyfully so and with the kind of ardor that only a newcomer to New York, excited by its diversity, might convey. "The things you see in this city!"

Annie only let go of Ives' hand when they'd reached Scully's bar. There the group took a table, ordered up pitchers and pitchers of beer and sandwiches, and forgetting, for the most part, the recent tragedy, enjoyed something of an impromptu show—actors taking turns singing by a piano. Quite unsettled by what had happened, Ives sat with Father Tom ("I also noticed the stockings," he told Ives) and looked up several times to see that Annie seemed much more interested in her corned-beef sandwich than in what her companion, Carl, was saying to her.

Now and then she caught Ives' eye across the table, and smiled sadly. And later, about a quarter past midnight, when Carl had gotten up to use the men's room but had dallied by the bar, where he'd struck up a conversation with another woman, she came over to sit by Ives. And because she had perhaps begun to feel something for him, she leaned close to him and whispered, "Would you hold me? I'm feeling a little cold.

"I still can't get over that woman's death," she told Ives. "And the thing that kills me is that every time I close my eyes, I see how easily it could have been you or me or anyone. I mean have you ever stood on a rooftop and thought to yourself how easy it would be to jump off?"

"Yes."

"Have you ever doubted the point of all this? I mean, Ives," and she sipped her drink, "has all the nonsense ever tired you out?"

"Yes, at times it has," he said sincerely. And maybe because of the way that he looked at her, she wrapped both her hands around his, and leaned her head against his shoulder as if they'd known each other for a long time.

When they stepped outside together, the snow was already more than six inches high and rising. A beautiful night, the streets in every direction impassable to traffic. Hardly anything moved save for the occasional snow plow on the avenue, bus engines whirring, strained, somewhere in the distance, little else. To the west, over the rooftops, through the immense, agitated hive of falling snow, a kind of violet light puzzled them. Down the street dozens of children, who'd swarmed out of their apartment houses, were in the midst of a snow fight, the scene lit by wrought-iron street lamps, snowballs bursting against hooded, gleeful faces, and dropping, soft as flowers, behind them.

Annie could not help but hide behind a car like a child, red-faced and laughing, trying her best to smack Ives on the head. Ives received her shots with joy and mounted his own assault. Raising his portfolio like a shield, he shouted at the top of his lungs, and, charging toward her, pulled her down into a drift of snow, where they briefly kissed and he felt the first fleeting heat of her tongue. Then they rested, side by side, on the frigid pavement like dummies, wistfully looking upward at nature's swirling activity. A kind of magnificence, heaven, as it were, coming down on them.

Perhaps it was the Christmas season, or because they had encountered death, or because the storm was very bad, or because they had been stopping on nearly every street corner, kissing, or because the place she shared with a couple of roommates up on Columbus was so far away, it seemed natural that they go to Ives' apartment. And so, just like that, they were in the dank and unkempt entranceway of his Tenth Avenue apartment house, an air of intimacy about them already, Annie climbing the stairs ahead of him, Ives pushing her up with his hand pressed to the small of her back, up five flights and into his cluttered clank-piped rail-road apartment. He did not have much by way of fancy furniture: an old drafting table, which he kept by the fire-escape window, a record player, a few chairs, radio, bed, and all manner of crates and boxes in which he kept books, artist materials, and personal memorabilia, or used as tables. Now and then he got something out of an office where he'd been working, a lamp, an old filing cabinet, about to be discarded. Otherwise, his furnishings, like the ratty, bottom-heavy sofa, he had brought up out of the street, with the help of neighbors.

He turned on the radio, finding a jazz version of "Jingle Bells," and discovered that Annie had an open way about her. Could she use the bathroom? Yes, and used it without really bothering to fully shut the door. Then she came out and asked, "What's to drink?" and Ives poured her some scotch on the rocks. Looking around, she noticed that the place was a disaster and began to tidy up a bit. Then she paused over a dense pile of pamphlets and thin books of a religious nature. When she'd finished her drink, she moved over to Ives and gave him another kiss, and before long they were rolling around on the floor, half drunk, necking, his hand finding the tenderest parts of her body under the material of her cotton dress. Shortly, at three in the morning, in the half-light of the bedroom, he threw a towel over his lamp, the windows loose and whistling from the force of the storm, and he and Annie MacGuire made love. A few details? He found a packet of ancient condoms that smelled like bicycle inner tubes, their elastic rims torn twice during her first efforts to put them on him. Her thin crucifix settled upon his navel. Then she straddled him, talking dirty, her pupils dilated, her head tilted back as she moved her hips slowly and assuredly over him. She moaned and her teeth chattered as if in an arctic chill; then she shook all over and screamed for a long time, as if breaking up into pieces.

*   *   *

Ives and Annie began seeing each other regularly after that. An informal union that suited both of them for the moment. They'd meet after work, go to the movies, and take long walks. They would even go up to the League together. And she got into the habit of assisting Ives with his drawings and with the organization of his chaotic life. On some days, she would pose nude for him, in his apartment, the sessions never lasting very long, as they quickly ended up in bed.

Independent-minded, she divided the world into two categories of people: those who were introspective and gave true thought and consideration to others and those who were not. She considered Ives to be the rare case of a man in the first category and the men in her family in the latter. She once told Ives, while they walked along the boardwalk of Coney Island, that, in her opinion the troubles in life were started by people who never looked into their own souls. He walked along holding her hand and nodding. He was astounded, a woman nearly as introspective as himself, who loved him.

THE KAMASUTRA

A pile of books, a Bible among them. A calendar: 1949. The bathroom door ajar, Ives listening to his future wife drawing the bathwater. He always found an excuse to slip into the bathroom to spy on her brunette beauty, stretched out in the tub. She usually read a book—science fiction, the stories of Zane Grey, Dickens.

Years later he would lie to his son about the reasons why he had wanted to marry her: because she was a Catholic and a schoolteacher. What he didn't tell his son, or anyone else, save Ramirez when he'd been a little drunk, was that sex was a large part of it even if he found it hard to reconcile his piety with his feelings of passion for her. She, quite simply, made him feel wanted. He'd tell himself he'd loved her for her brains and watercolor and gouache technique, but when he noticed her blue eyes dilating at the very notion of sex, all restraint fell away. Even though he did not consider himself a man of this world, his head up in the clouds, his virility and sexual exuberance surprised him. On one otherwise torpid and bleak March day, he and Annie made love seven times. (Or so he remembered.) Somehow she had become enamored of him. She loved his body, did unheard-of things with him, the mystery of her love expressed in entangled, twisted positions. Having read all the plain-covered marriage manuals and Greenwich Village books like the *Kamasutra*, Annie ground the bottom of her body into his uplifted maleness and made him feel that he was sinning. And then Ives, forgetting guilt, behaved like the most wanted and desirable man in the world, giving his all and losing himself in the little paradise of his orgasm—the release of such lust producing, like a settling mist, a new shroud of guilt, for Ives remembered the metal crucifix with its dark patina he kept on the wall just above the bed, and the anguished face of Christ.

FAMILY

He took her down to Brooklyn to meet his sweet-natured sister, Katherine, who operated a candy shop on a street corner in Brownsville. She loved her brother for many reasons, among them the fact that, when their father died, Eddie had turned over his share of the small inheritance to her, so that she might buy that little business and get an apartment, maybe have a normal life. She wrapped her arms around Ives, as if she had not seen him in a hundred years, and treated Annie MacGuire, from the start, like a good friend, greeting and accepting her as she had once accepted Ives when, shell-shocked, he had been brought into their household from the foundling home.

And he introduced her to Harry, not yet thirty-five and already smugly successful, an attorney in the real-estate business, who never lost a night's sleep about the sufferings of the world. In town from California to arrange some kind of bank loan, he, in his own way, welcomed Annie, taking them out to the Chambord restaurant and spending a small fortune as casually as if he were taking off his hat. He was civil enough. And he would have introduced her to two other brothers, Johnny and Michael, if either had been alive. (One, Johnny, the oldest, whom Ives had hardly known, was a petty criminal, who had made his father's life miserable, his time on this earth ending badly when he was thrown off a rooftop by some thugs over a bad loan, having nearly every bone in his body broken and lingering for twenty-eight days; and his brother Michael, to whom Ives was closest, killed in the Second World War, whose passing was a powerful source of grief to his father.)

For her part, Annie took him to meet her family in Glen Cove, Long Island, a family of cops. Her father, uncles, brothers did not quickly take a liking to Ives. Not only were they of the school that believed artists were bums, but they also weren't quite sure of him ethnically speaking. Ives had gotten quite defensive one night when one of her brothers, Brian, talked about stopping a carload of "spics" in town because they looked as if they were up to no good, and Ives said, "But they're fine people . . ." and started a long running argument about how decent working-class people had to put up with all the shits in the world, and that it didn't matter where people came from, if they had breeding and manners. Voices rose, recounting bad incidents, which mainly involved persons of color.

Even though his last name was Ives and he was not "swarthy," he did not quite pass for white. Though, in his mind, he was thoroughly so. Accordingly, Annie's brothers took him for a Jew or an Italian and gave him a hard time, a running joke, when they'd had lots to drink, being, "Come on, Mack, what's your real name?"

Later, walking along with his head downcast, his face flushed in humiliation. He'd thank his mother and father for the trouble they'd given him. And even though he should have been more thick-skinned about it, a depressed feeling would remain. He'd pass a dance hall at night, and hearing the music, envision the crowded floor, people involved in their own society and feeling that they belonged. He'd peer into a restaurant doorway during a party, and, seeing people having fun, feel as if life were passing him by.

At least Annie knew with certainty what she had come from—from strong Irish-Scottish roots. Her grandparents had come over to New York at the turn of the century, at a time when people spit on their kind of immigrants, and now they could sit on their porch watching their grandkids spit on other kinds of immigrants. Their prejudice against Ives turned her stomach. When she told her family to treat him well or to forget about her, they nodded, smiling, and went along with her as if it were a big joke.

For the most part, they saw each other on weekends. There was very little they did not do together in their spare time: they went to jazz clubs in the village, visited galleries, haunted bookshops, had picnics in the park, and sometimes, with a borrowed car, took drives upstate, along the Hudson and beautiful wooded areas, through quiet towns and countryside, where they fantasized about living one day. They got to know each other's friends, Ives the greater loner. Annie had a lot of friends from her job teaching school and seemed to know many more artists than did Ives, who tended to keep to himself. His bedroom sounding sweetly with a nearby church's bell-tower clarion on Sunday mornings, he would take her to Mass. He wore a blue suit with white shirt and red tie, and she wore a dark dress and a white felt hat, with a ribbon about its brim and a veil that fell piously over her face. At Mass she found Ives' reaction to the service more moving than the service itself. Indeed, she saw that as the priest raised the Host during the consecration he seemed beside himself with emotion, his eyes reddening and his face quivering from his attempts at restraint. She found it oddly intriguing that he would tip his head back and shut his eyes during certain moments in Mass as during the act of love. Afterward Ives, knowing all the priests, would take her around to the rectory to talk things over with Fathers Byrne and Dwyer and Vitale. He'd almost feel like a child again in their presence, safe and secure and welcome. For her part, she was ever polite but would make a joke as they headed home, "My God, Eddie, I'm almost jealous about the way those priests make you happy."

They had fallen in love their first year together and had spent so much time in bed, as if catching up on all the years they hadn't known each other, that sooner or later it had to happen: she became pregnant. And with it she had the pleasure of exasperating her family with the announcement that she would marry that "funny guy" with strange attitudes and unmanly demeanor sometime around that coming Christmas.

WHEN HER SPIRITS WERE LOW

As Annie might have told their son, Robert, she never let on to certain of the darker events of her past, but Ives knew when her spirits were low. One of the compromises she made in her life, after marrying him, was to contend with her family, who treated her poorly. Aside from their feelings about Ives, they were so conservative in their outlook they disapproved of her own life apart from them. There was always a tinge of envy and animosity in nearly every one of their telephone conversations, as if she'd moved not to Manhattan but to Paris, France.

The family tottered between extremes, even before their marriage. At first her father, beside himself with grief, demanded to have a talk with her. And so one Sunday afternoon she took the train out to Glen Cove and met with him in a local bar, where, drinking too much, he went from a sad discourse about losing the daughter who would always be his little girl, the softest and best part of his heart, to "Really,

Jesus, how can you want to hook up with such a loser?" And when he left to use the men's room, she walked out and went back to Manhattan.

There had followed a period of several months when she heard nothing from them, and then one of her older brothers called to tell her the family had made a decision that all was forgiven. How could they now take charge of the festivities and do things up right? All she and her man wanted was a quiet little Christmas wedding. It turned soon enough into a plan for a much bigger event, to be held in a rented hall and for more money than they wanted anyone to spend. It got to the point where Annie, unable to bear the notion of the future discussions about all that had been done for her, refused to hear a word more and demanded that her family cancel the reception, something that did not sit well with her father, who lost his deposit and never let her forget it.

Not that she didn't love them, but she could not stand their meddling ways, all in the name of "family," nor did she like the way they treated her like a child and the accomplishments of her life as a lark. She had been the first in her family to attend college, which she had arranged herself. She had gone to Queens College by day, studying painting as a minor and literature as a major, and in the years when she had fallen in love with Ives, took occasional courses at night at Hunter, until the kids would put that on hold. Even so, she had gotten her bachelor's degree without the slightest encouragement from them. And yet when the family attended her graduation ceremony they were both wildly proud and disapproving. Such changes landed the hardest on her father, who thought a woman belonged in the home and not in a classroom studying whatever on earth she studied.

(He had no idea about the kinds of books she read. One day, when she came home from college, she saw him examining her copies of *Bleak House* by Charles Dickens and a book of poetry by Langston Hughes. He had stood over the books, set on a table, for several minutes, without moving. After reading a page or two of each, his face took on a displeased, puzzled, and then bored expression. Then he left the room without a word.)

She had five brothers and several married older sisters, and they treated her like the odd one out and talked about her with pity, as if at the age of twenty-one she was on her way to old maidenhood. Annie MacGuire was anything but that. She came home from her college classes, her hair up in a bun, without a trace of makeup on, only to watch her father stomp about their house disapproving of her looks and muttering things like "Now, why don't you make yourself look a little nicer?" as if she were the ugly daughter for whom he'd always have to provide.

She found the whole business rather funny. She had her boyfriends here and there, and although she was not promiscuous, if she liked a fellow there was very little she would not do for him. When she was a student, one of her lovers had been a married adjunct professor, whom she liked because of his starved sexuality and his quiet demeanor, characteristics that she always looked for in her men and found abundantly in Ives. Her family was so out of touch with her they would have believed her a virgin when she married, had she not been pregnant. And even then they would not have believed that their bookworm daughter had already slept with a few men, that she was far from a prude or squeamish about being a woman. That she loved the idea of being a Catholic who could take lovers without blinking an eye. They would never have guessed that she had once earned extra money posing nude for artists' classes, that in the days when she first got to know Ives, he had seen and drawn every square inch of her lovely body. And if she was a bit more outrageous about the act of love than they could ever have imagined, it was because in her own headstrong way she wanted to act as differently as possible from her own mother, whom she could not imagine ever experiencing a bawdy kind of love or getting lost in the throes of passion, especially with her father.

There were things about her father she never told anyone, not even Ives. She had primitive memories about him that were disturbing. She'd recall how in a house where doors were rarely locked, he thought nothing about coming in to use the toilet, while she, his four-year-old daughter, was taking a bath. She did not like to think about it, but there were times late at night when she would remember feeling her father's hands caressing her in the most intimate places. Even years later the sensation of his index finger circling lightly about her breasts came back to her. He did these things when he was drunk, nearly to the point of falling, and perhaps forgot that she was a young girl who happened also to be his daughter. Perhaps he thought himself in some whorehouse with a young woman whom he paid to touch. But Annie never said a word, because it was *she* who tempted him and *she* who had not been able to help him out of his drunkenness.

For his part, if he remembered touching her at all, he never let on.

EXALTATION

Long before she had become pregnant with Robert, she and Ives had gone through a phase of exaltation, like the angels who expected the coming of the baby Jesus. The boy or girl would be a reflection of their love and carry forth into the world the very best of their qualities. His kindness, quietness, his artistic talents, and his small measure of faith; her intelligence, strong-mindedness, her versatility. He would have a history: a mother, whose roots could be traced back to the north of Ireland, and the Grampians of Scotland and the Isle of Skye. They browsed in maternity shops and bought little silly toys, bibs and pacifiers, and were happy, until after a few months, out of nowhere, Annie went into a deep depression.

One morning she left her bed and, while standing before the speckled bathroom mirror, she looked into her eyes and realized that if she was not careful her life would turn out like her mother's, one of family servitude. She would forget about her own interests in literature and painting and her own dreams of one day teaching in a college—and become this ever-smiling vision of aging Celtic prettiness, her blue eyes aglow. She would learn to smile when she did not want to because sugar got more than vinegar in this life. Time would go by quickly. Her life would be defined by a predictable sequence of events: children, birthdays, holidays, and land-mark days, such as graduations and weddings, and then she would become a sweet and plump grandmother, crying her-self to sleep, as her own mother did at night.

One morning, when they were in bed, her arms wrapped around his shoulders, as she rested on her side, she surprised him by breaking down and telling him that she had serious doubts about having a child. Ives went for a long walk, down to Greenwich Village and then over to the docks, where he watched some ships from the Caribbean unloading their great nets of green bananas, wandering back in the rain, with a bou-quet of flowers, and telling her: "Look, if a baby would be too much for you right now, we could find someone to take care of it." Then, sadly: "We could put the baby up for adoption. It's not what I would want to do, but I would do it."

And for weeks she thought about what he had said, fear tingeing every hope for happiness. She saw mothers pushing their baby carriages who seemed wonderfully content, and mothers who were glum and remote. She had memories of the house in Glen Cove reeking of her brothers' diapers, the safety pins nicking her fingers, their cylinder-shaped washing machine chugging all day, babies crying all night, the young boys running their mother ragged. But whenever she even came close to making a decision, her thoughts always returned to Ives and how he had been a foundling, and how much it must have hurt him even to consider giving up the child to make her happy, and she felt more in love with him. With that she thought how having a family would not be so bad a thing to do with this considerate and moral gentleman. And knowing about his past, she could not imagine giving up the child. He never raised the subject, maneuvering those waters quietly. He simply treated her well, and in time, despite her doubts, she let the issue drop. They married in December, as they had wanted.

HIS SON WAS BORN

There had been quiet afternoons when Ives would come home from a job and decide to visit his local church, Saint Andrews. He'd walk in with his portfolio in hand, dip his fingers in the font of holy water, make the Sign of the Cross, genuflect before entering the nave, and then dally over the table on which there were dozens of prayer candles, their little flames dozing, as it were, in their blood-red glass cups. He'd put a few coins in the slotted box marked FOR POOR SOULS, and make a wish that his adoptive father would find all the happiness and glory he'd wanted in the hereafter. He hoped that his brother Johnny would not remain too long in the purifying blue fires of purgatory. He wished blessings for the kids with whom he had grown up and who had somehow not made it. He had known, for example, the stupid kid who stood up in the roller coaster in Coney Island in the thirties, and had his head lopped off by an overhead sign; he had known friends hit by trains while sneaking along in underground tunnels at midnight, friends done in by fire. He wished for the parents he had never known, his softest feelings for the mother, why he did not know. He emptied coins from the pockets of his coat and lit candles for all the others like himself, who, for one reason or another, had ended up in orphanages and foundling homes—he was always certain that so many of the bums, hoods, and prostitutes he saw on the street started out that way. He stared at the fluttering tongues of light, moved the thin burning taper from one candle wick to the other, before blowing it out. In a slightly hypnotic state, he would kneel down in a front pew observing the statuary, the crucifixes, and the triptychs above the altar. A scene of Christ turning water into wine in ancient Judea; Christ ascending into heaven from his tomb near Jerusalem; a star rising in the east over the Syrian desert—these scenes of times and places, so far away in the real world, seemed, in the context of a church, immediate and accessible. In some moments, Ives would close his eyes and imagine those distant places, and in a flash he would feel certain presences. And he would think that was all the travel he'd ever need.

He'd prayed for a good son, and when he was born named him Robert, after his adoptive father.

HEIRLOOMS

He'd been living in his walk-up dump in Hell's Kitchen since 1945, after his father had died and he and his older adoptive brother, Harry, had sold the house on Carroll Street. Despite its cracked floors, falling ceilings, bubbling bathroom walls, popping radiators, clanking pipes, despite its mice and insect life, it had suited his purposes. All he needed, by way of physical amenities, were the basics: bed, sink, toilet, a little heat and hot water, which were what he got in the winters, and a place to work. He did not worry about burglaries, because the only things he had of value, to Annie's delight were some old editions of Charles Dickens' books, several signed by the author himself, which his adoptive father had come by years before as payment for some job. He kept the books, wrapped in layers of shipping paper, in boxes, hidden in a closet. He had first-class editions of *A Christmas Carol* and *A Child's History of England,* and signed copies of *Oliver Twist* and *The Pickwick Papers,* the latter of which he'd admired since childhood for its engravings by Hablot Knight Browne, its title page bearing the inscription "With the sincerest best wishes and deepest feelings of gratitude, your friend and servant, Charles Dickens, Doughty Street, Christmas, 1847." He knew the signed editions were valuable—a book dealer said the "family edition" of *Pickwick* was worth about five hundred dollars. And although Ives could count on making good money from selling them, in the event of a financial emergency, he had no plans to, and considered them heirlooms, as it were, from a family line that never existed.

And he loved those books because not only did they emanate the spirit of a different time, when, it seemed to Ives, people were better, but because they reminded him of his father. They seemed to have been a great source of pride to the older Mr. Ives. He had been fond of collecting well-made books, and kept a modest library of them in a hallway bookshelf, books that seemed to bring him as much pleasure and solace from the world as did books on religion and the Bible.

Over the years they had become part of Ives' legacy, as had a big, fat German Bible, which he could not read but kept for its beautiful gothic illustrations (another gift from his father), and an English Bible, which, in the most secret recesses of his mind, glowed with the sanctity of God. There were his Spanish books and a few rumba records, which Dominguez, who'd passed on in the late 1930s had left him. Otherwise, with Annie's scant few possessions—a closet of schoolteacher dresses, her own little library, and such other items as reflected her tastes and interests (drawing materials, notebooks, and jazz recordings)—they lived quite humbly.

THE NEW NEIGHBORHOOD

In those days—his son was born in 1950—it bothered Ives that the neighborhood was not quieter or more genteel, that they would wake up sometimes at three in the morning because some drunks had spilled out of the corner bar to fight, shouting and breaking glass and with police sirens wailing, or that, from time to time, one heard the prostitutes yelling at their pimps, or the occasional gunshots being fired off from on high, as if from the rooftops. There had been the night when Ives had come home late and was walking along the sidewalk in front of the old Madison Square Garden, over on Eighth, when two men had come up behind him, one sticking a gun in his back and taking the whole fifty dollars he had made churning out little newspaper ads for a shoe company that week, hour after hour having been spent hunched over a drafting table until all the muscles in his neck and the small of his back had become knots. Ives had lifted his hands up over his head and had told the men, "Oh, can you give me a break? I've got a wife and a kid to feed." And one guy laughed and said, "Yeah, well I've got three kids to feed," and that was that, the story of life in the city.

Then he conked Ives in the head and the two men ran away, leaving Ives slumped in the gutter. Later he found himself being helped up by two other rather diminutive men, who were part of the Ringling Brothers Circus "menagerie" of freaks, then performing at the Garden. They'd been out all night drinking but had managed to give Ives a mighty pull, and when he had gotten to his feet they had consoled him, one of them saying, "Believe you me, buddy, things could be worse."

Around five-thirty one morning, after one of his restless nights of odd dreams about heaven and spirits, he had gotten up to fiddle around with a drawing and to look in on his six-month-old son, Robert. He happened to glance out the window and saw that three stories below, in front of a bar, a prostitute was kneeling before a man. In that moment he decided that it was time to get out of the clouds and to become serious about moving. So he and Annie began to go through the classifieds for a new apartment, Ives advocating something near a park, which was what he had been used to in Brooklyn, and Annie thinking more in terms of local schools and hospitals.

During a torturously hot summer they looked around every weekend without success, for they had a certain budget and the more suitable places seemed beyond their means, but then they received a tip from Ramirez, who was friends with the superintendent of a building in his neighborhood uptown.

The building itself was six stories high and stuck clustered in a row of other such buildings on Claremont Avenue, near Columbia University. Ramirez himself lived nearby with his young wife and two young daughters, and while it was not an entirely quiet or genteel street, the building itself was an improvement over what they were accustomed to. It had a laundry room, and hallway lighting, and mailboxes that hadn't been pried open, and a back courtyard in which garbage had not been dumped for plump rats to frolic in. It had an elevator, and its lobby had stained-glass windows that glowed with a chapel's serene light.

When they'd first walked in from a hallway on the first floor they could hear jazz piano playing, someone composing. A doctor, a sturdy-looking black man in his early forties, in a suit and derby, with his heavy black bag, was entering his office on the first floor; and from another floor, someone could be heard taking voice lessons, the superintendent, Lopez, telling them, as they waited for the elevator: "That's Mr. Fantusi teaching opera singers." They liked Lopez, a handsome fellow with a family of his own, who'd seemed a little weary and pleased at the same time when Ives had asked him, in his carefully practiced Spanish, *"Y de donde veniste en Cuba?"* to which Lopez answered in English, "A place called Cienfuegos. On the far eastern part of the island."

Deciding to move up there, they took a two-bedroom apartment on the fourth floor overlooking a street that saw no major traffic. In fact Ives liked the liveliness of the neighborhood and its odd mix of professorial types and students, working-class people and hoods. And in that neighborhood there was a racial mix that he had not seen downtown. It appealed to some sense of the cosmopolitan in him, especially when he would see an Indian exchange student walking about with a Hindu dot upon his forehead, or two tall and regal-looking Nigerian gentlemen walking down the street. The landlord was Jewish, and the tenants themselves a mix of ethnic backgrounds.

And best, despite the distant rumble of the subway, pulling in and out of the 125th Street station, on Sunday mornings all the church bells for blocks around began to ring simultaneously at eleven. When Ives asked how many churches there were in the neighborhood, Ramirez told him: there was Riverside Church on 120th Street (a Protestant church where John D. Rockefeller himself attended services); the Cathedral of St. John the Divine, the largest gothic church in the world, also Protestant, on 112th Street and Amsterdam; and all kinds of small churches further downtown. There was Corpus Christi on 121st Street, where their daughter, Caroline, would be baptized in 1954; the Church of Notre Dame on 115th Street on Morningside Drive; and finally, among the Catholic churches that were within walking distance, there was the Church of the Holy Ascension on 108th Street off Amsterdam, where, one day, years later, their son would die.

Once settled in, Ives decided, having so many new expenses, to find a full-time job, and eventually began his long tenure with the Mannis Advertising Agency. He had a connection there, having occasionally free-lanced for them over the years, and was already known to their art directors when he formally applied for a position on the staff. From the beginning he liked the talented people who worked there, the small scale of the operation, more "mom and pop" than much larger agencies. And he loved the architecture of the building itself, famous in its own right, for its majestic Art Deco flourishes, the marble inlaid floors of its lobby, and the iron grillwork. Over its revolving doors, there was a large Masonic "third eye" set in the center of a pyramid, an image that intrigued him greatly at the time, for sometimes when he was sleeping and tried to visualize an image of God, beyond the normal depictions of a benevolent, or wrathful, Biblical patriarch—such as one might find in the engravings of Gustave Doré—he sometimes envisioned a watchful eye, floating serenely and invisibly, observing every moment of life; an omniscient God, who knew everything and was everywhere at once.

At first, the job in itself, as an illustrator, was not so hard as tedious, his hours spent with some rather dull assignments. But, after he had been there for a few years, one of the bigger, more highly paid staff artists abruptly left the agency in a huff, and the bosses—a certain Mr. Crane and Mr. Silverman—agreed about giving Ives one of his assignments. That was to draw some eye-catching representations of the Imperial Floor Polish housewife, for a print-ad campaign. Given this big chance, he wanted to excel for the family. He racked his brains for weeks, before finally coming up with a quite realistically rendered drawing of a woman in a mink coat, in her kitchen, applying makeup and, ever so glamorous, using the shiny kitchen floor as a mirror for the copy—"Let Imperial Make Your Floors Mirror-Clear." That was the beginning of a sequence of variations on the same: a vain neighbor coming to visit the wife, unable to keep her eyes off her own reflection; an elderly grandmother seeing herself reflected as a young woman, bits that Ives had fun drawing. In time, he became the artist whom they went to if they wanted something with a twist that would zip up a campaign.

But even his more straightforward renderings of postwar all-American housewives, depicted in the bliss of domestic life, somehow conveyed a hint of something else that was hidden, sex perhaps. Because whenever Ives drew these ladies, whom he depicted in a variety of household activities, he based them upon the appearance of his wife and the intelligent and slightly naughty cast of her face. Not overtly erotic like the women drawn by Antonio Vargas or Earl Moran, his aproned strong-bodied females had an understated seductive air about them, in short, like Annie MacGuire. And they were such successes with the clients that within a few years Ives' renderings of these women would grace many a national magazine—*Look, Life,* and *The Saturday Evening Post*—many an outdoor billboard advertisement, poster, and car-card ad to be found on rail-station platforms and on buses and trains, in every major American city. (A typical Ivesian illustration: A woman in a blue dress is in her kitchen preparing to put some detergent into her washing machine, her world the confines of an ad. Her lips are full, her hair auburn, her dress snug around her breasts. White cloth-covered buttons run down the front of her dress, and vaguely through the fabric, at a point where one would find the center of a brassiere cup, the suggestion of a taut nipple, nothing explicit, but somehow sexual. Ives worked hard on these illustrations and then brought them home to show Annie, who would sit by the fire-escape window, working over the drawings, softening his lines, adding a touch here and there, changing the curves of a mouth, the expression of the eyes, and most often, the hands, which always gave Ives trouble. She drew long, slender hands, elegant and inviting fingers, hands that were like her own, sensitive, anxious to touch.)

Slowly he began to earn more money, to dress better, and finally to settle into a series of relaxing affectations that defined the creative people in his field. While he arrived at work, say on a crisp December morning, in a London Fog overcoat, black brimmed felt hat, and woolen suit, by midday one would find him sitting by a drawing board or light box in his office, fussing with the mock-up of an ad, his jacket slung over a chair, tie loosened, the sleeves of his Arrow shirt rolled up, shoes off, feet tapping on the floor. Save for his vaguely foreign air, he could have passed for a Yale or Harvard fellow, commonly found in advertising in those days, but Ives had been, in fact, a lowly Brooklyn College dropout, having left after two years. He wore suspenders, a red or green bow tie, and smoked a sweet-smelling cherry-blend tobacco, his pipe often left poised against the bottom rim of a two-tiered ash-tray on top of his supply cabinet. If someone came by, say

Tilly the receptionist, in her ever-friendly manner, Ives, out of habit, would swivel in his chair, reach for his pipe, and light it with one of the safety matches he kept in a jar, while saying, "And how are you today?"

There was more that he would recall about that job, most of it unspectacular, and, in fact, after his career at the agency was over, when he'd finally left some thirteen years after his boy's death—years spent to mark time—he recalled that if he made any contributions to the business it was in his influence upon their hiring policies, having been responsible, in his own small way, for bringing in Spanish-speaking copywriters and executives, long before it became the fashion, and in encouraging accurate representations of that culture, as if that would have made any difference in the course of his son's life, in the end.

He had his habits. In the office by eight-thirty, lunch at one, home (God willing) at six, though quitting time often varied. Once a day, usually at four in the afternoon, he'd call his wife, careful not to disturb her between noon and three, when one of the next-door neighbors would watch his son, and Annie might do whatever she liked: pursue her studies, go to a library, see old friends, or, if she liked, try some drawings herself. He liked riding elevators up to his office on the tenth floor, and one morning had the fantasy that the elevator would continue onward like a Jules Verne / Wernher von Braun rocket to the stars. Many daydreams.

Most often, he'd go to the lobby diner and get a sandwich (Virginia ham and Swiss on rye, lettuce, salt and pepper, mayo and mustard), take a quick jaunt around the block to get some fresh air, and then head back up to the office, where, as he and his colleagues knew, the work never seemed to end. Still, Ives had days when, having finished a job, he could step out for several hours if he so liked, and on those occasions he would sometimes walk over to the Horn & Hardart's on Forty-sixth, or to a Turkish restaurant called

Iskanders on Third Avenue and Twenty-eighth Street. Sitting by a corner table, with a newspaper or book—science fiction or his book of Spanish grammar, his studies slowly progressing—he'd much enjoy the hypnotic Islamic music that the portly owner played out of a phonograph in the kitchen, as well as the spicy food. In any case, he never spent very much, and, on certain days, in the interest of saving money, skipped lunch altogether.

Then he might drop in on friends at different agencies, fellow artists and favored employers whom he knew from here and there, like the cartoonist Otto Messmer ("the father of Felix the Cat"), for whom Ives had occasionally free-lanced in the past. In those days, Mez, as his friends called him, worked for a company that operated the biggest animated or electrically lit billboards in New York City, like the Real-Smoke-Rings-Come-Puffing-Out-of-a-Giant-Man's-Mouth billboard on Forty-seventh Street, or, in this instance the flickering, animated Bulova Watch sign overlooking Times Square. Eight stories up, Messmer's small office, on the north side of a building on Forty-third and Broadway, was filled with control panels and circuit breakers, ticking gears, all exciting to watch. A narrow but long room, with slotted windows, such as one would find in a movie projection booth, his office looked out onto crisscrossing girders. Beyond that, a complicated patchwork of tangled wires and cables were jammed, here and there, into the back of the electronic billboard, large as a movie screen. Inside, the booth walls were warm to the touch.

Sometimes he'd bring his son with him, the kid no more than three or four years old and delighted by the futuristic machinery in that room. Messmer, stoic, reading a newspaper, even as Ives, against a backdrop of flashes—the afterglow of two thousand flickering lightbulbs seeping in—moved toward the control board. Fascinated, watching a gear or switch move, levers shifting, cylinders and piano rolls turning, and, at certain intervals, a whole new deluge of light: the walls suddenly pinkish or azure or carnival yellow, those colors flashing across his face; Ives remaining still, but ever tempted to push a lever or button or two, as he thought God might with men.

HIS FRIEND RAMIREZ, ROBERT'S GODFATHER

Afternoons and evenings found Ramirez working in the Biltmore Men's Bar, a large mahogany-paneled room, with tulip-shaped fixtures, high gloomy windows, and many a dimly lit corner. That important people came and went was indisputable; along the bar mirror rim and along the walls were various signed photographs: Joe DiMaggio's, Douglas MacArthur's, Milton Berle's, Cesar Romero's, and Ronald Colman's, to name a few that Ives would remember. There were others, but most of the autographs were carefully, if inexpensively, framed. Some were just signatures, scribbled out on napkins or beer coasters. Some with messages: *"Para Luis, con amistad, Ernest Hemingway,"* on a bar menu.

Hundreds of famous people had gone through there, but after a while they made no great impression on him, unless they left big tips. Otherwise, Luis had to pass his days taking care of ordinary hotel guests, many a European tourist and businessman and the usual clientele, advertising executives and middle-management types from corporations, book and magazine publishers, and a contingent of free lancers, mainly commercial artists and jingle writers who would swarm into the bar at five during the cocktail hour.

When Ives had first made the acquaintance of Ramirez in 1946, the Cuban took him to be just another one of the lowly paid commercial artists and copywriters who fed themselves from the hot cocktail trays. In those lean times, when he subsisted on donuts, the occasional Horn & Hardart sandwich, a few pieces of fruit, Coca-Colas, and mooched cigarettes, he'd brave the merry but boisterous atmosphere of the Men's Bar, order a stein of tap beer, and then, with black portfolio in hand, and an empty growling stomach, slip off to the table filling steamy little plates up with Swedish meatballs, cold cuts, and stew. Not yet working full time, Ives wore the same pinstriped suit nearly every day, the same scuffed shoes, and a black brimmed, flattop hat that he fancied gave him a more carefree, rather than dourly poor, air. Dressing better than his pay, Mr. Ramirez had a tendency to look down on these college-educated kids, who, having had all the breaks, still did not know how to comport themselves like gentlemen. In his late twenties with his hair already thinning, he felt annoyed by the abundance of fair, full-headed, cocky Yale and Harvard college boys, inheritors of the earth, who jammed the bar, called him Pancho, and were pushy getting their drinks. Of course some were courteous, some patronizing, but every night there was someone to make him feel bad about waiting on him. To protect himself, he remained professional, neither aloof nor overly friendly, feeling that he had little in common with his regulars.

Still, Ives had struck him as a curiosity. Although he never seemed to have much money, he was extremely courteous and sheepish about ordering his one- or two-quarter beers from the tap while eating his dinner. And he must have felt some shame about leaving his dime tips, which Ramirez contemptuously flipped into a brandy snifter by the register. Yet he had come to appreciate Ives' quietude and sympathized with his sadness. And there was one thing that Ramirez, lacking it himself, admired: a degree of introspection. Ives always turned up, after making his day's rounds, with his black portfolio and books from the Forty-second Street library. Titles varied: sometimes they were novels, sometimes art books, but one evening he came into the bar with a book of Spanish grammar, which he studied ever so carefully, even in the midst of the clamor.

Ramirez, his curiosity provoked, leaned forward, and setting down a bowl of peanuts, asked Ives, "And what do you have there?"

"Just something that I'm studying."

He held it up, to show him, Ramirez' eyes scanning the title.

In a good mood, he asked: *"¿Habla usted español?"*

"No mucho. But I hope to."

"Yes? Then can you tell me why Spanish?"

Ives sat back and took another swig of beer before answering.

"I don't know why but it's something I've always done. My father used to have Cubans and Puerto Ricans working for him, in the printing business, and—" Ives shrugged "—the language began to rub off on me a little. *Pero no sé si puedo hablar bien.* So I try, you know."

"Pero habla bastante bien, ¡hombre!" Ramirez told him approvingly. "What's your name, anyway? *¿Cómo se llama?"*

"Edward Ives."

"Eduardo, okay," and he extended his powerful right hand. *"Bueno. Soy Luis Ramirez. A su servicio, señor."*

At first, from the Cuban's point of view, seeing the world nightly from the dimly lit confines of the hotel, their conversations had been nothing more than a way of passing the evening more quickly. The bit of Spanish he spoke with the "kid" amused him. He would greet him each evening, putting a beer and coaster on the counter, and encouraging, *"¿Señor, qué hay de nuevo?"* and Ives would nod in a friendly manner and say, *"Nada, no mucho, amigo."* Usually their *lecciones* came down to fragmented exchanges that were lost in the noise of the room, but when business was slow and there was nothing better to do, Ramirez, from boredom, would listen to Ives' Spanish and make an effort to correct his phrasing and pronunciation. In this way, over several years, Ives came to develop, with the few words he had, a good Cuban accent, better than that of the businessmen who paid large amounts of money for private tutors and who dropped a phrase or two in the bartender's lap: *"Por favor, amigo, dame un whiskey."*

Actually, though, he did not have much in common with Ives, save for the fact that he had spent part of his childhood in an orphanage in Cuba, run by the priests in the town of Belén. His mother had died of malaria when he was little, and his father, who had fought against Machado, more of a dictator than a president, during the late 1920s, had been killed by machine-gun fire, in gangster fashion, while coming home from a dance. There was something of what Ives would describe as a nearly imperceptible "glow" of sadness which they had noticed in each other. Perhaps, without knowing why, Ives' own spirit had touched Ramirez in unexpected ways: odd, Ives would think, how one just "knew."

As much as he may have liked Ives, enjoying his respectful attitude, Ramirez had much that he kept to himself: even other Cubans found him a private man. He was, however, distantly admiring of Ives' ability to draw. Whenever Ives came into the bar after work and would show his portfolio to some of his fellow advertising friends, Ramirez would take a peek. And the occasions when Ives would kill time, fiddling around with tracing paper or a drawing on a sketchpad, Ramirez' attention seemed riveted on him: not so much on the pencil or ink lines, but on the motion of his fingers—the hand, healthily intact. Anyone who'd taken a close look at Ramirez from top to bottom would have known why; they would have noticed that beyond the superficial details of his appearance— the beige jacket with white trim and dark buttons, the "Biltmore" in curlicue script embroidered over the left pocket, the fresh, nearly fresh, and then wilting carnation that he'd wear in his lapel and change every few days, his scent of brilliantine and cologne, his precisely clipped mustache, and his gentlemanly bearing—that aside from a few other things like his Cuban accent and his tendency to tap his right foot when he felt impatient about something, in the course of executing his myriad duties, Ramirez often tried to conceal his right hand. Wiping the bar clean, or shaking a pitcher of martinis, or drawing some draft beer from a tap, he drew attention away from it by asking a question, "Are you all set, *señor*?" or by letting the cloth of his sleeve cover it.

Once upon a time, when he was a kid, Ramirez told Ives, in scrappier, more youthful, and pain-loving days, he had been a welterweight boxer. After winning a dozen or so professional fights in Havana, most of those held at the Arena Colón, and had a little money in his pocket, he got into "gambling troubles" as he would put it. For all his troubles he had been a carefree and hopeful enough young man back then. One night he had been climbing the stairway to his flat near the harbor when four men jumped him. And while two held him down, a third spread his powerful right hand out on the stairs, and a fourth took a sledgehammer and broke every bone in his hand. He was nineteen years old at the time and might have had a chance one day to fight a champion, like Rene Sanchez or Baby de la Paz, if he could have fought on, but with the hand destroyed, he changed his ideas about his life.

"That's one of the reasons I came to this godforsaken country," he said. (And if he were drunk enough, he would lower his head slightly and hold his hand up, slowly, slowly making a fist, his crushed, deformed hand filling with blood as he tightened his grip, as if trying to restore his fingers to their former state. He squeezed it until his head turned a dark purple and began to tremble, his eyes in those moments somewhere else, no doubt in some glorious moment of his past in which his fists served him well. A glint of sudden pride would come over him as if, in those moments, he was a young man dancing away from an opponent, a betting favorite whom he had flattened with a sudden left hook and who lay on his back, unable to rise.)

On occasion Ives had seen him standing off in a corner with his back to the room, shaking his right hand wildly in the air for a few minutes, to get the blood going. And he had seen him sitting ever so carefully trying to write on an inventory sheet, his hand unsteady and disobedient. He had watched him sitting, brows creased in concentration, as he tried to thread a needle, as if for the practice. It would take him a long time.

Even after Ives had started to date Annie MacGuire, he still dropped by the bar a few nights a week for a few quick drinks. One evening after sitting down with his beer, Ramirez came over, and leaning close, said in almost a whisper, as if ashamed, "I wanted to ask you something, a favor, my friend. There's something I want you to do for me."

"What kind of thing?"

"Well, there's this woman from Cuba and, well, at my ripe old age I think I'm going to marry her."

"Congratulations."

". . . Anyway, I'm wondering if you would be able to come to my apartment sometime, to make a portrait of us for the future. You make oil paintings? Yes?" Ives nodded.

Then dreamily, as if grateful that anyone could fall in love with such a hard case as himself, Ramirez added, "Her name is Carmen Flores and I met her at a festival last year when I was in Cuba for a visit."

"A portrait?"

"Yes, you can do it, can't you? I mean, of course, I'd pay."

"No, I don't want any money," Ives told him. "I won't take it from you, my friend."

"But you'll make it good?"

"Of course."

"Have another drink," and he extended his damaged hand to Ives in agreement.

A VISIT WITH RAMIREZ AND HIS LOVE

Ramirez lived up on the far end of Claremont, just off 124th Street and Broadway; in the mid-1950s it wasn't a bad neighborhood. Just blocks and blocks of tenement buildings, and then you hit Teachers College on 120th Street and a few blocks south, the campus of Columbia University. A few blocks uptown, Harlem proper: from 125th Street north, the neighborhood, mainly Irish and German in those days, really started changing. While East Harlem was still largely Italian, Jewish, and black, further uptown there were more blacks, more Puerto Ricans, some Irish, and a lot of friction. Certain of the young men who lived in those neighborhoods, with dim prospects for the future, formed gangs and thought in terms of "turf." There were the Assassins, the Sinners, the Imperial Aces. Street fights had become common enough events, particularly once you got above 122nd Street.

But the building where Ramirez lived had seemed peaceful enough to Ives. It was nothing fancy, smelling even back then of that strange combination of odors particular to tenements—dog hair, insecticide, wet newspaper, leaky plaster, and incinerator ash—and there was a handyman who kept the halls clean. Mainly people minded their own business and lived as quietly and as well as their salaries permitted.

Up there· for the first time Ives met Ramirez' fiancée. Because they hadn't yet married, Ramirez had gotten her a room with a Puerto Rican woman upstairs. Ives would come over for a few hours on a Saturday, and Ramirez would stick his balding head out the window and call out, in love-struck tones, "Carmencita, can you come down? It's time. The artist is here." She must have felt ridiculous but looked spectacular, coming down the narrow stairway in her elaborate ballroom dress—its skirt noisy with layers and layers of embroidered fabric, her face made up and her long and delicate neck glittery with heirloom jewelry. She was about twenty-five then and had the nearly weightless gait of a ballerina. In fact, she prided herself on her dancing, but had never studied it formally. She had been a seamstress from a family of seamstresses, whose great hope was to marry her off to someone of a better class. He had gone back to visit an old friend, in a little town west of Havana, flashing the money he had earned at the hotel, meeting her at a dance in the town square. Her family hated him for leading her astray. She was so pretty, her face soulful and pensive, that he lied through his teeth to impress her. Ramirez, who considered himself an unspectacular-looking man, had given Carmen and her family the impression that he owned the Biltmore rather than worked there. He seemed so casual about money; during his visit, he bought presents for every single one of her sisters; and when he had asked her to come to New York to visit—his intention to propose marriage—he had cabled her the funds.

She must have felt shocked, because even though he did not live in a slum, his building was far from the mansion she might have imagined. More than once she had looked out the window at two in the morning, feeling heartsick for home, and watched someone urinating on the sidewalk. Another time she saw two drunk men in a fistfight. And she must have been afraid, at least if she believed the wild stories that Ramirez told her, in the interest of keeping her at home. He had told her again and again that she was a beautiful woman but, because she had some black blood, certain people would despise her; and that if she walked out into the street without him, rough and hateful men would go up to the rooftops and drop bricks and garbage cans on her. He told her that, while walking along with a friend, sightseeing in the Bronx, he had been set upon by an Irish gang who tried to beat him into a pulp—only his boxing skills and the sudden appearance of a few cops had saved him; and that, while coming out of the subway at 125th at three in the morning, drunk, after a party, he had been picked up by some kids with pistols who didn't want no "spics" in the neighborhood, and that they were driving him upstate to kill him and dump his body in the river. On the outskirts of Riverdale, when they had pulled over to relieve themselves, he had managed to get away, running for his life into the night.

For her part, whether she believed him or not, or was afraid, or loved him or not did not matter. She remained with him because, quite simply, she didn't have the money to go home. And although she enjoyed the way he was courteous and doted upon her, bringing her a fresh bouquet of flowers every night and often taking her to buy clothes, she was a virtual prisoner. She had to be careful about keeping her distance from certain of the other Cuban men who lived around there, particularly a pair of suave musicians he had gotten to know. Without Ramirez she rarely went out, unless to accompany her landlady on an errand or to church on Sundays, and never alone at night.

One Saturday she came down the stairs, her silk dress rustling against the bannisters, and strode proudly into Ramirez' cluttered but orderly living room, where an easel had been set up. Ives was waiting on the couch. Ramirez had put two chairs together and draped a piece of linen over them, as if they were one love seat. He wore a blue serge suit and tie and posed with the seriousness of a man facing a death sentence. No matter how often Ives said to Ramirez, "Relax," and "Smile," his expression only became more severe. But as Carmen got to know Ives and feel more comfortable around him, she began to radiate a truly pleasant sense of inward joy. She was a beautiful and good-natured woman with a dazzling smile, and Ives could see why Ramirez had fallen in love with her.

She was so lonely that she looked forward to those days when Ives would come along, and even though he couldn't speak much Spanish nor she English, those painting sessions were quite festive and gay affairs, even if Ramirez would look over the canvases and demand that Ives have the decency to add a little more hair to his head.

As subjects they were a disaster. To Ives' exasperation, Ramirez shifted his position constantly, and Carmen, having overcome an initial shyness about saying a word to Ives, used these sessions to practice English. ("Mr. Ives, where do you go to get the subway? Is there a time now? When you have been here long?") And every so often he would try to speak

Spanish, the banter making Ramirez embarrassed and uneasy.

Around her delicate neck hung a medallion of the Virgin Mother and a crucifix, which Ives took extra pains to capture. And, in those days when he believed strongly in God, he wanted to show her his own crucifix. It was just a black-beaded rosary-crucifix, an antique that his father had given him. Inside, the crucifix contained a glass vial in which were set a few tiny bone fragments of a saint, which impressed her very much but was a difficult thing for Ives to explain. (*"Come se dice* 'bones of a saint' *en español?"* he had asked Ramirez.)

It took him several months to get the portrait done. In it, Ramirez' right hand is hidden under his left; he is leaning back and regarding the artist or world with weary suspicion, while, because of the way Ives gradually came to see her, Carmen is nearly "saintly," with an otherworldly glow.

When Ramirez and Carmen did marry, eventually having a son, Pablo, Carmen invited Ives and Annie to the wedding and banquet, held down at the Biltmore. And there the women became friends, and so much more easily than did the men, even over time. Ramirez tolerated Carmen's love for going out, and Luis tried to become something of a dancer, much to his chagrin whenever they made their way out to the dance halls. When his son, Robert, was born, Ives surprised and honored the Cuban by asking him to be his boy's godfather.

A HANDSOME BABY

Ives was twenty-eight when Robert was born, and from the start Ives had been surprised by his paternal instincts; it was almost inconceivable that someone so good and pure could have come from him. He was a handsome baby, with big, blue intelligently cast eyes, and a hint of sadness that must have come from his father. He had Annie's Celtic coloring and a symmetrical, pleasing, high-cheekboned face. Well behaved from the start, a baby who never cried much and had, like his parents, a quiet disposition, he would naturally become Ives' favorite and grew into a loving and considerate son.

It was as if he, and later Caroline, were meant to bring more light and cheerfulness and love into a family that was, in its way, very small and closed off from the world. Uncle Harry was a fleeting presence in the house, a disembodied voice on the harsh, clicky-sounding telephone, long distance from California; and Ives' sister, Aunt Katherine, who owned the candy shop in Brooklyn, visited as often as she could, mainly on Sundays, which was never enough (for she would come to the apartment laden with candies and gifts).

As for the MacGuires, they were scattered and lived so far away and were, in essence, so disapproving of Annie's choices in life that the Iveses usually saw them only once a year, at Christmas, when Ives would take his wife and children out to spend the day with his in-laws on Long Island, an ordeal that always left them depressed and low-spirited, because the once-a-year-only affections shown them always unraveled by the New Year. Even so they did it for the kids.

Not to say that there weren't "uncles" around. There was the occasional visit from Father Tom Bernhardt, who would sit drinking with Ives in his living room, and, as well, Ramirez and Carmen, who sometimes came over for early dinners on Saturday nights. Afterward they'd leave Robert in a neighbor's care, and go out to see some Broadway show like *Silk Stockings* and *Cat on a Hot Tin Roof,* compliments of the agency. There were trips to the Metropolitan Opera, the tickets coming from Ramirez, who had gotten them as tips from hotel guests like Jussi Björling's manager. During those visits, "Uncle" Luis, a dapper man, always impressed Robert with his suave yet manly presence. They were his immediate "family," as it were. To be sure there were others he would see from time to time, people coming over to the apartment:

some wonderfully helpful neighbors like Mrs. Malone, who used to look after the kids, or Mr. Spinelli, the tailor, from whose brother, a florist, they bought all their flowers and Christmas trees; and occasionally, some of his father's advertising-agency and cartooning friends came over.

When Robert was born a murmur was found in his heart, and although the doctor told Ives that such conditions were common enough, Ives still had suffered, his morbid fantasies getting the best of him. Thinking not just about his own past, but about the myriad possibilities for disaster, Ives found it quite impossible to sleep, and would spend half the night sitting by his son's crib, fretful when he cried or had normal digestive problems, colic and the like. And while he delighted in the mystery of life, and his newfound status as father—an identity he could embrace with even more fervor than he did his career—his imagination often led to severe bouts of anxiety. It had not helped to hear about one of the secretaries in the agency who had a newborn child, a boy, about six months old. Because the baby was allergic to tobacco smoke she had left him alone for five minutes, stepping out to smoke a Lucky Strike and chat with a neighbor on her stoop in the Bronx. By the time she had gone back into the kitchen, where she had set him down in a cradle, he had stopped breathing, having choked on some small bit of regurgitated food. Hearing about that, and seeing the mother's grief—she would wear black for a year—Ives got into the habit of pressing his ear against his son's chest nearly every time he held him.

Prepared for the worst and having heard even more stories—everyone he knew seemed to have a story about a baby falling out of a window—Ives was truly amazed that no disasters had struck.

Determined to show Robert the same kindness that his father had shown him, Ives would teach his son about religion, for which the boy truly seemed to have a talent. They would go off to church together, and the boy learned how to put his hands together in prayer, to kneel, to bow his head, and to make the Sign of the Cross. And Ives would tell him, "All this may seem confusing to you now, but when you're a little older it will become clear." He told him about how tongues of fire and soaring doves symbolized the spirit. He told him about the notion of a soul and guardian angels, and about the Holy Trinity.

He would hold a tarnished bronze crucifix, which he'd taken down from the hallway wall: "This man was called Jesus and He lived like all other men until the time He was called into the service of His Father, who was God. . . . He was part of the Trinity. The Father, the Son, and Holy Ghost, who were all one and the same. Now He took a human form for a time so that He could better understand human beings and He chose to give His life, in a painful way, so that He would know suffering. . . . He was crucified . . . nails driven through His wrists and feet. . . . A soldier had lanced Him in His side; He had been given vinegar to drink when He was thirsty on the Cross. He died so that our souls would go to heaven one day. . . . We will be judged . . . for God watches us and provides us with what is good in this world. . . . He closed His eyes and cried out, 'Why hast thou forsaken me?' And He was buried and after three days rose and took His proper place in heaven. . . ."

He would watch his son nod and think and think and think, contemplating the things he'd heard and looking around the church as if he were waiting for the statues to move, for the Christ to come down off the Cross. He'd remember how the boy had always loved all of that from the very beginning, that he had, in some sense, two homes: their apartment and the church.

Mr. Ives' Mystical Experience

Robert once had a dream when he was about ten years old, just after the family had returned home from Italy and he had received the Pope's blessing. He and his father were strolling in Riverside Park, as they sometimes did in good weather, and even though there were no streams in that park, in his memory of it a stream came flowing down the hill south of Grant's Tomb. He would remember seeing Jesus Christ standing waist high in the water, not as a grown man but as a boy of his own age. And Jesus turned to him and beckoned, and that was the first time, he supposed, that he thought of becoming a priest.

Now Ives, while always having a great pride in his son's piety, had, all the same, felt startled when Robert approached him and sought out his advice on the matter. Ives had been sitting around on a Saturday afternoon, by his drawing board, which he'd rigged up in the living room by the window, from which he could see certain of his friends, like Ramirez, walking by below, cheering him immensely. He also turned the television on and much enjoyed working with the sound of shows in the background. The afternoon Robert walked in to have a talk, he had been watching one of his favorite films, *The Last Days of Pompeii,* starring Preston Foster, on the *Million Dollar Movie,* anything set in past times somehow comforting to him. Vesuvius had just blown up and the sky was filling with voluminous clouds of ash, smoke, and molten stones, sizzling into the Bay of Naples, when Robert leaned his thin and lanky frame into the doorway, his face handsome and sincere.

"Can I talk to you about something, Pop?"

"Roberto, Roberto, anything for you," Ives cheerfully answered.

But when Robert stood closer, and it would kill Ives to remember this, there were tears streaking down his son's ruddy cheeks, his eyes blue and damp.

"Son, what's wrong?"

"Just something, Pop."

Ives turned off the television, and because it was a nice autumn day, said, "Why don't we take a walk? What's the point of being cooped up?" And soon enough they were making their way to Riverside Drive, and were walking around the hedge-enclosed gardens near Grant's Tomb. Then entering the park, they descended a stairway at whose foot a college girl had been recently raped and, with tennis courts to their right, and boats passing on the river, they sat on a bench, not far, as a matter of fact, from where Robert had seen Christ in his dreams. But there was no little stream flowing down: just a couple of strong, tall black kids with bandanas around their heads and enormous hands bouncing a basketball back and forth. In fact, one of them lived down the street, a nice kid named Owen, who, at six feet four, would try to make a professional team, the New York Knicks being his favorite. He called out, "Yo, sir!" to Ives and Robert and smiled ever so happily. Knowing him from the local church and from the Stone Gym, where he had sometimes taken his son to play, Ives waved back.

Ives knew that something was up. For two weeks, the year before, his son had walked the garden paths of a Catskills religious retreat and meditated, gone to religious talks and vocational question-and-answer sessions, had shared a dormitory with boys his own age, some of whom had surreptitiously masturbated while lying on their stomachs and pretending to sleep in the middle of the night, others who talked to themselves, others who put pictures of Saint Francis or Jesus Christ or Mother Mary up on the wall and said their prayers in loud whispers so everyone would know just how devout they were. Attending Mass nearly every morning and prayer sessions later in the day, he sat for hours reading inspirational pamphlets about the Franciscan order. He met with monks who had felt so blessed it seemed as if they could not stop laughing, and he encountered an older monk, sitting in the corner of an herb garden, in the shade of an arbor, weeping. When Robert came home he seemed normal enough. On Saturday nights he would go down to the Riviera movie house on Ninety-sixth Street with some friends and get in for free, because Celeste, Robert's girlfriend, worked in the ticket-selling booth. The other kids would storm in and carry on through a double feature, while Robert would sit on a stool, set against the open booth door, and keep her company, until she was done around 9 P.M. Then they'd go inside or get a hamburger platter in one of the local dives and, if the weather was nice, walk home together, holding hands.

But then a few months before, Robert broke up with her and on Saturday nights chose to stay home. She had called a number of times, asking for him. On occasion, Ives had looked down from the window and noticed her waiting for Robert on the stoop below, and it had confused Ives because he had thought them something of a couple.

Now Ives and his son were sitting on a bench when a long coal- or garbage-filled barge floated by on the Hudson; it was then that his son told him, after much fidgeting about: "I don't know how I got myself into so much trouble, Pop. I mean, I'm completely torn up about the future."

"Is it that girl Celeste?" Ives asked, wondering if his good-looking son wanted advice about courtship (or more outlandishly, what if he had gotten her pregnant?); or perhaps there was someone else and his son did not know how to choose.

His son nodded and said, "That's part of it. Celeste is definitely a big part of it, Pop. But it comes down to this." And he slouched forward, looking at the ground through a kind of open diamond he'd made with his hands. "I've made a decision to go into the Franciscan order. I'd been talking a lot to the monks downtown, and, after coming back from that retreat, I think that's what I want to do. But," and he let out a laugh, "I'm not one hundred percent sure. I've thought about it for two weeks in a real serious way, and every time I tell myself 'yes,' I get all messed up with doubt. I mean, what do you think I should do?"

"Well," Ives said, "can I ask you something a little personal?"

"Okay."

"Does knowing Celeste get in your way?"

"Oh, yeah," he said after waiting for some New York Central trains to pass on by in an underground tunnel, their fumes filling the air. "I'm not seeing her anymore because when I'm with her I start losing my grasp on the things I think I want for the future. On the other hand, I have it really bad for her. I just don't know whether I should try to stick it out as a lay person and see what happens, or to give the order a real try now. Celeste is really nice to me, and she is as sweet as anyone can be, but I just don't know. It's killing me, Pop."

People were passing by, some of them friends.

"Hola, señor," a gaunt man called out. "Hey, Eduardo"— someone whom Ives knew from around.

People fully involved with the world were passing: athletic college runners, a track team at practice perhaps, broadchested, long-legged, in damp rayon tops and sweaty trunks; a trio of high-stepping black men in velvet-pinstriped jackets and denim bellbottoms with leather Beatles caps, huge afros, and high-heeled hooker boots, like pimps in the movies; and then some Columbia University love children, whom Ives always found amusing, when they'd make their peace signs with their hands, in a neighborhood where that did not often go over well. Among them a quite beautiful woman, a brunette, in a flowered, long-skirted dress, headband, and brown suede boots turning rapturously in circles under the sun. Robert just looked off into the distance. He did not move.

"What do you think?"

What Ives thought was that he was happy his son had decided to confide in him, unhappy that he wanted to make that kind of decision when he was still so young, and that, deep down, he knew what his son wanted, but had reservations. . . . A secular life of good deeds, with an allotment of mistakes, seemed a reasonable enough way for his son to live if he chose to, and, as Ives had observed, the church was not what it once used to be. Every day, it seemed, he read a news item about yet another priest in trouble for some indiscretion. And yet what else could he expect after having been so adamant in his own faith?

Though his son had always been guileless, attentive, and considerate of others, in fact, almost priestly in the best sense of the word, the thought of him joining an order had initially disturbed Ives. He had imagined his son attending a university, perhaps to study medicine; hadn't he once shown a strong interest in that profession? And what about the idea of denying himself—and his father—children? Had he thought it all through?

"Well, as you know, son, there are many ways of doing good. But to be a priest . . . Have you spoken with anyone about it?"

"The thing is, Pop, I've decided to give it a try; it just feels like something I'm destined for; it's something I've thought about since I was a kid, and it just won't go away. I guess what I'm asking you, Pop, is for your blessing. I know you can give me that, can't you?"

Ives would remember nodding, but not really being sure if he'd meant it.

HIS MOTHER'S PATIENCE WITH MEN, AND A TRIP TO THE CLOISTERS

Although he had confided in his father about his decision regarding the seminary and it was hardly a secret in their household, Robert could not bring himself to tell his mother about his doubts, for the young man truly believed that one of his jobs in life was to seem independent. So even though he suffered through many a bad day, even after talking it over with his father, when a vague depression came over him, as if he already knew about his true future, and wanted to rest his head upon his mother's lap, to feel her reassuring hand on his head, he kept his feelings bottled up inside—at least around her.

For her part, Annie had known about his feelings for Celeste for some time, but she refused to interfere. In her opinion Robert would have done quite well to eventually settle down with her, but she kept that opinion to herself, even after Celeste had come to the apartment on a number of occasions with the hope of somehow changing things. Fond of Celeste, but protective of her son, she came to accept his choice, which, given his spirituality and sensitive mind, did not surprise her.

But the whole business of Robert's future life in the priesthood rekindled a maternal streak in Annie. Normally occupied with her own interests, the knowledge that her boy would be leaving the household for good, drove her toward him and sent poor Robert running. She liked to straighten his tie in the mornings, to give his thick hair a good comb, and to hug him before he stepped out into the chilliness of the world, as if he were a soldier going off to war. She got into the habit of calling him "my handsome young man." Once she told him, "Don't squirm so much around your mother, one day you'll be an old priest remembering your mama with love and wishing you were back here again."

He had nodded, blushed, and walked out of the room with his ears burning red. Acutally, none of that behavior bothered him, as long as it took place in the apartment, but when she became publicly affectionate, especially when his friends were around, Robert, in the name of independence and manliness, would pull away from her.

Mainly, he treated her with due respect and affection.

There had been that Saturday in late October when Ives was in the office and Caroline was off taking an afternoon dance class, and Annie, never prone to strong bouts of depression like her husband, had started to think about her own family and how the men had never taken her too seriously. She was not crippled by a debilitating sadness, but for a moment, a sensation of terrible melancholy, over the fact that the world was presided over by men, came through her and she trembled and sighed. A great number of exasperating, flattering, sad, frightening thoughts regarding men resided painfully inside her, and she found it oddly strange to be married to one, even a good man like Ives. Then something else happened: standing by a rear courtyard window she recalled the chilliness with which she had always been treated by her father and nearly cried.

Then she heard a voice. Her son, Robert, had been by the door watching her.

"Mama, what are you up to?"

"Not much." And realizing that her eyes were wet, she dabbed them with the back of her hand. "I was just thinking about my life when I was a young girl."

"Well," her son said cheerfully, "I'm going up to the Cloisters in a little bit to check out the choir. They've got something going on with All Souls' Day, would you like to come with me?"

"Why, I would."

And in a few minutes they were standing around on Riverside Drive waiting for a northbound bus, its last stop Fort Tryon Park. Shortly, around two o'clock, they were sitting in a crowd in an echoing gothically ornate hall listening to a group of choristers singing in Latin about the transformations of the soul and other such autumnal subjects, and in the midst of one such song, Robert, reached over and took hold of his mother's hand, holding it gently. And he had looked over at her, his expression saying, "I will always be with you, Mama, from this day onward."

Or at least that was how she would choose to interpret that look, in retrospect, long after he was gone.

A year later, Ives awoke, a few days before Christmas, feeling pleased by the general drift of his life. Fulfillments had been slow but steady in coming, and though he had experienced many a torpid moment when he found his earlier daydreams slipping away from him, life had unfolded in a more or less orderly way. After more than fifteen years at the agency, he had been made a vice-president of the creative division, and he spent his days overseeing and approving much of the print and outdoor advertising artwork that came through his department, his initials, in blue pencil, on the corner of a proof, his occasional correction marks, the extent of his artistic legacy in those days.

Although it depressed him that he had not made more out of his painterly ambitions, his talents had still led him to a secure and comfortable life. Mr. Mannis himself was quite fond of Ives and paid him a good salary: if he'd wanted to move up to an area like Westchester, he probably could have afforded to.

He would leave the apartment, catch the 125th Street El train downtown to Times Square, scoot over from Seventh Avenue, cut through the garment district, the streets and sidewalks already chaotic with people, get his daily blueberry muffin and two cups of coffee from the lobby diner, and make it to his cramped office.

For years he found working late dispiriting, for he lived to see his kids. On his desk, among the piles of mechanicals, memoranda, purchase orders, magazines, and page proofs, and upon his walls were a number of photographs: a shot of himself and his father and brother and sister taken years ago in front of their house on Carroll Street; a picture of Robert, ten years of age, shaking hands with Pope John XXIII during a general audience at the Vatican, "the greatest moment of my son's life," Ives used to think; and a third and favorite shot, of himself and Annie and the kids when they were small, about 1956, posed in the park before Grant's Tomb. Ives was in suit and tie, and Annie beautiful in a coat she'd received the Christmas past and a brilliant blue scarf, standing behind a stroller in which sat Caroline in a bonnet; Robert, age six, was dapper in a little bow tie and jacket, his flaxen hair falling over his innocent lineless face. That had been taken on a late autumn day when shortly they were to meet with Ramirez and his family, all of them piling into a big roomy black Oldsmobile and driving up along the Hudson to get a look at the changing leaves, their picnic that afternoon taking place on a grassy hill overlooking the river, just north of Tarrytown and the Sleepy Hollow Cemetery (where Robert and Ramirez' kids had earlier played like ghosts among the tombs). He loved that photograph because he and Robert were holding hands, and although they did not look particularly alike, they were standing in nearly identical positions, their feet planted wide apart, and each regarding the other with a slightly tilting head, eyes a little sad and enchanted at the same time, smiles nearly forming on the edges of their mouths.

Ramirez, face twisted, a cigarette oozing smoke into his squinting eyes, had taken the shot.

Those were his happiest years, Ives would think, when the kids were small. He'd walk down Claremont with his hand on his son's shoulder, his other hand gently guiding his daughter along. He would stop on nearly every corner and make sure that the light was green and cross himself quickly as they passed every church, trying to teach the children to do the same. And if his daughter's bonnet straps were undone he would kneel down and retie them, careful not to pull too tightly, and while doing so, he looked at her angular face with its slightly jutting chin as if she were the most precious thing in the world. During such moments his daughter regarded him as if he were the most kindly and godly man alive, and he would smile, as that was just what he wanted to believe about himself.

Ives and Annie seemed to epitomize, with their well-behaved children, a wondrous example of what a family should be like, especially in that neighborhood, where many of the kids were rough and got into trouble. In a London Fog overcoat, with his pipe in hand, Ives would lead his little family along the streets, toward the park, ever pleased by the attention that passersby seemed to pay them.

He lived for their excursions out. Trips here and there around the city. Brought them into the office, showed them the photographer's studio, a television commercial being shot, a printing plant. Took them to triple-feature movie shows at the Nemo on 110th Street and Broadway (*Creature from the Black Lagoon, The Time Machine, Hercules Unchained*— in one bill!) and to see the museums: ostriches posed as if in a gallop at the Museum of Natural History, and Egyptian sarcophagi over at the Metropolitan. During their walks he led them into many a church, which he thought of as museums too. Hustled them onto the subway, down to Brooklyn to their aunt's candy store on Marcy Avenue, where they sat in a corner reading comic books and drinking egg creams from the diner next door. They attended the circus and visited the Bronx Zoo and did most of their shopping on 125th Street, where he led them on jaunts through crowds of black faces when they'd walk over to Lenox Avenue to an Army-Navy store (where one could buy, if one wanted, World War II bomb casings) or Grand Central Station to catch a train north to Scarsdale or Larchmont, when they had been invited up to visit one of the executives from the office, like Mr. Freeman.

He bought a parlor grand piano from an elderly Italian woman on the third floor, hauled it up by pulleys that hung off the roof and brought it in through the living-room window (a huge spectacle which took hours and drew crowds that watched from the street). He sent each of the kids over to Corpus Christi for their fifty-cents-an-hour piano lessons, Caroline being the one with a small gift for playing. He watched his son (with the better voice) start out in the pipsqueak section of the choir (even then Robert was envying the altar boys for their proximity to the altar), and was proud that his children always passed their grades easily and had won the general appreciation of the Dominican nuns who taught them.

Wherever they went, Ives found himself preaching about the misfortunes of others; poor people broke his heart, and though things were not as bad back then as they would be in the days of Ives' old age, on their walks they would often come across someone begging on the street or sleeping in the gutter, folks left over from the depression, for whom it was never over, or who were just unprepared for life in the modern world. And in those instances, Ives always made a point of giving a dollar to whomever he came across, as that was the right thing to do, he would say. The Christian thing, he'd say. And he made them aware, early on, about how certain things worked in this life. He did not often talk about the sort of tragedy that was common during the great depression, when shantytowns abounded in the city and people lived in the streets, but made it clear that the unfortunates of life, like the poor on welfare, or the public school kids who were sent for classes to their local Catholic school on Thursday afternoons, who dressed poorly and cursed and sometimes had mournful scowls in their eyes, and who often were "of color," were to be treated with compassion. They could not help being born poor, any more than the rich could help being born rich. Even Ives, looking back, would feel amazed about his fair-mindedness in those days.

Remembering the wants of foundling children, one of the things he did out of the office was to produce and oversee much artwork and advertising to raise money for different funds, especially for Harlem kids. Working with the local church, Ives headed clothing and food drives, and whenever he could wrest free sporting-event tickets from the agency, or any number of products like reel-to-reel tape recorders, transistor radios, toys, books, and writing implements from his advertisers, he did so—the fruit of his labors dropping like pebbles into a sea of the city's growing troubles—but perhaps making a little bit of difference in the end.

He would remember coming home and how Robert and Caroline greeted him at the door, or waited for him on the stoop. There were always kids playing on that street, dozens of them—stickball, running games, tag. Several times a month, he would come home with a big carton of comic books from one of the agency's printers and distribute them on the street, *Superman* and *Tom and Jerry*, two of the titles he remembered as being most popular, the neighborhood kids swarming around him and shouting, "Mr. Ives! Me! Me!"

Yet while a lot of the street kids wanted to be Superman or like the Paladin character on *Have Gun Will Travel* on television, his son's mind always drifted in a certain direction. In those days, anything regarding the church seemed to fascinate him. He remembered how one of the old Puerto Rican ladies who lived in the building would say, *"Su hijo es un angel."* How the boy had memorized his Baltimore catechism, memorized all the altar-boy Latin for the Mass in the good old days before it was changed by the reforms of the Ecumenical Council, how he had actually dressed up as a monk on Halloween one year.

No intellectual himself, Ives took an enormous pride in the fact that he had books in the house. And not the kind of science fiction or fantasy or religion that he liked to read, or books that were beautiful just for their physical production, but the books that he and Annie thought would help their children develop as adults. Those choices he left mainly to her. She was the "educated one," and besides she was an expert in literature. Once both the kids had started school, in the late 1950s, she had gone back to work as a substitute schoolteacher of art or English, a job that took her into some very bad places and situations. The pay, however, was money she could put away for the kids and future vacations and to cover the courses she occasionally took at night at Columbia University, those credits toward a master's degree in Lit so that she could teach college. In any event, it was she who advocated a number of purchases: an *Encyclopædia Britannica* and a bookcase of novels, everything from the *Hardy Boys* to the books of Ernest Hemingway. Oddly enough, neither Robert nor Caroline was particularly bookish, despite their exposure to such works, but the presence of two full book-shelves in an apartment on a street where most people would rather spend their money on movies or baseball tickets gave their household an air of culture, and one that made a great impression upon certain of the kids on that street, like Ramirez' boy Pablo, who would not recall having many books in his house but, coming over to hang around with Ives' children, always left the apartment with several of their books as loans.

RESISTING TEMPTATION

At certain times of the evening, a young Hispanic woman who lived across the courtyard dressed with her window cur-tains open, so that if one cared to, it was easy to glimpse her walking around in her bedroom. She wore black and frilly underwear, with garters and nylons, and undertook a nightly ritual of sitting half-naked before her mirror, applying her makeup. But Ives only noticed her because of the occasional skittish behavior of his son's friends, who would come over to watch TV, and, later, going into his son's room and pre-tending to play hiding games, turn off the light. There would be long periods of silence, then laughter, then mad scram-bling. One night they were making so much noise that Ives knocked on his son's door to see what was going on. When his boy opened the door, his face was flushed as if he had been getting too much sun. Like a detective Ives saw that the window shade's lower rim was crumpled up, and so he moved the shade aside just in time to see that young woman rolling a nylon up her shapely leg. Otherwise she was wearing only a pair of skimpy black panties. She had a large and shapely bot-tom and pendulous breasts, which she covered with talcum powder and stuffed into an elaborate too-tight brassiere, her state of undress thrilling, even for Ives in his fatherly guise.

He ended up giving them a lecture about respecting people's privacy and writing the lady a discreet note, and although she must have known what she was doing in the first place, she kept her window curtains closed from then on. And Robert? Trembling, he later approached his father, as Ives sat by his drawing board, saying, "It wasn't my idea, Pop. I swear it."

"Well, even if it was, it's natural to want to look at a pretty woman." Then he added, "Temptation's a difficult thing in life, with anybody, and sometimes more so with priests. You know that, yes?"

"Yes."

And he was about to say, "So, if you ever want to change your mind . . ." but told his son, patting him on the back, "Well, you do whatever you have to do."

He returned to work. Above his drawing board on the wall, he kept a small crucifix, and could not avoid the image of Christ's body on the Cross: the musculature of the legs, the tensed arms, the tormented chest, the downturned head, sculpted in metal. For a moment, Ives imagined the actual body of Christ and wondered what He would have made of the woman in the courtyard window. Would He have been thrilled by the sight of that woman's alluring body? Would He have felt a momentary queasiness in the belly, or lingered for a moment, as his son and his friends—as Ives himself— had done?

"BUT HE'S YOUR ONLY SON"

Walking back from the park the day he had been told of his son's decision about the priesthood, he went upstairs to his apartment. His head aching, he drank a glass of whiskey with water and took a couple of aspirins, a twisting feeling shooting through his stomach when he realized his son was serious about his vocation. Two whiskeys and Ives almost started to feel better. Then he decided to watch some television, with its unpleasant war news, and—just like that—a quickly consuming bout of stomach cramps came over him. Washing up, he decided to visit with Ramirez.

When Ives walked in, a little beside himself, Ramirez was having an early dinner with some of his wife's relatives, whom he had helped to bring out of Cuba at great expense during the past several years, and who were staying with him. The apartment, meant for about five or six people, had twelve living there, nearly all the rooms ringing out with activity. (*A family*, Ives would think!) In that jovial, somewhat chaotic, atmosphere, Ramirez' relatives had gotten to know Ives from his occasional visits, and always made him feel welcome. His visits were always greeted with inquiries about job prospects, as Ives, knowing the difficulty of their situations as Cuban refugees, had promised to look into his connections. The year before, Ives had gotten one of Carmen's cousins, Manny, a job driving a truck for one of the printing outfits the agency used. And he had helped to arrange a summer internship for two of the younger men, Jose and Miguel, putting up advertisements in Long Island railroad stations. These gestures were appreciated—Carmen's great-aunt, an ancient Cuban lady, who slunk about the apartment with a cane and a pagoda-shaped shock of white hair, always took Ives by the arms and held him in the dark hallway, regaling him with their appreciation of his good deeds, saying that God would bless him in heaven. Then he would end up in the kitchen, where his plate would be heaped with food, even if he had already eaten.

Ives always liked it over there, as it reminded him of happy times when he and his father used to visit Dominguez' house in Staten Island. But on that afternoon he was maudlin and only grew more so, sitting with Ramirez, when, having explained his mood, he heard Ramirez' main objection: "But he's your only son. And once they have him, they'll never let him go. They'll control him and he'll never be the same." He heard his son's godfather declaring this again and again. Ives nodded, wondering if that was so. Finally, the evening took an odd turn when Ramirez proposed that they call a certain woman to bed down the boy ("You would not believe what she can do for a man," he confided), so that he would know for sure whether to choose the spirit over the flesh.

A FEW REFLECTIONS ON GOODNESS

Sometimes he thought of God as the father on the throne in heaven, the ever-powerful deity, a great Hercules stretching across the sky, as Michelangelo had depicted Him on the Sistine Chapel ceiling, which they had seen during their trip to Rome, or alternately like one of William Blake's wizened spirits, with a long flowing beard and fiery eyes. And there had been times when he thought that *Dios* looked like a forlorn figure by El Greco, a Lazarus newly awakened from the tomb and forced to look through saddened eyes again at the world.

Once, when his son was only five or six and they were sitting on a beach by Lake Sebago, watching the water, Robert had asked him what God looked like. It was that time of day when the changing light and wind had made the water choppy and mysterious, when the silt had risen like clouds of dark milk from the lake bed to just below the surface. In those moments, when Ives told Robert, "God is a spirit," he imagined Him as a vaporous goodness inside people's being.

His strongest feelings about Him, it seemed, came about on Sundays, when, at around eleven, all the church bells in the neighborhood rang. On his way to High Mass with his family, he always felt as though they were partaking in a special ceremony, like a royal wedding or a pharaonic rite out of ancient Egypt. In the good weather a crowd always gathered on the church steps, the ladies in their bright dresses and white gloves, their light blue and pink and white hats with bird pins and veils; the men in suits; a special occasion, the marriage of the spirit to the flesh, Ives would later think in those dramatic moments when, closing his eyes, he knelt by the communion rail and awaited the Eucharist.

God's most common form? The goodness and piety of others.

Ives had seen a kind of piety in the faces of Jewish scholars in their long black coats and squat hats, dressed like undertakers or gun slingers from the old West or like Amish farmers. They were always coming in and out of the high doors of the Jewish Theological Seminary on Broadway, like secret agents, their valises filled, as Ives imagined, with sacred scrolls and ancient writings about the propagation of good, not evil, in the world.

One afternoon, when he had slipped out of the office into Iskanders for a late snack, at around four o'clock, he had been surprised to see the Turkish owner, a certain Mr. Barokas, down on his knees, in the narrow foyer between the dining room and kitchen of his small restaurant, kneeling in worship on a prayer carpet, praying furiously, the word *Allah* repeated dozens of times.

Of course, there were the pious priests and nuns, but, among the Christians, no one had more impressed Ives, through their own goodness, than some of the black congregationalists walking along Broadway on the way to their churches. The serenity, the blissful sense of faith, that he saw on their faces was not the evidence of a wrathful nor vindictive God—though many of these people, from what Ives knew of history, would have had good reason to believe in one—but a kind and loving deity. When Ives formed a mental picture of their God, He resembled the nineteenth-century engravings of a great African king from the time of Solomon and Sheba, a deity who would rather laugh than destroy the world. . . .

His mind would drift to Italy and the several weeks the family spent going here and there, to Florence and Siena and Assisi, down to Tivoli and little hillside towns, where time had seemed to dissolve, and it was a joy to take long and quiet walks in the countryside. It was Easter, on the cusp of poppy season, and wisteria and almond blossoms and morning mists ruled the world. There had been innumerable pleasant moments and exchanges, mainly with the people of the small towns, wonderful meals for next to nothing, long carriage rides through the gardens of the Villa Borghese, and lost afternoons in Trastevere visiting every kind of shop, when they loaded up on Christmas presents for the next year.

And visits to churches and churches and churches.

On that occasion, during Holy Week, Father Tom, transplanted from the Bronx and studying advanced Latin at the Gregorian University, had told them about a tenth-century church in Trastevere where some of the most devout Catholics in Rome gathered on Wednesday evenings for services that would "tear one's heart out," as he had put it. So they went, and no sooner had they entered its candlelit gloom than Ives did feel the presence of early Christian spirits. That night worshipers took turns giving testimony to their faith and strong belief in Him before the congregation. They wept, beat their chests, they lay stretched out on their bellies on the floor, praying. Others crawled on their knees, hands folded in prayer, toward the altar, their shadows thrown high against the vaulted walls. Chanting in Latin, their eyes wide open, they seemed to be seeing something—the presence of Jesus or the Mother or the Holy Spirit—that Ives could not.

But he had noticed that Robert's face had taken on their expression of insight and submission; tears had come to his son's eyes as if he were kneeling before the actual Cross. What was it that his son, then ten years old, had asked him later that night when they were walking back to their *pensione*?

"Do you think that if you die just after receiving communion you will absolutely go to heaven?"

"Yes. Without a doubt."

And his son gravely nodded, then smiled.

There were the activities of Holy Week in Rome, Holy Thursday at Saint John Lateran, Stations of the Cross on

Good Friday evening, held on the *viale* outside the cavernous, floodlit Colosseum, Easter Sunday at the Vatican. There had been that morning in Saint John's, when, through a mist of frankincense, a procession of skullcapped cardinals in scarlet robes, and priests and altar boys carrying elaborate candles and antique bronze crosses swept in toward the sacristy. And among them, as a choir sang and an organ shook the floors, *Il Papa*, John XXIII, blessed the crowd and, touching the heads of the faithful, laid his palm upon his son's brow.

Ives, standing beside him, with his arm around Robert's shoulder, felt a surge of inexplicable energy rushing through him. . . . The goodness of God? he had wondered.

THE SYNCHRONIZATION OF CLOCKS

Now, one of the things he had picked up here and there was a bit of information from a building engineer, about the synchronization of clocks, as it occurred in just about every single office-building in Manhattan, from the Empire State Building to the Chrysler, to the building in which Ives worked. He told Ives about a signal that was electronically transmitted from a central command unit located in Rockefeller Center. At a quarter to the hour, the minute hands, whether slow or fast, were magically readjusted. Some afternoons, while waiting for an elevator down, Ives would point this out to a distracted and rather bored young secretary, more concerned with love or her waistline, Ives saying: "Look, even though the clock says twelve-forty, it's wrong, but just watch, any second a signal will make the minute hand go forward."

And even the bored secretaries sort of looked up, intrigued, their eyebrows rising when, indeed, the minute hand sprang to its proper time, almost miraculously.

He was on his way out for lunch one afternoon in early December, and had pointed this out to a certain Miss Feingold when the elevator arrived with a *ding*. Ives, tipping his hat, ushered the young Miss Feingold inside. Smiling civilly at each other, they were waiting for the car to move when a buzzer went off and the elevator suddenly lurched upward, shooting toward the roof.

"Oh, Christ," she said, rolling her eyes. "What's wrong with this thing?"

And though they pushed all kinds of buttons, the elevator continued to rise without stopping, each floor upward marked by scraping noises and buzzes and *dings*. As they were just reaching the penultimate floor, the twenty-eighth, a smell of burning wire seeped from the control board, the lights went out, and instead of continuing its ascent, the car hung suspended, then something let go, it dropped some five or six stories, and, lurching, jammed to a stop.

"Oh, Christ. Oh, God," she said, wrapping her arms around Ives, and quietly weeping. "What are we going to do?"

There were fumes in the car, and as he and this young woman started crying out with calls of "Help!" he felt almost embarrassed.

Then he took a lighter out of his coat pocket and, guided by its flame, got on his tiptoes. With a kind of mercury shooting through his bones, he found some screws in a ceiling hatch, which opened to more darkness. Still it helped to let in some air. And while it was impractical—and dangerous—to climb out, they were momentarily heartened by the voices above, snippets of a conversation about a "control" key and a "jimmy" to get the doors open. Then the man in charge said two things that were something of a comfort: "Hey, down there. We're coming, you hear?" And: "Yeah, Tommy, don't forget the fuckin' ladder."

They waited in the dark together, neither saying for several moments what each thought: that when the elevator was falling, they might have been killed.

"Well," he told her, "I'll be happy when we're out of here."

"Me too, I thought my heart was going to pop out of my chest. Did you feel that too?"

"Yes, I did." He crossed himself.

"Could you light my cigarette? I'm so nervous I can't find my matches." Her hand was shaking when Ives used his lighter again, the car interior bright with a wick's blue flame. She inhaled, sucking, and then dropped the cigarette on the floor. And she laughed, and let out a deep breath. "Forget the cigarette. Oh, God, I can't wait to get outta here." She sighed. "Where were you going anyway before this happened?"

"You know, I can't even remember." Then: "Actually I was planning to walk up Fifth and get a little Christmas shopping done. I'm thinking about getting my wife a nice coat—you know that furrier up on Forty-sixth? Gardner's?"

Odd thing, talking to someone in nearly complete darkness, a shaft, gloomy as a grave, above them; the two waiting silently, hopeful when they heard tools clanking.

In his coat pocket, Ives had a book of Spanish grammar, his plan having been to walk to the furrier's and, time permitting, to head over to Horn & Hardart's for a quick bite and a few minutes of study.

In the elevator's darkness, Ives, aware of Miss Feingold's presence, felt something out of the ordinary happening inside him, what he did not know, but in that moment, Ives had the impression that the interior of the elevator had somehow expanded, that Miss Feingold, not a yard away from him, was, in a sense, a million miles away. He felt as if he were floating alone and lost in the middle of a treacherous and dark place. Devoid of God. Trying to understand his feelings, and barely aware that Miss Feingold was speaking to him, Ives was making a journey, within himself, so to speak, to where he did not know.

He remembered a time long ago when he was a kid of fourteen and nearly drowned out at Coney Island. It had come down to this: Harry had been riding him all day about the fact that he was a lousy swimmer and had dared him to swim out to the horizon. After all, the water was dense with people, and there must have been a dozen lifeguards to save him, if he got into trouble. He hadn't wanted to go out, and stood in the shallow water, watching Harry, with his long and muscular arms, adept in baseball and boxing, rising in wide arcs over the cresting waves, and, on an impulse, had bounded further into the murky, pissy sea. At first he stayed on his toes, then floated around—people were surrounding him, it was almost impossible to avoid them—and because he was feeling kind of relaxed he decided to float on his back, and closed his eyes before the majestic light of the sun. Then, just like that, he had slipped off into a kind of sleep; when he next opened his eyes he was much further out. Suddenly, when he tried to stand and found the water too deep, and waves began to slap his head, and he could not see the shore, he began to lose his composure, with his hands flailing the surface wildly about him, his thin body twisting as if that would somehow lift him out of the water. The harder he fought, the more he tensed. Then his lungs constricted, his body seemed weighted by lead, and he began to swallow water and drown.

In the falling elevator, he recalled how stupid and hopeless he had felt that day at the beach, and in his supposed last moments, though the sun loomed through a late-summer haze like a god, he had no thoughts of comfort, and simply wanted to be saved. If the truth be told, he cried for all his faith, doubting there would be another life ahead of him. . . .

And when he had been pulled out by lifeguards and brought back to shore, he walked dazed on the burning sand through the crowds, feeling both relieved and ashamed of himself. With that it occurred to him that, for all his posturing, his faith was false, at least in those moments when it should have really counted, because when the elevator had started to fall, he had only experienced fear, and something else—he had wanted to grab Miss Feingold's breasts.

Whatever, in those moments, his faith seemed nothing more than a construct, that he had merely learned to mimic the spirit and mannerisms of his truly devout father, that deep down inside he was nothing more than a fake, an actor, a sense of worthlessness coming over his foundling soul . . . and though he did not feel this all the time, he regarded such feelings as one of his little secrets.

REASSURANCE

And just like that, through the elevator exit hatch came a beam of light—the service workers having pried open the doors—and with it, the base of a wooden ladder, its rubber "shoes" thumping against the roof. A burly man climbed down and was followed by another, who carried a stepladder; shortly they heard a voice: "Just be careful coming up now." Soon enough they were up on the twenty-first floor (one of the service workers catching a satisfying glimpse of Miss Feingold's shapely legs and the slightest intimation of her lacy, plumply filled undergarment as she climbed).

Miss Feingold then became the center of one service worker's attention—not the boss, not the fellow who had shined the flashlight up her legs, but a rather handsome, low-keyed fellow, who had pleased Miss Feingold with a simple line, "Statistically, it'll never happen to you again."

With a smile that slayed Miss Feingold, the handsome fellow was in the process of asking her out for a beer, when Mr. Ives, still floating on a sea of inward sensations, happened to notice that the building clock, whose hands now read one-fifteen, had become oddly aglow with a kind of benevolent, supernatural light. Then he looked around: the nine or so people gathered on that floor—service personnel and curious office workers—seemed to be radiating what Ives could only define as goodness, as if they were angels, sent to reassure him during a crucial moment of doubt. Though another elevator was waiting, Miss Feingold wanted to walk down the stairs, and Ives, off in his own journey, placidly agreed to go along. In the building lobby, smelling sweetly of a large decorated fir, Miss Feingold gave Mr. Ives a peck on his right cheek and went off with the handsome fellow to have a beer and hamburger down the street. As she disappeared out through the lobby's revolving doors, she told Ives, "Thank you so much for being so calm about things. Jeezus, I was scared." And then cheerfully, "See you around."

ON MADISON AND FORTY-FIRST STREET

Buying a chocolate bar in the lobby, Ives stepped out through the revolving doors into the street: the sky was a clean wintry blue—the blue of deeply processed magazine ads, the blue of poster art for seaside vacations in Hawaii and Havana, a blue that, reminiscent of water, seemed dense and inviting, a blue of light diffused through crystal. It was bitterly cold, the temperature way below freezing, thanks to some northeasterly winds that had come down from Canada, he remembered, cold enough so that clouds of steam billowed out of the manholes of the street and oozed out of the very pavement. But a good and clear day, all the same, in fact so clear that Ives had the surprising impression that his slightly myopic vision, never one hundred percent—he disliked wearing glasses—had suddenly improved to a remarkable degree. He had eaten about half of the chocolate bar and was savoring its aftertaste when several of his fellow workers came out of the building, and while he nodded in his usual friendly manner, he could not even begin to entertain the idea of a conversation with them. When Tilly, the receptionist, saw Ives standing by himself, and asked, "Mr. Ives, you feel like taking a walk?" he could barely bring himself to answer. "Maybe tomorrow."

And she walked on.

Then something else unusual happened: walking down the street toward the impossibly crowded avenue, and standing shoulder to shoulder amid a throng of shoppers on the corner, Ives was waiting for the light to change, when he blinked his eyes and, in a moment of pure clarity that he would always remember, began to feel *euphoric,* all the world's góodness, as it were, spinning around him.

At the same time, he began to feel certain physical sensations: the sidewalk under him lifting ever so slightly, and the avenue, dense with holiday traffic, fluttering like an immense carpet, and growing wider and stretching onward as if it would continue to do so forever, an ever-expanding river of life. And the skyscrapers that lined Madison Avenue—beginning with the Young & Rubicam building just across the street, with its streams of employees rushing in and out of its revolving doors—began to waver, the buildings bowing as if to recognize Ives, bending as if the physical world were a grand joke. And in those moments he could feel the very life in the concɪete below him, the ground humming—pipes and tangles of cables and wires beneath him, endless ticking, moving, animated objects. Why, it was as if he could hear molecules grinding, light shifting here and there, the vibrancy of things and spirit everywhere.

In one slip of a second, anything seemed possible—had the moon risen and started to sing, had pyramids appeared over the Chrysler building weeping, Ives would have been no more surprised.

Then, not knowing whether to shout from ecstasy or fear, he looked up and saw the sun, glowing red and many times its normal size, looming over the avenue, a pink and then flaring yellow corona bursting from it. And then, in all directions the very sky filled with four rushing, swirling winds, each defined by a different-colored powder like strange Asian spices: one was cardinal red, one the color of saffron, another gray like mothwing, the last a brilliant violet, and these came from four directions, spinning like a great pinwheel over Madison Avenue and Forty-first Street. Leaning back, nearly falling, Ives was on the verge of running for his life when, just like that, a great calm returned, the sun receding, the blue sky utterly tranquil. The traffic light clicked on and the light changed, traffic and commerce resuming as usual.

*   *   *

As a cop in a helmeted, visored, vaguely medieval-looking rain suit directed traffic, waving pedestrians into the street, Ives's fear left him and he began to experience a thorough love for all things. In the glow of such feelings people truly seemed blessed; truck and car horns sounded like heavenly trumpets, the murmur of the crowds and all the other voices fell upon his ears like music; the enormous visage of a dapper-looking fellow smoking a cigarette in an advertisement on the side of a bus seemed like some evidence of the absolute. Then there were the swirls of green wire and Christmas lights, those that tipped over and bubbled, those whose glowing filaments pirouetted like ballerinas, those whose collars resembled cherry necklaces—those lights, entangled or cleverly strung, adorning store windows, twinkling with benevolence, and, it seemed to Ives, nearly breathing, like everything else in the world.

Catching his own reflection in a window, Ives, nonde-script in an overcoat, hat, and scarf, judged himself a most pleasant-looking, perhaps saintly, fellow. His face like a sphinx's in one moment, the next like Saint Paul's, as it might have been when he was stricken with a divine light. With a renewed appreciation he considered the mechanisms of his own body, the littlest turn of his artistic hands, the twitch of nose, all splendid. To hear, to smell, to see, to feel, all were miraculous.

It was on Forty-ninth and Fifth that Ives saw an old woman struggling down a stairway to a subway station, and he stopped to help her along. He was whistling and seemed so cheerful that the old woman said, "My, you really do enjoy this holiday, don't you?" and Ives said, "Yes, I do, very much, but you see, ma'am, it's just not this time of the year; you see, ma'am, I've just had the most unusual kind of experience, though it's not anything I can really explain, except to say that about half an hour ago I had a vision of God's presence in the world. And it still makes me feel joy." Then: "Well, good luck to you, ma'am. And Merry Christmas."

The woman, leaning forward on a cane, moved slowly through the turnstile, Ives a little hurt by her expression, which, as he read it, seemed to say that he was a very nice man, but one who was not playing with a full deck of cards.

An afternoon spent keeping things in. A vision was a vision, he supposed, not understanding why it had happened to him. It wasn't his nature to talk about such things. When he got back to the office, around three-thirty, and someone asked, "How was your lunch?" he smiled, shrugged, and said, "Fine, thanks." Someone, having heard from the doorman about Ives getting stuck in the elevator, had told everyone in the office, so that many a person came by to chat about it, only to find him sitting behind his drawing board, hands folded on his lap, a puzzled and troubled expression upon his face.

He tried to call Annie at home, but she wasn't there. Then, attempting to work and finding that he could not concentrate, he made his way out of the office, even though it was only four o'clock.

Heading uptown on foot, he decided to visit Saint Patrick's Cathedral, beginning to tremble the moment he approached its doors. Visiting the church on that afternoon seemed oddly difficult. Too many supernatural forces seemed to be swarming everywhere around him, and though he found himself doting, as he always had, over the benevolent images of Christ and the Holy Mother—particularly of the crèche—he began to feel a slight weariness and apprehension, partly harking back to his natural disposition, and partly due to a question that he had started to ask himself: "If I had a vision, then why did it not seem Christian?"

Like Saint Paul struck by a heavenly beam of light, or Teresa de Avila with her vision of the celestial mansions of God, or Constantine with his fiery cross in the sky?

Telling no one about the experience, not even his wife, after six months he wrote Father Tom, and the Jesuit wrote back recommending that Ives read certain books by Meister Eckhart, Saint John of the Cross, and Søren Kierkegaard, which Ives found impenetrable; thereafter he continued to keep it to himself. Though he seemed very much the same, prone to bouts of melancholy as always, and worked as conscientiously as ever, his first year after that event was torturous. As much as he tried to dismiss it, not a day had gone by when he did not have a powerful memory of the experience. Other recollections fell down a deep hole while the four powdery winds circled his brain like taunting apparitions.

At the time he had written it off to the fact that he had been overly agitated by his near elevator crash or that he had been so fatigued by overwork that his imagination had gone wild. And yet with each passing day, as much as he tried, his memory remained vivid.

He did not let it affect his life at home, especially with Annie. That very night mysterious things had happened. With the children asleep, they had opened a bottle of pink champagne that Ives had been given by someone in the office and, having decided to call in sick the next day, he and Annie decided to romp around in bed, the door sealed with towels and T-shirts to keep the noise from reaching the children, making love like newlyweds on the honeymoon they never had. After carousing for some time, she made the observation that he had seemed more self-assured, that his concentration was splendid; indeed, he made love to her that night as if he thought he were about to die and wanted to leave her with a wondrous and everlasting impression. Early in the morning, when Annie was sleeping, he could not begin to fathom a connection between his physical virility and what had happened. He decided it was the champagne and the fact that they had not made love for some time. And yet, at three in the morning, he found himself unable to resist another foray, and his wife found herself sleepily devoured.

He had endured a year of nearly sleepless nights, his restlessness getting to the point where Annie would send him off to the living room. There he would spend the rest of the night fiddling about the drawing board or just listening to the street noises. Now and then, a few hours before he had to go to work, he would close his eyes, only to have all kinds of spooky notions come to him. He had thought a lot about death, not so much his own, but of others. His thoughts were about his father, or older brothers, whose caskets he had helped to carry during their funerals in Brooklyn, and about the afterlife they had faced when their souls were whisked out of their mortal bodies. He had once been supremely convinced that in death one would enter a new world as intricate, elaborate, as mysterious and pleasing, as the embroidery of an altar mantle. The Garden of Eden— some kind of version of it—would be reentered. A perpetual childhood, lived in peace and with all the comforts of eternal love everywhere. Even orphans and foundlings would be welcome—or especially welcomed. And the good of the earth, as Ives had been told again and again and again, would be rewarded. But on those nights, while staying awake, imagining such an afterlife had become nearly impossible, sometimes, for all his initial elation, Ives came to believe that what he had seen—or imagined—was a picture of a bleak, otherworldly future.

Not one to read books on spiritual subjects, on out-of-body experiences, reincarnation, spiritualism, or mysticism, witchcraft or voodoo, Ives was left confounded by the strangeness of his vision. He sighed, wishing that he had seen the Virgin Mother floating over Forty-first Street and Madison Avenue instead. Somehow, in his mind, it all related to his ideas of afterlife. He would think of all the depictions of Christ on the Cross, his tortured eyes looking upward, heaven just beyond, and wonder, to his horror, just what Christ might have been seeing. What if he had looked up and seen the whirling center of a chaotic universe swallowing him up? He felt disappointed that he had neither the education nor intelligence to fathom what had happened to him. On some of those nights, he had concluded that death would not be a joyous ramble with ethereal and eternally pleasant angelic beings, but a chaotic, mysterious, and dark experience, as if a soul, in leaving the body, would alight upon the surface of Jupiter or Mars or some other mysterious planet, such as he had read about in *Astonishing Stories* magazine, or in the science-fiction books whose covers he had upon occasion illustrated.

Lost in a kind of delirium and frightened by the prospect of an eternal afterlife in such a world, Ives would begin to doze, and finally asleep, or nearly so, soon let out a shout, waking everyone in the small apartment.

EVEN AFTER HIS SON DIED HE HAD THOUGHT ABOUT IT

Whatever had happened, it reinforced his feelings that a God existed . . . and yet? Weighing the possible meaning of what he had experienced that Christmas season, he believed that he had been privy to the inner workings of God. He was not crazy and had not come easily to that conclusion, his route having been circuitous and riddled with doubts and terrifying thoughts. (Like the batty Irish lady on his street who spoke to garbage cans and sometimes lifted up her skirt to strangers, revealing her nakedness underneath and pointing down, saying, "Be praised for thee can worship the queen called Cleopatra!" or that Negro man he sometimes saw wandering dazed by the river, wearing a cardboard pyramid on his head and shouting at passersby, "Every one of you dead, dead, dead!" Or the priest, Father Smithee, whom he sometimes saw getting drunk in the bar, on those nights when he would stop by for a sandwich after work, the cleric explaining to those who would listen about the apparition of the Holy Mother who appeared to him at night, weeping tears of blood, because men had cruelly disregarded the words of her Son, Jesus. And what about the rich Argentine at the Biltmore Men's Bar? After downing several martinis, this otherwise sophisticated-seeming gentleman, sitting at the far end of the bar, moved down to tell Ives and Ramirez that just a few hours before, while walking across the Sheep Meadow in Central Park, he had witnessed the descent of a scarlet-hubcap-shaped flying saucer and that when it landed, not thirty meters from him, its door opened, its occupants, a pack of ordinary hounds. Or for that matter, what of the handsome drunk who worked as a messenger and, dressing dapperly, told the ladies in the office that he was the film actor James Mason? As he thought about madness, Ives, a long-time resident of New York, remembered other examples, all of which will not be mentioned here.) Articles on hypersensitivity, religious visions, and the spiritual suddenly appealed to him. And he began to attend lectures, held in New York City and sponsored by reincarnationist, spiritist, and psychic societies, and took Robert along. They would go as a kind of lark, Robert loving to do anything with his father. And yet even though Ives told his son that he got a kick out of hearing those crazy different theories, and rolling his eyes and looking askance at these proceedings, part of him took them dead seriously, no matter how outlandish the topic. He would listen to different lectures on the astral plane, past lives, love in the hereafter, spirit music, spiritual masters, and holy men, much of what he heard during these sessions, like the individuals involved, striking him as so much air. And yet from time to time someone would say something that would make the hairs on the back of his neck rise, tales about reincarnation, past identities, and their influence upon the spiritual life in the present. Terms he had never heard of, like *karma,* at a meeting of the Theosophical Society on East Seventy-second Street, nearly made the very Catholic Ives wonder if, somewhere in his ancestral past, or pasts, he might have had some far-eastern mystical blood in him. Did he not have an unusual vision?

He always thought about the last of these lectures, which he attended in the spirit of "fun" with Robert; it was given by a certain Indian writer, A. I. Explixa, whose pamphlet *The Mystical Experience Explained* Ives had found at a newsstand and read one evening after work. One paragraph that seemed to speak especially to him he had marked off in pencil. It said: "To commune with the divine, with the unseen, which is only an extension of what all people call reality, is to experience the world ashimmer. . . . One feels like a pebble at the bottom of a stream of rushing water, awaiting not just the warmth of the sun, but the very hand of God to seek it out through the current. And although that hand may well never come, which is not the point, the very anticipation of that possibility leaves one breathless and makes it seem as if life is without boundary and time eternal."

That pamphlet was resting on his lap the night he and Robert attended the lecture by its author, the two sitting in the back of an auditorium of an Upper East Side school. The auditorium was full, the crowd largely female, divided into two general groups—rather affluent elderly women who may have had a real craving for an insight into the next world, and much younger, sharp-looking women, college students for the most part, Ives concluded. Among the men present, many seemed rather cerebral, like professors; others seemed ill-at-ease or overly amused. All hushed and then gave a smattering of applause as someone from the Center for Spiritual Development, named Blaine Thomas, introduced the "master."

Wearing an Indian dhoti, his forehead anointed with a red dot, bald, slight, with a bony face, deep-set eyes the size of peas, his body skeletal, his feet in velvet slippers, he sat on a hard wooden chair, at center stage, tucking his legs under him in a yogic manner. Then, applause dying down, he called for a moment of meditation, and, speaking as if a wad of cotton had been placed just above his front teeth, he began.

"First of all, I must tell you that my name is not truly A. I. Explixa, but I use it because I one night dreamed of it, the voices of my subconscious mind instructing me to use this name, a way of telling me that the vanity of a name does not matter. My real name is Ranjit Gunanand, and for the time when I lived in England as a young man I had been called Raymond Gunan, but my dreams have led to Explixa, a name whose letters I saw being written on a wall."

Then in a serene and kindly voice, he sought to tell something of himself, for those who did not know his work. He told of how he had been the son of a wealthy banker in Bombay and that he had studied in London and Paris before the Second World War, living a life of pleasures and much disappointment. Driven to despair, he had wanted to take his own life, having little belief and respect for the spiritual aspects of his existence, disdaining, for example, the idea of reincarnation. He planned his suicide to take place in the very bed in which he had been born.

And yet, though he had gotten hold of a pistol and was about to pull the trigger, he noticed a dove sitting on his windowsill watching him with the most compassionate and tearful eyes. In that small moment, that simple act had made him falter, and when he had looked again he saw the Hindu god Krishna, "radiant and magnificent," standing before him: and even though he had never been a seeker or teacher of men, he had decided to henceforth give over his life, trying to understand the "un-understandable."

Then Explixa spoke of "existing outside of time." Each moment, as he saw it, one died only to be reincarnated again. With each "little death," one moved inexorably toward the eternal peace of a Supreme Death.

Later a woman who described herself as a "pragmatic Catholic" stood up and spoke of visiting the amphitheater of Ephesus, Turkey, where Saint Paul had once preached, and of being lulled into a kind of "glorious waking dream" because she was certain that his spirit was still a powerful presence there. (She went on to say that the oddest thing happened to her: she saw herself—or her "double"—as a little girl, walking hand in hand with an Italian tourist. "I felt twice lifted through time that day. Once to the time of Saint Paul, the other to when I was four.") Another, a gangly youthful looking man dressed in a business suit, who had walked into the hall with a pronounced limp, told of how, as an infantryman, lying badly wounded on a snowy hillside in Korea, he had experienced the visitation of a "being"—"an angel or, in any case, a manifestation of benevolence"—that had told him, in all his fear, "You will not die." Another man spoke of trekking in the foothills of the Himalayas and experiencing an overwhelming sense of "God" everywhere around him. ("Yes," Explixa said, nodding, "the mountains are permanent and remind us of how temporary and insignificant we are.")

A young married couple, students at the Union Theological Seminary in Manhattan, asked Mr. Explixa if, to his mind, religious manifestations were cultural entities—say, the sense that Jesus Christ was present, as opposed to the Buddha, and Mr. Explixa answered: "Yes and no. Yes, if these figures draw us further toward the wondrous. No, if all we are looking for are familiar apparitions to calm us in our fears."

Then, and this perked Ives' interest: "The question we must ask of ourselves is how we can learn to see that which will allow us entry. That state of mind, closer to God, becomes us. That is all."

What he next said remained forever with Ives: "Some men seek enlightenment, others not, but find it in any case. . . . In some the divine is present, a thimble's worth, in others, it is like a sea. . . . Buddha, the Christ, the prophet Mohammed—in other words, the great mystics—are but receptacles for the grace and wisdom of the Eternal Principle: 'God flows through all of us, to some degree'. . . a Mystery. His is a presence that is only an intimation of what stands outside of time and yet makes it possible."

He remembered how, afterward, he and Robert had

caught a bus uptown and stopped off at a pizzeria on 122nd Street and Amsterdam, picking up two pizzas to go, and that, while walking up the long hill toward Broadway, the moon lingered over the rooftops, watching them.

"You ever see anything weird, Pop? Anything mysterious ever happen to you?"

(He would have liked to tell his son how each time he walked along the street on a clear day he vividly remembered his mystical experience. He had wanted to explain how a sensation of impending glory came over him, and how for a few moments he became aware of a God that was like no God he had previously conceived. But when he thought about his son's clear-cut, lucid faith and the sheer abundance of physical evidence of His existence around them, he felt humbled and decided to keep his experience to himself.)

"Well, I've had dreams. That's about it. Sometimes I'll see an angel or just dream about floating through the sky."

"Yeah, me too," his son said. "But you know I've had lots of dreams about seeing Jesus."

His father nodded.

"And in the dream he always seems to be waiting for me."

Then they were silent. They walked up a stretch of the block, across the way from the projects, a nerve-racking experience, even with a guard in a booth, because people were always getting held up, sometimes stabbed on that street. They had reached Broadway when Robert added: "You know, sometimes I think about what it would be like to be dead. All I know is that He will be waiting. It scared me for a long time, but you know what, Pop? It doesn't anymore."

He said that with great self-assurance, a tone of wisdom, and with certainty, as if, Ives would later think, he had already known.

Christmas 1967

THE TREE PARTY

It was a Tuesday evening, the week before Christmas 1967, and Mr. Ives and his children had come back from Amsterdam Avenue and 119th Street, where the local kids sold trees outside a stationery store called "Jack's." As in previous years, Ives bought a balsam fir, its spectacular forest smell and pagan benevolence filling not just the living room but all the rooms of the apartment, called by the local kids a "house" (as in "You going to your house, Tommy?"). They put up a large wreath on the front door, smaller wreaths and strings of lights in the windows, blinking at all the other windows with their wreaths and lights, even those windows from which came loud, raucous, and tinny Latin music at night.

Earlier in the day Ives had walked over from the office to Ninth Avenue during lunchtime, to buy boxes of Italian cold cuts and pastries, and these were set out on a table as a buffet. Around eight some friends came over: Arnie, a bachelor grocery counterman, whom they felt sorry for; their down-the-hall neighbors, the Chevaliers, a Haitian family; and one of Annie's schoolteacher friends, a nice lady named Esther, past forty and unmarried, whom they hoped to fix up with Arnie. Then there were some of the neighborhood kids, friends of their children, who, each year, came to devour the first-rate food and to help decorate the tree. Finally, the bell would ring again, and Ramirez and his wife and kids would be at the door with boxes of pastries and several bottles of Spanish wine or chilled nickel-refund bottles of Rheingold beer, dark brown glass sweating. Ives would put some Perry Como or Bing Crosby on the big RCA console with the twenty-one-inch black-and-white TV, radio, and phonograph that his boss had given him as an extra-special bonus one year, and the tree-decorating party would begin, the adults chatting on the couch, eating, everyone smoking cigarettes and watching the kids at work.

They decorated the tree with sets of blue, red, yellow, and

green lights that resembled medicine droppers or dragonflies, bubbles undulating through their shifting liquid centers; the kind of lights whose wires often overheated and started many a fire in tenement apartments all over the city. They put up strings of lights with angel sconces and holly-colored beads. There were ornaments from the closet, snow-sprayed and clumped with strands of last year's tinsel clinging to them. Several were holdovers from Ives' Brooklyn childhood, battered, flaking, and chipped, but royally old and precious (along with different pieces of a crèche set) and some had come from Annie's home. And there were the ornaments Ives and Annie bought in antique shops and street markets, and some ceramic *putti* that they had found in a small shop off La Via di Penitenza, near the Vatican, on a rainy afternoon in Rome, during their trip to Italy years before.

Now, Ives watched one year turning into another and had already begun to miss Robert's and Caroline's childhood, perhaps more than they did themselves. As he sat on the couch with his adult friends, half listening while Ramirez spoke about the changes that had taken place in Cuba, to which he'd hoped to one day retire, Ives became ever more nostalgic. Not so long ago his children were infants and he and Annie had lived to make their Christmases happy. He recalled his pleasures at giving his children just what they wanted at Christmas, *nearly* spoiling them, and nearly so because even though he would have done anything to make them happy, he and Annie had seen to it that they earned their way in the world. Robert had passed many of the mornings of his youth, before going off to school, delivering newspapers or working for a neighborhood laundry service, watching the shop while the boss made his runs. In the late afternoons when he was not studying, he often went to work in a pharmacy on Broadway. Odd jobs here and there, and his duties as a student, altar boy, and choir tenor, had kept him felicitously busy. And Caroline helped an old woman in the building, Mrs. Myers, to keep her apartment clean, occasionally baby-sat and worked behind the counter of Party Cake bakery. She was all of thirteen.

But he made it a point of telling his son, "Never take your good looks or coloring as something better." Although many of his son's classmates at Corpus and later high school were black and Spanish-speaking kids, Ives went a step further and encouraged his quiet son to join a Harlem baseball league. For several years Robert had the distinction of being the only white boy, playing left field, on a softball team called the Harlem Ravens, which made it into third and fourth place in the city two years running. He eventually had to quit because he was always getting jumped and coming home covered with bruises and with other injuries, about which he never complained but which broke his parents' hearts and tested Ives' convictions.

That evening passed festively enough. The tree had been decorated with great aplomb and by ten-thirty everyone had left and the children were in bed. Buoyed by the companionship of his friends and family, Ives had consumed a few more drinks than usual. In the dark of the living room, with only the tree lights on and Bach playing on the hi-fi, Ives and Annie had remained on the couch, relaxing. He would remember certain things about that gathering. That Arnie had seemed jittery about Esther, but had gotten along well with her anyway; that Ramirez and Carmen had been in especially good spirits. Ramirez had talked about one day opening a restaurant in midtown, serving good Cuban cuisine, and he had told Ives that he had better save his money and could count on becoming a partner. He would recall being ever aware of Pablo's interest in Caroline, as they sat in a corner talking quietly about the Beatles, and how later they stood before the bookcases where Pablo noticed the addition of several Robert Louis Stevenson novels and *The Plumed Serpent* by D. H. Lawrence. That his son and daughter had kissed him goodnight. Before leaving for his bedroom, Robert had, in his sunny way, reminded them that he had choir practice scheduled at the Church of the Ascension the next day at four.

"We'll be singing from a program of Praetorious and Bach," he said.

At around eleven that night, a predicted snowfall had come. He and Annie looked out about midnight before pulling the plug on the tree lights and going to bed, and mutually agreed how peaceful and clean the streets of New York seemed in such weather.

THINGS WERE NOT WELL WITH THE BOSS

The next day, Ives was in the office by eight-forty-five, the last business meeting of the year before the Christmas holidays, with various art directors and executives, scheduled for half past nine. Afterward there would be a company luncheon, and then the office would close for a pleasantly long weekend at three, and the parties, held here and there at different agencies and suppliers, would begin. There was always work to be done, but aside from the billing and accounting departments, the agency had in effect closed down a few days before. Gifts—bottles of booze, boxes of candies, and other items—circulated around, the high point coming when Mr. Mannis himself, jovial and friendly, made the rounds, robustly shook each employee's hand, and gave out the Christmas bonus, which usually consisted of two or three weeks' pay. His employees were used to seeing a virile and handsome man in his midfifties, but this year, his manner was rather downcast and despondent, an intense sorrow about him, even when he, a thoughtful employer, tried to seem cheerful, given the holiday. A few months before, his nineteen-year-old son had lost both his legs in Saigon, and since then he had been in a mood that would later mirror Ives' own. His boy would die in transport on his way to Australia.

Mannis had given out the bonuses early that morning,

and when he had come into Ives' office, he dallied for a moment over some of the pamphlets Ives had picked up at a spiritist lecture. One of them, entitled *Will There Be a Tomorrow?* with its cover of a soul in flight through the cosmos, seemed to have intrigued Mr. Mannis, and when Ives asked, "Would you like to take that with you?" he told him, "Thank you, Ed. Do you mind?"

And he'd tapped Ives' shoulder thoughtfully and, maintaining his composure, had marched out of the office, shoulders back, chest out, a look of devastation upon his face.

TEACHING HIGH SCHOOL

Just as the agency meeting was beginning, Annie MacGuire was standing in the front of a public high school classroom in Upper Manhattan. She had agreed to help out a friend by substituting for her that morning, and although she usually had a strong sense of control about these kinds of situations, this particular group of kids were about as badly behaved as any she had ever encountered. She walked in with a copy of Dylan Thomas' *A Child's Christmas in Wales,* which, given the season, she thought might be appropriate to read aloud. But no sooner had she introduced herself and begun than a shouting match between two students over a pack of cigarettes started, each calling the other a motherfucker and a liar. Just a few years before she would have interceded. She had friends, female teachers, who'd been spit at, had been "flashed," had their teeth knocked out by students they'd tried to discipline, had cigarette butts put out in their hair, friends who had been raped under stairwells. She herself had watched a young man expose himself and slap the table to draw attention to himself, had seen young girls making out wildly, and had once shouted at a young woman busily masturbating her male friend in the back of a class. The very worst jobs always started out badly, with the kids smoking and carrying on and throwing things around, spitting at each other and exuding such menace that she'd wish she were a man, or teaching in some distant and beautiful place that perhaps only existed in her mind, a quaint country school in England in 1904.

She sometimes gave a talk about what hard work would get someone, and the kids either responded by clapping or they shouted insults, the most common being, "Oh yeah, if education is so good for you, than what are you doing here?" Because to some of them being *there* was the worst thing in the world. And sometimes the kids laughed at her and cursed, or they stared at her blankly and she'd realized that many of them did not speak or understand English.

Honor classes were her favorite, because faced with attentive students she could give talks about writers like Lawrence or Charles Dickens, the latter a favorite of hers to teach. She would point out to the poorest kids that not all writers were upper-class fops, as was their impression. Dickens came from humble stock, as did Lawrence. She would tell them about how Charles Dickens had the greatest sympathy for the poor because he had known suffering himself: his father had gone to the poorhouse and died young, and he himself had worked as a kid in a "blacking house," the deprivations of that time something he would never forget. Dickens, she said, had lived for his fame and wrote out of a need for acceptance, but he had also deeply believed that a man's life's work might bring about social change.

She liked to talk about the circumstances of his most famous story, *A Christmas Carol*. Dickens was in the habit of taking very long walks through the city of London at night, she would say, and had seen so many poor children working in sweatshops and starving in the streets that he had been moved to write a story about a rich man who has a change of heart toward the poor. And if she had the time, she would read parts of it aloud, and always reiterated that tale's moral: *There can be no greater reward than goodness to your fellow man.*

"He had a kind heart," she said to one class in East Harlem. "He believed that only a heartless society would leave its unfortunate poor to its sad fortune."

And a kid with a coy expression raised his hand and asked: "And what country did this man live in?"

Later, there had been an afternoon assembly and the special speaker had been the writer Piri Thomas, the heart of whose message to the kids had been, "It's cool to hang out, but there comes a point when if you want to get out of the barrio you can't hang out on the stoop anymore," advice met mainly by jeers and boos. She'd remembered that the next morning, while discussing his talk with a different class, her defense of Piri Thomas' sentiment was met with derision. As she thought of her own high ideals, their reaction had brought her to tears: she left the classroom and had fled into the faculty ladies' room, where she stood over a sink crying her eyes out for half an hour, until she realized why she had taken it so hard: something in the expressions of those students reminded her of her own brothers and other members of her family who used to laugh and give her a hard time just because she wanted to escape a world of ignorance. It struck her just then that there was no escape, with or without a Dickens or a Piri Thomas in the world, that ignorance just went on and on and on.

THE NATURE OF THOSE PARTIES

Some years it was Le Pavillon or the Chambord or the Waldorf-Astoria or the Oyster Bar in Grand Central or Keens Chophouse or the Biltmore Men's Bar, but that December the agency held its Christmas party-luncheon at a Cattleman steak house on Lexington Avenue. By two-thirty in the afternoon a number of employees, who had earlier stormed the open bar and drunk champagne and wine with the buffet lunch as they toasted the coming holiday, were hanging around a cocktail pianist, arms locked around each other's waists like college protesters, swaying, smoking cigarettes, drinking, and singing Christmas carols.

Packed in that room, a dense crowd of employees and invited friends and associates; among them Mr. Ives, who spent much of his time talking with one of the account execs, a certain Mr. Freeman, with whom he went back many years, a ruddy-faced, red-haired old-time advertising man, who dressed like a college professor in tweed suits and red-dotted bow ties. Ever civil, they mainly talked about their familes, and tended toward great silences while taking in the proceedings with amused expressions.

Ives and Freeman were two of the more respectable higher-ups. "Family men," whom the slightly looped secretaries tended to praise to death at these parties, for their gentlemanly natures and fidelity to their wives. With thirty-nine years at the agency between them (seventeen for Ives and twenty-two for Freeman, who had started at the agency just after graduating from Yale in 1945), they, in their forties, represented something of the composed and more refined "old guard." Over the years they had been privy to the not-so-private craziness induced by too much holiday drinking. One could go hopping from party to party, drinking all day, if one liked. Many did. For the young unmarried—and married— wolves, who lurked about, Christmas drinking afforded the the best opportunity to whisk a young "lamb" off to bed. The previous year one of the secretaries, drinking too much, had been goaded by a crowd, men and women, into taking off her clothes. She had stripped down to her brassiere and begun to expose one of her large moon-shaped breasts, when Ives, feeling morally indignant, marched over and, like an angry, concerned father, pulled her down from the table, saying: "Come on, child, you don't know what you're doing." And to the others he'd chided, "My God, are you crazy?" At that same gathering, a young Italian secretary, who was engaged to be married in the New Year, fell momentarily in love with a handsome account executive from Y & R, and hid away for hours in a corner drinking stingers and kissing him. Afterward, she went off with him to a bar, and that was all, until, three days later, she woke up naked on a beach in Puerto Rico, without a memory of how she had gotten there.

Forty-five years old, Ives was considered well into midcareer, and was already thinking about retiring in another ten years or so; there was a grind about the job that was slowly wearing him down, even if he no longer put in the kind of hours he had when he was in his late twenties and early thirties. That is, he had "spent" a certain amount of his ambition and drive for the agency, proving himself, and now, as with others like Freeman, he'd hoped to eventually reap the benefits: buy a vacation home in the country, travel, paint, look after his children. And grandchildren if Caroline married and started her own family.

Proud of what he had done to change the company, as with the Spanish division, he now mainly supervised and okayed artwork to which he could not particularly relate, his bluepenciled initials and corrections appearing in the margins of work produced by the newer, younger artists, who were in touch with the latest fashions. Ives, in his middle age, had spied the sixties from afar, and while he knew about the Beatles and Carnaby Street and Andy Warhol from magazines and the news and *The Ed Sullivan Show,* in his mind what advertising should look and feel like still had to do with the emerging postwar America of the Eisenhower years. While his own style of illustration went by the wayside, a new kind of "free-form" creativity started to show up in advertising art—a style that Ives could not, nor wanted to, adopt. As too conservative an artist to offer anything fresh, Ives might have had reason to fear for his job had Mannis been a different kind of employer. From his office, he watched the company slowly change. They'd even hired several young black college graduates as account reps and there was a buzz regarding the possible hiring of a woman to run promotion. Those were changes that he liked, but, just the same, Ives had moments in the office when the sense that he had wasted himself creatively would come over him, and he would feel nostalgia for his younger days, when he had fantasies about the creative life. On the other hand, he was not Michelangelo and knew it, and would feel a kind of inward gratitude toward his own resources and toward God, and had already started to daydream about other options—syndicated comic strips, children's books, and perhaps paintings themselves.

He refused to give in, to become something that he was not, like those garment-district executives who were his age and older and had grown their hair long and had taken to wearing Nehru jackets and love beads (Ives thought, to convince themselves that they were younger or to get young women). He still wore suits or blazers and put on a tie and a hat, got his hair cut once every two weeks at Juanito's on 123rd and Broadway, caring less what the young hip executives in the office thought, as if a fashion statement, a uniform, could really define an identity or inward soul.

That year he and Freeman talked about how the kids were doing. He had two boys in college and a third about to graduate from high school the coming spring, all red-haired and freckle-faced. Once they were all out of the house he was going to buy a place down in Palm Beach, where he hoped to live the life of a gentleman. Ives told him, a fellow Catholic, the news that his son had decided to attend a seminary.

"Are you happy about that?" Freeman had asked.

"Yes, how could I not be?"

While standing there they were aware, and sadly so, of certain absences. Not of the young cocky, job-hopping execs who barely stayed a year and left, or some of the old-timers like Mr. Palluci, a big-billboard man who had retired, nor of the secretaries or file clerks who came and went, pleasantly enough, but of several executives, one of them not yet forty, a certain Mr. Gianni. He had run the television division and was so tense that just standing next to him one could feel his aggravations. He had died during a lunchtime indoor tennis match at the New York Racquet Club in Grand Central Terminal, a few months before. There had been Saul Zimmerman, another art director, who seemed particularly obsessed about reading the *New York Times* obituaries with his morning coffee, and each Christmas always commented, "My God, I can't believe how quickly all this time is going." He had died from cancer that past spring, not yet fifty-two.

They toasted those departed friends and their fellow workers who had good fortune. Like a certain Mr. Shinn, who had won five thousand dollars earlier that year in New York State's first "scratch away" lottery, or Miss Feingold, now Mrs. Mallon, down from Coop City in the Bronx to show off her twin three-year-old daughters, telling them, when she introduced Mr. Ives, "See, this is the man Mommy was stuck in the elevator with." They greeted one of the mafia printers, who wore four diamond rings on his hand and told everybody, *"Buona festa!"* And there was the oldest employee at the agency, a Mr. Myers from the mailroom, going on about some past glory. (He'd started out with another agency as a messenger back in the late 1920s and had a memory for odd New York events, like walking down Madison Avenue making a delivery the morning that a B-25 bomber collided with the Empire State Building.)

Eventually one of the senior vice presidents, Mr. Crane, Mannis' right-hand man, gave a speech on the boss's behalf; Mr. Mannis, his spirits low, had left the office shortly after noon and was preparing to go off to London with his wife that evening to spend a week in the chilling English cold, catching East End theater shows. In any event, through Mr. Crane he thanked his employees and wished them the best for the coming year. Then a raffle was held, many small gifts handed out by an actor playing Santa Claus, the grand prize a week in the Virgin Islands. Gradually the crowd started to drift off, to attend other affairs, or to go home, or to meet up, as Ives did with Annie, with their spouses. She arrived shortly after three, so that they could get in some shopping.

So, Ives would remember, he and Annie had dallied at the office party just long enough for her to wolf down a quick plate of food, to say hello to some of his fellow employees, before heading downtown along Fifth Avenue. They passed the remainder of the afternoon making their way through crowds and going in and out of department stores, before ending up in Macy's.

Roaming through the aisles, Ives had picked up some half-dozen ties and wallets for certain male friends, a scarf for his brother, and a nice French hat for his sister Kate. That year he had decided on buying Robert a good watch and prevailed upon an overwhelmed saleswoman to pull some twenty watches out of a case, before he settled on a black-banded gold Hamilton with Roman numerals, suitable, Ives had thought, for a young man headed to a seminary.

Finished with their shopping and on their way out, Ives had asked one of the old security guards if a certain Mr. Frankie happened to be around. For three years, from 1938 to 1941, Ives had worked alongside him each Christmas season, painting backdrops and helping to set up mechanical displays in Macy's windows. As it happened, they found Mr. Frankie on the Sixth Avenue side of the store, in a cluttered workshop off one of the hidden stockrooms, trying to repair a female automaton. A slender and slight man with delicate features and the smallest hands, Mr. Frankie seemed nearly doll-like himself. His hair, dyed to a nearly golden color and rippling like the sea, appeared stiff, as if from lacquer; seeing him, Ives remembered that even on the windiest nights Mr. Frankie's hair never moved. Of a rather coquettish demeanor, as was typical of window dressers and display artists, and with a perpetual tan, Mr. Frankie behaved around Ives as would a beloved eccentric uncle, wrapping his arms around him and giving Ives a kiss on the neck.

Putting aside his work, he sat his guests down, made

them hot rum toddies, before filling them in on the events of his recent life. Ives would remember feeling especially amused and a little confounded by him that evening: while Ives himself had aged more than twenty years since they last worked together in 1947, Mr. Frankie, ever delicate and small, in a light blue V-neck cashmere sweater, white trousers, and violet scarf around his neck, seemed not to have aged a single hour.

A MALAISE

Earlier Caroline and her brother had gone to a Sam Goody's in their mother and father's old neighborhood, to Christmas shop. Afterward, they took the subway back, and while Robert went to his choir practice at four, Caroline had gotten off at 116th Street. But instead of going home to Claremont, she had met a friend and they had taken a bus down to Eighty-fifth Street and walked over to Central Park West to a boy's apartment. His name was Kirk and he was a fifteen-year-old prep-school kid who acted as if he had lost his virginity; he had long hair, bangs that fell over his brow, and a chiseled pretty-boy face, with high cheekbones, clear blue eyes, dimpled chin, the kind poor kids love to smash up, and he was tall and a sharp dresser. His father was a professor at Columbia, and she had met him at a square dance over at the Horace Mann School on 120th Street one Sunday afternoon. She had gone there at the suggestion of a friend, who thought she might get an idea of what hipper, more refined, and worldly boys were like. That translated into English as non-poor, non-working-class boys. At that dance he noticed the way that Caroline, smitten by his appearance, had looked at him, and thinking her older, as she rarely smiled, he had called her friend and invited them over for some "fun."

His parents were not at home, and he and his friend set up a table with Coca-Cola and rum and ice and potato chips. Because he had talked to Caroline long enough to ascertain that she liked groups like the Beatles and the Zombies, as opposed to groups like the Rolling Stones, he put these albums on a turntable, offered her hand-rolled cigarettes made out of tobacco, and then held out a pipe filled with burning marijuana. She took a few puffs, coughed, and rolled back onto the couch, feeling slightly nauseated: when she got up and looked in a mirror she thought she had never seen anything so funny or ugly or homely in her life. Then she dallied in a corner for a long time before joining the party again. She was wearing a brown skirt and brown turtleneck sweater with a black belt, high black boots, fishnet stockings, and a Portuguese mariner's cap, made popular by the folksingers she had seen walking on the streets during her excursions with her father and brother to the bookshops of Greenwich Village.

They had gotten there about a quarter to five, and she had to be home at seven. But when she checked the time again it was twenty to the hour. That's when Kirk brought out a paper bag and filled it with the contents of a thirty-cent tube of DuPont model glue. Burying his nose in the opening, he suddenly flew back as if someone had smacked him in the head with a two-by-four, laughing wildly. Then he gave her a whiff and she found herself circling overhead, her thoughts whipping along, propelled by the chemicals, the feeling of strangeness multiplying when he clicked off the light and lit a candle, and then brought her out of that dark blue and black atmosphere into reality. She opened her eyes and realized that he had his hand up her skirt and that the crawling sensations inside her were caused by the clumsy groping of several of his fingers, and while one part of her seemed interested and flattered and excited, another part of her disliked every last bit of what was happening. And she would remember how, at about seven-fifteen or so, as she had stood up and pulled down her skirt and looked for the light, a sensation of utter and complete sadness abruptly rushed into her, lingering there and then suddenly vanishing.

Thinking that it had to do with sinning, she quickly made

her way out of that apartment, leaving her friend behind, rushing across Columbus Avenue to catch an Amsterdam bus uptown, her stomach and heart in knots. Happy and relieved to be getting home, she was mainly concerned that her father might have started to worry about her. She leaned her face against the window and noticed a battery of police cars and ambulances around 107th Street, their red lights flashing, building façades flickering on and off like neon signs, and she hoped that nothing bad had happened. Her thoughts focused instead on how she had been stupid and allowed herself to get carried away by a handsome face, and that the marijuana had not sat well with her, that the glue had a depressing aftereffect, even if it had been exciting to embark upon an adventure.

ON CLAREMONT

Leaving Macy's, they spent an hour walking uptown and lingered by the Rockefeller Center ice-skating rink, on the promenade, directly across from the bronze statue of Prometheus reclining, the great tree, a Maine pine, some fifty feet high and as wide as a house, covered with thousands of lights, towering cheerfully over the scene. Down below, a hundred skaters, of all ages, circled the ice, some gracefully as professionals, others clumsily, their faces and twisting bodies in colored caps and suits, vivid in the surrounding floodlights. Leaning against the railing, Annie and Ives were caught up, as were so many others, by the romance of the setting, and, ever so happy, held each other tightly, nudging one another with their chilled noses and stealing kisses, until laughing, she said, "Oh, Eddie, you make me feel like a kid again."

As they happily walked to the subway, they were looking forward to spending a lot of time together at home during the holiday, in the company of family and friends. Ives and Annie had stopped to peer into a window display of French linen when, just like that, a terrible darkness entered them, and they could not move and stood looking at one another stupidly, on the crowded and busy sidewalk.

NOT ENOUGH WINE OR SCOTCH

They were in one of those states that come from having had enough to drink but not enough to ward off an early hangover, and as they made their way from the 116th Street station toward Claremont, Ives began to suffer from a headache and was thinking that he would have a nice glass of scotch at home and take a couple of aspirins. Maybe they would order takeout from the Chinese joint on 124th, or go to the local bar, Malloy's, whose big sign he himself had designed and painted, where they had good tap beer and hamburgers rated among the best in the city, Ives in the mood for its unsavory atmosphere every so often. But as Ives and Annie passed 120th Street and were approaching their building, they could see people milling about in front of their stoop—dozens of their neighbors, among them Ramirez and his son, who came solemnly toward them, Ramirez' face a mask of grief. Two police cars were parked in front. The first thing Ives thought was that something had happened to Caroline: she was getting strong-headed lately and might have gone off to the park by herself, which he had warned her about a hundred times, but soon he saw her on the stoop, her head buried against Carmen Ramirez' arms. And then he saw Mr. Ramirez' stony face, eyes wide open: with Ives' forearm in his grip, he squeezed it more tightly than it had ever been squeezed before, and he said: *"Hermano."* And shortly, as Annie stood atop the steps with her daughter, shopping bags by her side, Ives found himself walking between two plainclothes police officers. Ramirez followed behind them and got into the front seat of an unmarked police car, sitting beside one of the officers. Then, leaving Caroline with Mrs. Ramirez, Annie got into the back beside her husband.

As the automobile pulled away from the curb, another green-and-white police car followed. Ives and Annie did not say a word and just watched the streets and lights flashing by as they made their way along Tiemann to 123rd, and then uptown again. A train pulled into the elevated station and his wife, nestling her head against his shoulder, sighed. He noticed that in a first-floor window on Broadway a family had put up a lovely display of the Holy Mother posed in a Christmas setting, with a wreath of red and pink and light blue electric lights blinking crazily around her, and that she was flanked by two oversized electric candles, which gave off a tremendous pink light, the kind of gaudy but pleasing display one generally found in the poorer parts of the city.

Then the cop behind the wheel offered each a cigarette, and Ives said rather matter-of-factly, "No thanks, but that brand is one of my company's biggest advertisers."

In the back of that police car, he remembered a four-color ad he had drawn one Christmas, about 1954–1955, for a toy company: in it, a young sleepy-eyed boy, newly awakened on Christmas morning, stands before a richly decorated tree, gasping with delight over an electric train set, an illustration he had based on his son. The boy looked just like Robert, and Ives could see him crawling around the floor of their old apartment on Fiftieth Street and exploring the lowest boughs of the Christmas tree, strands of tinsel, lights and ornaments glowing like majestic stars above him; his son reaching up, his son's fine lips slightly parted, heavy-lidded eyes wide.

And then Ives blinked and found himself standing on the sidewalk beside his wife, across the street from the Church of the Ascension. On the pavement, just by his feet, was a large piece of canvas, and under it a body, stretched out. Then the officer lifted off the canvas and shined a flashlight onto the face to reveal the shocked and bewildered expression of his son.

WHAT A COP HANDED IVES

One of the kids would say that Robert had showed up in generally good spirits around a quarter after four, a little late, and that they joked about the prospect of getting hired to record the theme song to a cartoon show about outer-space hounds from Japan in the new year, work that Ives had gotten them through a connection; that he walked in with a Sam Goody's shopping bag as well as another bag filled with different items, mainly paperback books. Dressed too lightly for the cool day, he had worn a long black-hooded raincoat and a cap that he didn't like because it messed up his fine dark hair, brown penny loafers and galoshes, a Cardinal Spellman High School senior ring. During the break he sat around with a couple of his friends in the choir room, showing them the 33rpm records he had bought as Christmas presents that afternoon, about fifteen albums in all.

The records were in a Sam Goody's shopping bag, which a police officer had retrieved from the scene. He handed it over to Mr. Ives, saying, "I guess these were his." In his shock Ives stood under a street lamp going over his son's purchases: he'd bought albums by Thelonius Monk, Art Blakey, and the Jazz Messengers, and John Coltrane for his mother; a Dixieland recording and a Nonesuch anthology of Gregorian chant for his father. There were recordings by the Dave Clark Five, the Young Rascals, and the Beatles for Caroline. A Temptations record for an old pal, Richie, a Golden Oldies anthology for Pablo. He had bought a recording of the Goldberg Variations by Bach for his choirmaster at Corpus, and a Mass by Palestrina for his choirmaster at Ascension. He had bought Perry Como and Rosemary Clooney albums for his Aunt Kate.

GOD HAS CALLED HIM TO HEAVEN

His murderer took ten dollars from the other boy and walked over to Amsterdam Avenue, not one hundred yards away, calmly hailed a gypsy cab, and went up to 136th Street and Broadway, to a block that once was largely Irish but that had become, over the past few years, mainly Puerto Rican and black. When a five-hundred-dollar reward for any information regarding the crime was offered, the taxi driver, a Dominican who had not liked the boy's arrogance, decided to call the cops. He told them where he had picked up the kid, where he had dropped him off, and how, incidentally, he had been stiffed on his two-dollar fare. The boy was a mulatto, about five feet seven inches in height, solidly built, maybe 180 pounds, with a short haircut, mustache, about fourteen to fifteen years old. He was wearing a striped turtleneck sweater, an army jacket with a 1st Cavalry patch sewn onto the shoulder, and a woolen cap. The cops found him the next day.

He was so arrogant and cocksure that he had not bothered to hide or even to change his clothing and, in fact, had been bragging to his friends in the neighborhood about having popped "a rich white boy," and showed off his .22-caliber pistol, which he carried around in a paper bag and occasionally fired at night, leaving holes in apartment-house windows. Even though many a street below 125th Street was filled with tenements and junkies, he had the fantasy that rich people lived around there. The proximity of Columbia University gave that neighborhood, which had more than its share of problems, the allure, in his mind, of Park Avenue, even when some strips, say Amsterdam Avenue, running from 120th all the way down to the Nineties were pretty much working class or poor. There were projects on 125th Street, stretching from Broadway way east of Madison Avenue, and a row of New York City high-rise projects on the east side of Amsterdam to about 123rd, where the neighborhood, turning left, headed into the center of Harlem.

The cops found him in his aunt's second-floor apartment, sitting on her plastic-covered living-room couch, reading *Thor, the Thunder God* and *Fantastic Four* comic books, which he bought with part of the ten dollars. With a shrug, and hardly any fight, he went off with the cops, who hauled him down to the 126th Street police station, where they stuck him in the juvenile pen, before taking him downtown to Centre Street for booking at night court, where he met his Legal Aid lawyer.

Because the shooting had taken place so close to Christmas and the victim was so pious, "a young man about to enter the seminary," reporters flocked to Claremont. Ives' telephone rang constantly. A photographer broke the faulty door lock in the entranceway and went upstairs to get a picture of whoever answered the door. Camping outside, television crews and newspaper reporters competed for tidbits of information. The kids and neighbors who knew the family said little to the press, aside from generalities, in an effort to respect a gentle father and the memory of his son.

And when it was learned that Ives had been involved in the community on behalf of poor children, and in particular those of Spanish-speaking descent, they made him out to be a saint who had been betrayed by the very kind of young person he had tried to help. Despite his suffering and pain, reporters hounded the poor man as he made his way to church or to the funeral parlor or just to the store.

In the newspapers, he read that his son's murderer was named Daniel Gomez. His mother was on welfare. He had two previous arrests for petty theft. He was an eighth-grade dropout, his father in jail. He had seven brothers and sisters and an extended family (even he, a family!). Ives read that Gomez' thirty-four-year-old mother wept uncontrollably at hearing the accusations and denied that her good son could have committed so heinous a crime. He noticed the word "heinous" again and again. At the time of the incident Gomez had just been to a movie on Ninety-sixth Street with his girlfriend and had been in a bad mood because of an argument about money. She was thirteen. He had bought the gun outside Alexander's department store on 152nd Street and Third Avenue a few months before for twenty dollars and was known in the neighborhood for bragging about how he was going to use it to get rich. A school report listed his IQ as average; some concern had been expressed by a Jewish social worker, who said the kid had blamed his problems in school on his principal, who was Jewish, and that he was convinced that all Jews were running the schools badly on purpose. Some neighbors said that he was basically a good boy, but others said he had been prone to violence since childhood. He had once tied an "ashcan" to a pigeon's neck and lit its fuse, laughing when the bird had been blown to pieces. He too also went to church and had just recently spent a morning shoveling snow for his parish, for free.

At fourteen he would be tried as a juvenile and, if convicted, he would be out on the streets in four years, tops. And what did Mr. Ives think of that? a journalist asked him. Ives, on his way down the street and feeling hounded, shrugged and said, "Please leave me alone."

But they managed to get a quote from one of the local priests, and this was used as a headline in two of the papers: GOD HAS CALLED HIM TO HEAVEN.

THE VISIBLE MAN

Walking down the street, Ives could not look into anyone's eyes very long without his inward pain bringing tears to his eyes. He found himself wearing sunglasses all the time, night and day, and oddly, despite the darkness of his spirit, he wore a large crucifix given him by Carmen Ramirez and let it hang on his chest, visible to all. He remembered sitting for hours inconsolably in his son's room the night after he had died. He'd sat there examining a Revell model of a man that his son had kept on a shelf, the outer plastic shell transparent, the organs inside visible. He remembered when his boy, then twelve and wondering if he might one day become a doctor, had asked him to buy that model kit for Christmas. And when that Christmas had passed, Ives would find his son lying on his stomach in the living room, with a biology textbook open before him, dipping a brush into one or another small jar of airplane-model paint, trying to capture accurately the colors of the organs. He saw the miniature liver, kidneys, stomach, intestines, and all the rest set into place, and thought about his son.

The heart had been cut, the femoral artery in his hip torn in two, the coroner had whispered.

He saw the skeleton, the gallbladder with its deep purple coloration and the heart and all the veins shooting upward like tree roots throughout the body; for a few moments he imagined Jesus Christ himself on the Cross, Jesus trembling, as his son must have trembled in his last moments. . . .

Glorious life ending. There must have been a moment when his son had gasped for air, the last time, as Jesus must have. But as Jesus had risen, he wanted his son to rise up, organs and spirit and mind intact, and everything to be as it had been not so long ago.

He sat there in his son's room thinking about the time when he had experienced the presence of God, *or of something,* on Madison Avenue, and for the life of him, he tried to imagine death as something transcendent and beautiful, as he had been taught to believe and had wanted to believe in those moments.

And now, he thought, his boy was dead, and even if he were to rise, to be reincarnated in some other form, their lives would not be the same. What was that little quotation from the New Testament that had once impressed him when he was a boy? A quotation he'd at one time always taken to heart, from I John 2:17: ". . . The world passeth away, and the lust thereof; but he that doeth the will of God abideth for ever." Was that so? Or was it that the world, their life, the familiar, the comfortable would not ever occur again?

Suddenly he began to feel a sorrowful nostalgia for the kind of afterlife that he had been raised to believe in, when he used to envision a pastoral setting in the clouds. People wore white robes and walked on a road that led to an eternal city where they could live in harmony with God and the good saints, in a state of perpetual love and comfort. . . . He thought of a book he had purchased a few years back, in his "searching" days after his "vision": something called *Human Personality and Its Survival of Bodily Death* by F. W. H. Myers, in which its author argued that all human beings, good and bad alike, had souls that existed into perpetuity, in an afterlife that he called an "eventuality," a kind of painless darkness. Memories and personalities would pass intact into eternity. And yet there was a flaw in that theory, as Ives saw it. There would be no God, no further development of the spirit, no change of being, just eternal recollections of what had once been, as if all memory and thoughts attained during a life were sent up invisibly into the night air, to exist in a godless, lightless afterlife, the image of which struck Ives as a kind of eternal death. Then he thought about his vision of the four swirling winds and interpreted them as an expression of supernatural folly and grew further depressed.

At a quarter to two in the morning, he allowed his face to slowly lower into the chalice of his hands, and he wept until he could not see.

THINGS WERE IN THE AIR

The wake lasted only a day and was held at an Amsterdam Avenue parlor, Kennedy's, not far from the church. Everyone from the neighborhood was there. The MacGuires came in from Long Island, Annie's three policeman brothers in their dress blues, with their shoulder cords and medals, sat in the back. Her father and mother and various cousins came and went throughout the day, but her brothers stayed, and going outside to smoke cigarettes, marched up and down the street in front of the parlor, Ives by their side, regarding all passersby, street drunks and junkies as well as decent citizens minding their own business, with contempt. A lot of strangers came with flowers, and so many prayer cards, rosaries, and crucifixes were left in Robert's coffin that every few hours a lady who worked for the parlor would come up to remove them. Young seminarians and many priests came by. A lot of neighborhood fellows came in around two in the afternoon, half drunk, paid their respects, and stood about the parlor entrance in thin-soled shoes shivering. Flowers arrived from New Jersey, where his friend Mr. Messmer lived. And he got a telephone call from Mr. Mannis in London; he had called during intermission of the theater where they were presenting *Stop the World I Want to Get Off,* with Anthony Newley. A number of Annie's teaching colleagues showed up or sent flowers, and about twenty-five people from the agency came, among them Mr. Freeman, who traveled on that soggy day with his wife and one of his sons from Chappaqua; Morty Silverman, Alvarez, Martinez, Dinnerstein, and Fuentes from the Spanish division of the company; many people from accounting; and secretaries from the sales department, some of whom came in from the Bronx and Queens.

Ives wore a blue suit and stood by the door, speaking with one of the parish priests and greeting, ever so quietly, people as they came in. But now and then he would look off toward the casket and turn his back on the people, as the darkest thoughts overwhelmed him, and he would have to compose himself again. Every so often Ramirez went up to him, took him by the arm, and whispered, "You are all right, my friend."

Annie and Caroline were in black. She was taking her brother's death badly. She spent much of that day sitting with her mother, holding her hand. Just a few days before he was shot one of Caroline's girlfriends had teased her about how she thought Robert kind of looked like one of the Beatles, Paul McCartney: "Too cute to be a priest." And now? There he lay, against a backdrop of flowers, a black rosary wrapped in his curled hands, and dozens of Mass cards for prayers to be said for his departed soul stuck in the silken creases by his side. Every so often, Ramirez' son, Pablo, came by to sit with her. He brought her a candy bar and he kept saying, "If you're hungry, let me know, okay?" At one point they took a walk over to Riverside Park, so that she could stretch her legs and get some air. They stood in the chill wind in a field of stark trees under a sullen sky, watching barges float by on the water, and because she was cold, he wrapped his arms around her and they kissed and held each other for a long time.

Ives' sister, Katherine, came to stay in the apartment and cooked their meals; Harry had flown in from San Diego with his third young pretty wife, and he dealt with the situation by giving Ives a check for a thousand dollars to help defray the costs, and said things like "Why you brought the kid up around here, in these times, is beyond me," again and again, a sentiment that Annie's family shared. In their opinion it seemed incomprehensible that decent people would even want to subject themselves to the noise and filth of the city, let alone expose themselves to the potential for violence.

Ives listened, and while a part of him thought these notions small-minded, another part of him blamed himself for not having brought his children up outside the city, as in Larchmont in Westchester, when he could have afforded it. In those moments, his liberal ideals were disturbed, and he found himself distressed that they had not moved years before. There had been that autumn day when he and Annie and the kids had taken a drive upstate and, getting lost, had found an old house that had been built in the 1920s, in the style called "Stockbroker Tudor," the kind that one saw in ads about happy families with wag-tailed dogs and gardens in the springtime and warm, homey parlors, bountiful tables, and stone fireplaces at Christmas, the kind of place that Ives had illustrated dozens of times—images from "another America" that he had somehow disregarded when it had come to his own family. It was situated on a beautiful piece of sloping land, near a decent small town and a train station, and, at the time, the property was being offered for a very good price. But Ives had decided against it because he did not want to leave the vitality of the neighborhood, or expose his children to the kind of well-intended but nevertheless narrow thinking of small towns, and because he had come to love the Puerto Ricans and Dominicans and Cubans who lived near them. But now his boy was dead.

During this time Ramirez and his wife had been invaluable and among the most respectful and sorrowful mourners. Juanito the barber came by with his family, as did Freddie Alvarez, owner of Freddie's Bodega, as had dozens of Spanish-speaking people from the neighborhood, like a certain lady of great dignity named Mireya, a nurse, who like many others said to Ives and Annie, "I'm really sorry that the boy who did it was Puerto Rican." And Ives would nod and then hear the same thing repeated, even while some of the Irish citizens of the neighborhood stood about by the doorway, figuring out ways to exact justice and revenge.

They buried his son on Christmas Eve morning, 1967, out in Long Island, his marker a simple Celtic cross. The burial was covered by the press, despite efforts to maintain privacy. A lot of important people came, few whom Ives knew. Zoom-lensed cameras captured the scene, and in an unfortunate gaffe, they published a picture of Celeste, Robert's former girlfriend, who had fallen apart and kept her distance from the family until the funeral, being held in Ives' arms, and identified her as his daughter. . . .

Later, because it was Christmas, Ives had somehow felt compelled to leave the nice watch he'd bought his son in the room, instead of returning it to the store. He put it in his top drawer, as if his boy would come in anytime now to claim it. That drawer was stuffed with school paraphernalia, prayer cards, baseball cards, playing cards, a *Felix the Cat* comic that Ives had illustrated himself, years before. And pamphlets, a dozen of them, from different seminaries, clipped together, one of them with the sun's rays extending outward in the shape of a cross, the title: *In God's Service*. On a shelf Robert had an edition of the *World Book Encyclopedia*, which he had bought when he was ten with his own money; an *Oxford Book of Saints*, his marker left on the page describing Saint Francis of Assisi. A row of books on sciences, a picture book of pretty flowers from Celeste. A paperback novel called *Invasion of the Star Creatures* and a book on ancient Egypt. He saw that in a row on the inside cover his son had drawn three symbols: that of an ankh ☥, chrismon ☧, and crucifix †, one leading to the next. In a bag he found a copy of *Fanny Hill*, which had one of his son's friend's names in the margin, certain pages marked off. It made him laugh. Then on Robert's desk, where each night he had worked by lamplight on his school-work—what "good" youngsters do—he found an edition of *A Christmas Carol*, which Annie had given him, opened to one of the middle chapters.

He went to church and prayed for guidance, begging God to bring forgiveness into his heart. He would kneel before the crèche, the crucifix, and wonder how and why all these things had happened. At night he would dream of black threads twisting in the air and slipping into his body from afar. Though he bowed his head and trembled at the funeral, though he spoke kindly with the priests and repeated to himself a thousand times that God was good and that the manifestations of evil that come to men are ultimately explicable in some divine way, His wisdom greater than what any of them would ever know, Ives felt a great numbness descending over him.

What did it feel like? He felt the way that young girl whom he and Annie had once seen falling through the air had felt. Expression tormented, he spent a long time before the mirror, reading into his own face great foolishness. He did not like to look back and recall the last days of that *other* Ives. He wanted to be drunk. He had nothing to say. Getting two weeks' sympathy leave from the agency, he spent much of that time pacing up and down the hall and standing by the windows. It meant despairing about the supernatural and yet waiting every night for a supernatural event.

Ives and Annie slept, entangled in each other's arms, their daughter sleeping alone. Ives would get up a half-dozen times a night to make sure that she was resting. And every so often he would push the door open, intending to turn the radio off, but would find himself standing silently over her, his heart breaking whenever he would think about how much Robert's death must have pained her. And he would sometimes move closer, and, brushing aside the hair that fell over her brow, plant a tender kiss on her forehead. He would hear her sigh. . . . You know what it was like? It was like drowning.

THERE WAS A PHOTOGRAPH

There was another photograph that ran in the newspapers, taken a few weeks after the funeral, when Ives met the Gomez family for the first time. This "meeting" was arranged by a priest, a Father Jimenez, a nearly Chinese-looking Puerto Rican man of about thirty, who turned up at Ives' door, black hat and New Testament in hand. "Perhaps the pain would be diminished if you met these people," the priest told him. "There's a lot of poison in the air: it would say something for you to go there."

And although Annie would have nothing to do with the boy's family, Ives, in the spirit of reconciliation, agreed to think about it.

A week passed and Ives, out of a notion of decency, and after going back and forth about it, called the priest.

"I'll go and see them," Ives said.

The Gomez family lived on 137th Street, in a tenement down the steep hill from City College. Ives had agreed under the condition that no one know, but when they turned up at around three one Sunday afternoon, there were photographers parked in a car across the street. The boy's grandmother, holding a rosary and with a mouthful of prayers, had been waiting on the stoop for them, and at the sight of Ives, with tears in her eyes, she begged for his forgiveness. Ives nodded and embraced her before going in.

As they walked up a stairway, they passed a window that opened onto a backyard filled with the residue of a recent snow, lumps of garbage, the hard edges of discarded boxes and bottles peeking out here and there. Then the apartment on the third floor: loud television from the living room, promptly turned off when the grandmother opened the door and shouted: "Angie, they're here. *Turn off the television!*"

A humble apartment, Ives thought, a poor family as the newspapers had said. And apparently very religious: he counted three crucifixes, one in the kitchen, one in the hall, one in the living room. Led inside, he was introduced to the boy's mother, Angie Gomez. She was an attractive woman with a bouffant hairdo, long earrings, heavy rouge on the cheeks and lipstick. High heels and tight slacks, a long rayon blouse and bracelets, as if she were getting ready for a party. Three of her other sons were in the room, and it seemed to Ives, as the introductions were made by the priest, that none of them wanted anything to do with what had happened. He had the impression that he had interrupted them as they watched a favorite movie on television. When Ives shook Mrs. Gomez' hand, she could barely manage to smile, and when her mother chided her about warming up a little bit for the *hombre simpático*, she suddenly exploded in one-hundred-words-a-minute Spanish, unaware that Ives could understand: "Don't tell me I'm being cold. You know that I didn't want to be here, but I'm doing this for you, mamá, but I don't think my son did shit, and if he did do something, I bet you he was provoked because he's not so stupid to do something like that out of the blue; and who is this man, anyway?"—these lines broken by an intermittent, nearly gracious smile. Ives sitting way out on the edge of the couch, with his hat in his hand, looked at the priest, wanting to go, and at the same time, wanting to make a point that his intentions were good.

"It's a sad thing that's happened," Ives softly said. "For all of us."

"Yes, we're so sorry about this," the grandmother said. And she started up about how they had tried to raise him in a correct manner, but with times being what they were, and with his father "away," there was only so much they could do. Ives nodded in sympathy.

Then the priest asked them to pray with him, to ask God to fill their hearts with forgiveness and understanding. But while they prayed Ives could not keep from looking at the woman, his eyes boring into her, because in this woman's scornful expression he read the story of her son's life: he had seen women like her many times on the street, young mothers who had gotten pregnant as teenagers, and hating it, dragged their kids along, slapping their faces, and saying, if the kids complained or gave them any kind of "lip" or cried, "You keep on, and I'll kick your ass, junior."

And it was as if she could read his mind. Suddenly, as if she herself had been accused of something, she broke off from the prayers and announced: "Look, everybody, I gotta go." And to Ives she said: "Mister, you really seem like a nice man, but I've got to tell you something. I feel really bad about what's happened to your son, but the fact is nobody knows who really did the shooting. You know how many kids walk around here with pistols? I feel really bad, but we don't owe you nothing, and we don't need this . . . this show, okay? I've already got two boys who've gone to jail and now they want to put this one away too, and you come here without nobody proving a goddamn thing. You know why he's in trouble? Because of this." And she slapped at her own skin. "Because he's dark and Puerto Rican. I know he didn't do it, and that will come out. The cops picked him up beause they had pressure to pick someone up. You know it, Father here knows it, everybody does. But I don't believe any of it and can tell you that just the fact you're here makes us look bad. It's a dishonor, so forgive me if I can't apologize for something that my son didn't do."

Then to her mother in Spanish, *"No me mires así,"* or "Don't give me that look." And she lit a cigarette, and threw on a coat, and left the living room. Her mother, a tenor of shame to her words, said, "Ai, these young kids today." And, "I mean it sincerely, Señor Ives, that I will pray for your son's soul every day. I am—we are—so sorry."

There was little else that he could do except to leave.

Taken earlier when Ives and the priest had first arrived, the photograph showed the grandmother wrapping her arms around Mr. Ives, their expressions sorrowful, intensely sympathetic, perhaps even understanding. The headline above the photograph: "Forgiveness?"

THE DREAM

The kid had been released on bond, as he awaited trial, and that bit of information continued to distress Ives even after he had met with his family. He was not a drinker, but after work Ives would stop by the Biltmore to see Ramirez and have a few double scotches and then, on his way home, stop at Malloy's and have a few more and remain until he could hardly keep his eyes open. Such was his pain, at his lowest point, that he would tend to dally longer with each passing evening. Spending those nights in the bar, by the pool table, or lingering before the bathroom mirror, or watching the young men playing the pinball machine, he would find himself in that bar at midnight, conversations dimmed and then growing louder, images blurred before him.

Early one morning, with his eyes half closed, he listened as the men, with their own kids to worry about, speculated about what they could do to punish his son's murderer. He was so exhausted that it all struck him, or would be remembered, as a bad dream.

"What do you think, Ives, should we or shouldn't we?"

"Should you what?"

"Pop him."

"What?"

"Mr. Ives, like we've just finished telling you, and it doesn't have to go beyond my door. If you want us to hire someone to kill the son of a bitch who killed your kid, we'll do it."

Addressing Ives was Mr. Malloy, the owner. He was a burly, affable enough man, known as a small-time gangster, whom Ives would see in church on Sundays with his devout wife—Ives never saw her in the bar. Mr. Malloy then leaned closer and said gently, "Let me explain . . ." And he told Ives about how they had started collecting money for the purpose of hiring someone to "take care of business." Then he reached behind the bar and brought up a tin shortbread box, which was filled with crumpled five- and ten-dollar bills. Ives held the box for a moment.

"Listen, Eddie," Malloy continued. "We got nothing against the Spanish. Guys like Ramirez are okay with us, but we don't want any of these people to think that they can fucking come over here and get away with murder. You know that if you go uptown into a Cuban or Puerto Rican neighborhood and try to pop someone, they'll kill you like that. . . ."

"The Cubans?" Ives asked.

"And the mafia's like that too," another voice added.

"So the question is, what do we do? Do we take care of business? Or do we forget about it until this kid pops someone else? Come on, Ives, can we do it?"

Ives looked around him and found himself in the center of a circle of snarling wolves' faces.

"Please, I beseech you . . . "

"Beseech?" someone said indignantly. "Are we in the f—ing Bible?"

"Please," Ives was saying. "In good conscience I can't condone it. No."

But a part of him really wanted to say "Yes."

"Look, it wouldn't cost much to do it. We could even hire another spic to do it." Then (with sensitivity, for his closeness to the community was well known), "Sorry."

The word was that for a thousand dollars they could have a professional from Brooklyn shoot Gomez, but times were such that they could hire a kid for three hundred dollars off the street, and if they looked around, they could probably find someone who cost two hundred, maybe even one-fifty. . . .

"Think about it, Eddie. The kid's walking free while your son is in the ground. Just say the word and his ass is grass."

Ives got home around two o'clock, didn't know how he got there, and woke up with his trousers and shoes still on. That day he had vague recollections of further arguments, voices coming back to him.

"What if he gets off and kills someone else?"

". . . And just remember he'll be free anyway when he's eighteen. You think he'll have straightened out by then? How many kids you know who do time come back like priests?"

"What about justice for your son?"

"It won't bring him back, but at least we'll save the tax-payers money. And believe me you'll feel better, we all will."

". . . Just remember, if you don't take care of business, no one else will. Do you really think God gives a shit?"

At work he thought about it. Had someone really made the offer, or had he been drunk or dreaming and imagined it?

INCIDENTALLY

The "bench" trial took place in the early spring of 1968 and attracted further publicity. The whole proceeding took about an hour, and the young man was convicted of second-degree manslaughter and sent up to the Spofford Detention Center in the Bronx, where he would remain until he turned eighteen. That morning Ives and Annie showed up in court, and their photographs were splashed all over the newspapers again. Sitting erect, a white purse on her lap, and not once turning her attention from the front of the courtroom, Annie gave an impression of stoicism and strength. As for Ives? Eyes red, his face gaunt, he seemed on the verge of weeping, and looked out at the courtroom with the weary expression of a man who had not slept well for months. He tried to sit still, but kept fidgeting. He wore a wool suit and regretted it, because the fabric was driving him nuts. He kept scratching himself. As he sat there, his knees ached from his many visits to church, where he had tried to understand the reasons why He had allowed his son's death. He had knelt so much that a terrible rash had erupted upon his kneecaps.

But that's not what Ives would mainly remember. There was a moment when the young man was being led away by a correction's officer, and he passed not three feet from where Ives and Annie were sitting. He was wearing a blue suit, white shirt, and blue tie. His thick and wavy black hair had been cut short, and despite the violence of his crime, and the setting, he could very well have been a young usher at a wedding. Ives was struck by his lack of expression, and by how young he seemed. He was a boy. And because of that, perhaps, Ives stood up and wanted him to look into his eyes, to see the pain that had become well known to others in the neighborhood. But the kid averted his eyes, and it so upset Ives that he tried to grab hold of the boy's arm as he was being led out by a guard, but could not reach him.

The kid would serve out a term of three years and seven months, and Ives' hair would turn white in the interim.

Was There a Moon?

In the years after the trial, with all its publicity, they responded to nearly every letter and query about their son, save those from pushy reporters. At the high point, during the weeks after the Christmas of 1967 and through the late spring of 1968, they received twenty or so letters a day. And although many were well intentioned in their anger and indignation, each time someone mentioned that their son had been killed, each time they read about it, and found another letter of commiseration or outrage, their son died a little more.

Even when Ives became visibly distressed at hearing about that murder, people, particularly his Spanish-speaking friends, brought it up anew every time they saw him. Of them all, Ramirez, the boy's godfather, was the most circumspect and had gone around asking for silence on the subject.

People also sent them gifts and money, which they turned over to the church. The most heartbreaking letters, many written in Spanish, conveyed stories as sad as their own and came from all over the country and occasionally from abroad. These were kept separately, Annie spending her evenings carefully answering them as best she could. She did not know what to say to a forty-year-old mother from Cleveland, Ohio, who had lost her husband in a fire. She did not know what to say to parents whose son had shot himself. Or to a mother whose two-year-old drowned in a one-foot-high tub in the yard. Or to a man whose wife had been killed by a falling brick, dropped off a roof on purpose, while she waited in her car for a light to change.

With so much correspondence to answer, on many an evening, when she might have otherwise been studying, she sat in their living room, at their secretary, chain-smoking Chesterfields, sipping wine, and listening to music as she composed her responses. That she did not know what to say in the face of tragedy greatly vexed her. She would write sympathetic notes of response in her impeccable script and enclose an illustrated prayer card that her husband had made up in the office: Christ giving his blessing. Finishing with her signature, she handed each to Ives, as he sat by his drawing board, so that he could sign the notes too. She was not certain that he read each one over, but had often watched his face sadden when, as if wincing, he would sign his name.

On those nights, they did not say very much to each other. Occasionally he would get up and ask her, "Would you like a drink?" Or "Should I open the window?" and she would often say, "Thank you, but I'll do it myself." There was not much she let him do for her, and although they would walk down the street holding hands and attended church with their daughter, and sometimes made public appearances together before school PTA meetings or gun-control rallies, they drifted slowly apart.

Now and then, when they were in bed at night, they made a kind of love. They would wrap themselves up in each other's body, arms and legs entwined, squeezing tight as if to force the pain out. But, most of the time, nothing sexually intimate occurred, and they learned to be content with kisses and hugs. She came to regard her own sleep as a kind of refuge from the world. Somehow the loss of their son had undermined the expression of their mutual devotion, as if it were impossible to make love with a ghost, *his* ghost, in their bedroom. Books that cautioned them not to blame each other for what had happened, and to realize that feelings of guilt were psychological rather than moral phenomena, appeared on their bedside table, and although Annie read them and encouraged her husband to do so, in those days nothing penetrated the expansiveness of their grief.

She did not particularly enjoy talking on the telephone, but began to spend hours making calls to friends, and even called her own family, to whom she didn't have much to say. They'd meant well, trying to persuade her to move the family out from Manhattan to Long Island, but their tactics of bombarding her with attacks against her husband and the neighborhood and those "other kinds" of people had only succeeded in making her feel worse and annoyed with them.

Otherwise, if the phone hadn't rung, or if they didn't have their daughter to cheer things up, or neighbors like Luis and Carmen or Arnie or Mrs. Malone to come by to pass the time, they would spend many a night without saying a word to each other.

During the first year after Robert's death, when Ives worked late and Caroline was in her room talking on the telephone with her friends, or else listening to her radio and doing her homework, Annie played the jazz recordings that her son had intended to give her for Christmas and agonized over the notion that he would never hear jazz again. They had planned to visit the Half-Note Club on Spring Street to hear Art Blakey the next time he was scheduled to perform after Christmas. On many a night, she had watched him sitting in a stuffed chair in the living room studying for school, his left hand holding up the book, the fingers of his right hand cascading frantically along the side of the chair in time to the music. He had known enough about music to follow the different improvisations and melodies in his head. And although he was not a pianist, he had learned to pick out certain tunes like Dave Brubeck's "Take Five" on their tinny upright.

The phonograph music would fill the living room, and she would find her head turning and digging deep into the easy-chair headrest in rhythm to the beat, as if she were a 1940s bobby-soxer, and she would daydream about the time when Robert had used their living room as a rehearsal studio for a kind of jazz group he put together with kids from the neighborhood. Some knew what they were doing, others didn't, and the neighbors knew it too. During those sessions he played a snare drum with brushes and foot-tapped a high hat and felt so honored, so formal about jazz, despite his ecclesiastical training, that he used to shine his penny loafers and put on a tie before playing.

His friends—Rocco, Dazi, Bruce, Tommy, Richie, Pete, Kevin, Willie—played trumpets, saxes, trombones, and guitars and made such an eccentric sound that one of the more famous local musicians, the guitarist Kenny Burrell, who lived on Tiemann Place—down from Claremont and just off La Salle—stood fascinated before the stoop one day, looking up with wonderment. Then, knowing the kids, Mr. Burrell went up to the apartment and, putting down a sack of groceries on the doghaired rug, showed them an easy arrangement of "Caravan" on an old F-holed Gretsch. After an hour of "manglement" they got it out right, and no one could have been happier than Robert, who had been unable to stop smiling for hours after his friends left. Later, with his tie loosened, he had held forth in the kitchen about the intricacies of jazz to his father, and when he went to bed he hugged his father and then kissed his mother three times on each side of her face, in a *bap-bap-bap/bap-bap-bap* manner and had almost danced down the hall, something he rarely would do in front of them. . . .

On those nights, with dozens of other jazz recordings in a cabinet, all she played were Thelonius Monk and Art Blakey and the Jazz Messengers, again and again. She listened to them nearly every evening through the long and humid summer, stopping only when her daughter, Caroline, had started to throw fits about missing a favorite television program, or when Ives finally came home. And then, sighing, one evening during the autumn, Annie clicked the hi-fi off and never played those particular recordings again.

Gradually, she found that her most reliable companions were books, and decided that her best friends were people who loved them as much as she did. Among the gifts that came to their apartment in the outpouring of public sympathy were four copies of Margaret Mitchell's *Gone With the Wind*, which, along with other novels, she donated to the library or gave to Carmen, whom she always helped with her English, and to her son, Pablo. One of the joys of her life was to take walks with Caroline and Pablo down Broadway to browse in the college bookstores. Nothing pleased her more than to search for mysterious and new authors from different parts of the world, to find a cart filled with exoticisms recommended in Columbia literature classes. And because Pablo had always liked books and treated Caroline so well, and liked to show her the essays he wrote in school, she insisted upon buying him paperback novels, five or six at a time, crumbling, moldy, second-hand inexpensive editions that hardly made a dent in her budget. How could she resist a twenty-five-cent edition of *Sons and Lovers, Dubliners, Bleak House, Moby Dick,* or for that matter, *Don Quixote* or *Sonnets of Shakespeare* for the same price as a slice of pizza?

THE HEREAFTER

That had all happened long ago, and a few weeks before another Christmas Ives awoke in the bedroom of his apartment on Ninety-third Street as a much older man and recalled how for years he would get up for work at seven in the morning, and swear that he could hear his son, Robert, whistling the theme to *The Andy Griffith Show* in the hallway, as he used to in the days when he delivered newspapers. Ives would dress, half expecting to find the boy in the hall, ready to start his morning's work regardless of the weather; or he would hear Bach sung faintly through his door, or find one of the books his son had been reading in the living room, left casually open on the couch as if he had just been reading it again. And although he would think, "Caroline," another part of him imagined his boy, nostalgic for the habits of this life, materializing from the hearafter.

WAS THERE A MOON?

Walking down a hall, or waiting for the morning subway, on many a day he would imagine this scene over and over again.

His son had just slapped five with another boy in the choir and had walked out of the church and crossed the street to chat with another friend, Tommy, about their plans for the holidays. He was excited about all kinds of things. About how he would spend Christmas with his family and old neighborhood friends, but also about going away to the seminary that next June—to his "new life." In the evening wind, Robert kept shifting his weight from foot to foot, and rubbing his hands. He was jaunty and friendly, glancing quickly at passersby, individuals that, on any given day, could have stepped out of Nicholas Nickleby. Wasn't it so that he found something pleasantly amusing about just everybody? What was it that he used to say? "One of the reasons I want to become a priest is to help people."

Then this other kid, a brawny teenager in an army jacket, came walking along, jitterbugging, his stride so exagerrated and dancelike that Robert could not prevent his blue eyes from widening or his forehead from crinkling at the humorous affectation. Finding it amusing, he began to smile in a friendly, well-intended way, and, just like that, the teenager said something that Robert did not quite have the time to digest, and then pulled out his pistol and fired three shots, *pop, pop, pop.* . . .

On his back, Robert must have had time to see something beautiful, and not just the ugliness of a city street at the end of life. Even with the tremendous pain in his badly gutted belly he would have looked up beyond the fire escapes and the windows with their glittery trees and television glows, to the sky above the rooftops. A sky shimmery with the possibilities of death; lights exaggerated, the heavens peeled back—a swirling haze of nebulae and comets—in some distant place, intimations of the new beginning into which he would soon journey. He would have seen a few pale stars, maybe a planet or two, Jupiter or Venus. Remembering his Catholic schoolboy's mythology he might have imagined Apollo and his chariot, somewhere "out there." And he would have seen the moon and its sad expression and imagined in its pocked, luminous surface the faces of his mother and father and sister. . . . The moon? Was it out that night? Ives tried to remember.

He stood on the front steps of his building on a nice spring day, in checked Bermuda shorts and new tennis shoes, waiting for his wife and daughter, and for Ramirez and his family, so they might all go for a long drive and picnic upstate. He fell asleep one night with the television on in the background, his tattered nerves soothed by Bing Crosby in the movie *Going My Way*, and he thought about his son as a priest. He played bridge aboard a Circle Line boat, during an Advertising Club cruise, as it made its way down the Hudson under the George Washington Bridge, and won twenty dollars in petty bets. He wept while watching *Miracle on 34th Street*. He held hands with Annie during a James Bond double feature, down at the Olympia on Broadway, and recalled how, on one Halloween, Robert had gone trick-or-treating as Agent 007. He applauded his daughter in a performance of *The Story of Joan of Arc* at her high school in the Bronx. He came back with Annie late from a dance out in New Jersey with Luis and Carmen, and turned on the television to a program that kept replaying old film footage of Robert Kennedy after he had been shot in Los Angeles, the poor man lying on the floor, his eyes bewildered and glazed as life left him, as his own son Robert had looked, he imagined. He chased fledgling junkies from his stoop, requesting in his calmest voice that they go away. He went to a cocktail party in Westchester and drank too much. He collected donations at church, genuflecting quickly when he came to each pew, and then stretched way over so that people on the far end could drop their money into the straw basket. He sat in the rectory, tie loosened, counting out the change and bills, and then put the coins into rolls and tallied it all up on a piece of paper. (And he was the kind of man to throw an extra ten-dollar bill into the take in the end.) He received Holy Communion and did not open his eyes or move from the white crimson-cloaked railing until the wafer had completely dissolved on his tongue. He took his wife and daughter on vacations in the summer, but never very far, renting an inexpensive cabin at the far northern reaches of Lake George in Upstate New York. He heard cicadas and the wind sweeping across the lake in the middle of the night, and felt depressed because he had little sexual drive, and Annie, his beloved, had started to feel neglected and middle-aged. He went into women's dress shops at lunchtime and, on an impulse, often bought his wife dresses. He sat beside his wife in the front seat of a rented Impala without saying much and drove their daughter around to seven different college campuses so that she might better choose her future alma mater. One autumn when his older brother, Harry, came to New York on business he took Ives and Annie to the Waldorf for a fancy dinner. Later, feeling tired, Ives commented to Annie how prosperous, healthy, and happy his brother seemed to be. He attended the funeral of Annie's father, Captain MacGuire, who had died of a stroke, and was one of the more somber pallbearers, taking his death badly despite the fact that he and Captain MacGuire had not particularly gotten along. He held Annie in his arms for hours that night, as she cried, and then watched her expression change in a matter of moments as if she had decided "enough is enough." That same night, while stopping in the kitchen at about three in the morning to get a bottle of beer, he heard his new upstairs neighbors, a young college student and his girlfriend, making love so loudly that their cries of pleasure echoed in the courtyard. He closed the window. He sat in his son's bedroom in the half-light of the late afternoon trying to hear something in the silence. Home from work early on a rainy December afternoon with the flu he caught Caroline, on Christmas break from her junior year at Antioch College, sitting with Pablo Ramirez, whom he loved very much, necking in the smoky living room. In his hoarse, soft voice, he said, "I've got to talk to you," sent Pablo home, and asked his daughter, "Don't tell me you're smoking pot?" Then he shuffled along the hall, his heart heavy with weariness, took some aspirins, drank some organic

Indian tea, and, barely able to keep his eyes open, fell asleep. He became known in different neighborhoods for his charity work, but had his disappointments. Through a community outreach program, he became a "foster father" to a number of poor children, took them to museums and the circus, to movies and to play ball in the park, and at Christmas had them over to the apartment and bought them nice presents. He even formed an attachment to a gentle black teenager named Willie, who had some drawing talent. He was fond of the young man and could not understand why he had been foolish enough to use heroin, which, one afternoon in the summer, made him drowsy enough to fall backward off a Harlem rooftop. He stood on the subway-station platform with a newspaper in hand, the train approaching, and became suddenly apprehensive. He left his drawing board and by his window watched the stream of life, of buses, cars, trucks, taxis, bicycle messengers, pedestrians, and garment workers pushing their clothing racks on the street, and wondered what it would be like to stand out on the ledge. On some days he would loosen his tie, take off his jacket, and for some reason, his belt, as if these items were the encumbrances of his life. He entertained a group of Japanese advertising executives, showing them the huge four-color Kodak super-spectaculars in Grand Central Terminal and, with Annie, took them to Radio City Music Hall. He kept longer and longer hours, and people passing by his office got the impression that he did not want to go home. He won a special-mention citation for one of his illustrations. One night, while working late, Ives, in his fatigue, staggered out to Madison Avenue: for as far as he could see, the office buildings were casting eerie shadows, and he felt the world a lonely and dreadful place. He often awoke with a gasp in the middle of the night, his heartbeat acceler-ated, his breathing shallow, his heart filled with sadness, his head with memory.

While this small fraction of things went on, Ives thought of his son.

As a young man, Ramirez' son, Pablo, was cheerful and polite, and although he'd taken on certain of the affectations of rebellious youth, he worked, did well enough in school to get into a public college, kept out of trouble, and was "good." While his father, Ramirez, gave great importance to the events in Cuba, the very notion of "Cuba" was as remote to Pablo as Ives' uncertain ancestry was to him.

If he had been born in Santiago or Havana fifty years before, he would have had his father's life, but there he was, in New York City, in the early 1970s, a fairly handsome, dark-featured young man with a hawk's intensity, his black hair down his back. He had stacks of scratched American hippy records, books that he had accumulated over the years, radical pamphlets in his room, and two guitars. He too sang in the choir as Robert had, and on occasion they had sung together. He had other gifts; Ives heard from Caroline that Pablo (or Paul) had a talent for poetry—he wrote her love poems nearly every day. He was always closely observing things and had a natural curiosity about what people thought and had to say. . . .

His interest in the world reminded Ives of himself at his age, and he wished the boy well. Yet he saw that he had never gotten any support from his father. One night in Ramirez' apartment, Ramirez, in the most serious tone, asked Ives, "Do you think my boy may be a fairy?" And when Ives told him "No," Ramirez answered, "*Muchas gracias, señor,* but I wish I could believe that myself."

With his two daughters Mr. Ramirez had been a splendid, if sometimes overprotective, father, doting on them, but it seemed to Ives that he always picked on his son. Once he had outgrown childhood, there was little that he could do that wasn't wrong. Ramirez became impatient and unfair with him. He took his anger out on the kid; Ives once had to stop Ramirez from half beating him to death with a belt on the street, after catching him smoking a cigarette in the basement. On many an occasion, Paul would rap on their door late at night; they would let him in, to find his arms covered with bruises—no one could punch harder than his father. Waiting for the appropriate moment—they were watching Friday-night boxing on television—Ives decided that he had to broach the subject, before Ramirez went too far.

"You're a long-time friend," Ives told the Cuban. "But if you want to keep your son, and your reputation in this neighborhood, and the friendship of my family, you have to let your boy alone."

Luis sat in silence for a long time and, without a word, got up and left Ives' apartment. It was never spoken of again and he seemed to have stopped hitting his son, for a time.

Still Ramirez, from another generation, his heart and imagination somewhere between Cuba, 1938, and Manhattan when it was Manhattan, R.I.P. 1960, seemed to convey embarrassment and disappointment with his son and had nothing to say about him that was good except that "his teeth are his mother's, not a cavity."

Annie, having experienced a similar kind of derision with her own family, was particularly sympathetic to the boy and had him over quite often, even in the days before it was obvious that he and Caroline had become something of a couple. He was welcomed into the household in the same way that Ramirez and Carmen had welcomed Robert when he was alive. Ives, in fact, somehow took comfort in having Paul over for dinner. While Paul would grab for the chair closest to Caroline, Ives always asked him to sit to his left, in Robert's old seat. Shrugging his shoulders, he'd move over, and Ives, bowing his head, would lead the family in prayer.

Although Ives was not always sure what to make of the young people of that time, he liked to bump into Paul on the street. One afternoon, a few days before the fifth anniversary of the shooting, when Ives felt like taking a walk in the park, as he used to with his son even on blustery days, he ran into Paul coming out of the subway and fresh from a part-time job at the *Village Voice* newspaper. Buoyant in his stride, Paul went with Ives. As they walked along, an odd feeling almost immediately came over each of them, as sometimes happens between people of emotion, a feeling that they were not entirely alone.

For a few brief moments, in the company of Paul, who wore a long army coat and a woolen cap with a fuzzy ball on top and looked rather strange that day, Ives felt as if he could have been talking to Robert. And that was all right with Paul—who'd felt Robert's presence too.

Inhaling the West Side Highway pollution and the frigid air off the river, Ives noticed that Paul was carrying several books, as usual, and asked: "What are you reading these days?"

And he rattled off the titles of three D. H. Lawrence novels, *Lady Chatterley's Lover, Sons and Lovers,* and *The Man Who Died,* works he called "far out and passionate."

"Take a book like *The Man Who Died.* You know of any other authors who would have Jesus come down off the Cross, head to Egypt to make love to an Egyptian priestess of Osiris?"

Ives could not say he did.

"The thing about that book, which always amazes me," he went on, "is that Lawrence wrote about Christ as if he somehow knew him. I mean it's a believable book, in that sense. I figure that the only way he could do that, and pull it off, was by having some sense of God. I mean Lawrence was no atheist, even if he was a little outrageous.

"Sometimes when I run into your missus," he added, "we'll sit down and have a nice chat about writers like him. She's into a lot, you know?"

That's when Ives thought to inquire about how things were going between Pablo and his daughter. But, as if speaking to Robert, he suddenly decided to tell him about that other afternoon on Madison Avenue, years before, when he had his little "vision": and as they were walking along the drive, down toward 110th Street in the deserted park, Ives told Pablo what he had never told Annie.

". . . And I can swear to you, on the Bible, when I looked up over the avenue, I saw four distinctly colored winds, coming from four different directions. They were colored powders and swirling and so vivid. You believe it?"

"Oh, yeah. Definitely. Why not?"

"The thing is," Ives added. "Even after what happened with Robert, you know I wake up every day wondering if I'll ever see anything like that again, and what it was supposed to mean."

Nodding, Paul rapped Ives on the shoulder and for a moment, as they stood near the wall overlooking the river, something benevolent and fleeting passed between them, but neither said a word. Then, as they started homeward, the sky began to darken; over the river, low to the horizon, a bank of bottom-heavy clouds, shaped like a man on his back. Later, within the hour, there would be a storm and heavy rains and hail would begin to fall.

PLAYING CARDS

. . . And he would think about that pretty woman in his office named Maria, with her air of permanent sorrow, and how she would cry in the middle of the afternoon with memories of the people, especially the children, she had watched die in Auschwitz; she had been only a child of ten when the Russians liberated the camp. One afternoon, back from Christmas shopping, Ives stopped by her desk and showed her the items he had purchased: a mirror, a camping knife, and for one of the small children in the building on Claremont, a Mickey Mouse puppet. The very sight of it, however, made her break down and cry; in a moment she was hurrying off to the ladies' room to collect herself. Later, she found Ives in his office and apologized: the Mickey Mouse doll had reminded her of a Russian tank commander, who, with tears in his eyes, had found her huddling in the corner of a shed. He had lured her out with a funny-animal doll, perhaps a Mickey Mouse, that he himself had found earlier during his survey of the camp.

Before his son died, Ives had asked her if she was at all religious, and she had told him, "If you mean do I believe in God or in a nice old man in a white suit taking care of things, the answer is no." Even though she had told him she would never set foot in any church, she had shown up for his son's funeral. Sitting in the very last pew near the door, she did not kneel or stand or make the Sign of the Cross but had broken her rule all the same. To thank her without directly saying so, he took her to a restaurant called Maurice's, where he had hoped the food and a little wine would help her spirits, and yet his very kindness seemed so touching, in the context of his circumstances and his tragedy, that, by the time she finished a half glass of wine, she was crying for him and all the horrors of life. . . .

Later on, Ives spent the evening playing bridge with a few neighbors from his building but he was not concentrating well and angered his partner, Ramirez, by making careless choices, his heart and mind elsewhere. "What's wrong with you?" Ramirez chided him. And Ives shrugged and continued to go over certain thoughts that had nothing to do with the game: that He was of the Spirit and He did not interfere in human affairs; that He provided a light toward which to aspire. . . .

THE SWEET SUMMONS

Sometimes when Ives worked late, he chatted with Clarice Towers, the cleaning woman, the man much enjoying her straightforward goodness. She was typical, it seemed to him, of those men and women—Baptists or Seventh-Day Adventists—he sometimes saw on the subways or on certain bus lines on their way to church: well turned out, dressed sportily but respectfully so, the ladies in pink, light blue, and yellow dresses and flowery hats, the men in wrinkle-free suits and brilliantly shined shoes, an air about them of sanctity, cleanliness, and goodwill toward others. (He remembered how much Robert loved them, how he had thought of them as being "more Ozzie and Harriet than Ozzie and Harriet.")

Splendidly devout in their beliefs, they always impressed Ives, whose curiosity about them was such that, in the days before Robert was killed, he often thought about asking Clarice if he might accompany her to church in Harlem one Sunday, but somehow he never got around to it.

Over the years, they were friendly; knowing that she had a big family, Ives always passed on to her whatever promotional items he thought she might find useful at home—soaps, perfumes, candies, magazines, or books that came to him through the agency, courtesy of the advertisers; and sometimes, when he ordered up some food, he would buy her a sandwich, a Coca-Cola and an apple, too. She often brought Ives homebaked spice cakes and pies and, as well, pamphlets from her church, their usual theme the travails that men must endure in order to eventually find a place in heaven. He would bring the pamphlets home and put them in a box in the closet, with his collection of pamphlets from every religion: Eastern, Christian, Judaic, Islamic, Transcendental Meditation, Jews for Jesus.

One of the pamphlets was called *The Sweet Summons*. Its cover depicted clouds that were bursting with light, a chorus of gospel singers standing before them—"The Good Light of Eternity" awaiting all, the "sweet summons" that came at the end of a life.

While they were sitting in his office, Ives asked Clarice if, indeed, she thought that death would come as a relief.

"Oh, yes!" she told him cheerfully. "The sweet summons of God to man. That's when He calls you up to His arms. And it's the most beautiful thing, a rebirth, a new life. But, just the same, I'm in no rush to find out."

On one of those evenings, just as he was getting ready to leave the office, Ives saw Clarice, and feeling low of spirit, he decided to finally ask her if he and his wife might have the honor of accompanying her to church. That Sunday they arranged to meet in front of her church on St. Nicholas Avenue: Ives and Annie decked out in their Sunday best. Clarice Towers, splendid in blue, with a little Jackie Kennedy pillbox hat, a fluttery veil over her face, proudly escorted them toward the front, where her friends and family occupied a row of seats. Conspicuously, Ives and Annie sat quietly, delighted when a tall and handsome deacon, fragrant with colognes and dapper in a tan suit with a white flower in his lapel, came by and said to them, with a Jamaican accent, "Welcome to our church," so affably that he left Ives in a better mood; and then some others came by, just to say hello to Clarice and nodding toward her guests.

Once the service started, with a chorus of gospel singers bringing the Lord's message to the gathering, Ives and Annie knew soon enough that it was nothing like the solemn Catholic Mass. There was a great communal rejoicing in that service, and many got carried away with the breathtaking goodness of their collective purpose, to praise the glory of the Lord and to celebrate their faith in Him and the Kingdom awaiting them. Pretty young girls and their grandmothers beside them were swaying in place and clapping, some people were even crying, as Ives used to. He was so moved that he, nothing of a dancer, found himself shifting from foot to foot in a kind of abbreviated jig and swaying with the crowd and clapping his hands and trying to sing along with their spirituals, so uplifted did he feel, which made Annie smile, for it had been a long time since she'd seen him express even the smallest joy.

And there was the husky, quivery, thunderous voice crying from the pulpit: "As the Lord died on the Cross which is this world so shall we; and there will be a reckoning. . . ." And as he stalked across the floor before his congregation, in long, flowing blue robes and quoted from the Gospel according to St. John, there was in his voice a ferocity; stricken by the reverend's faith, Ives daydreamed about heaven and hell.

Impressed, he could barely wait for the church social afterward, a breakfast held in the basement. Later, Mrs. Towers, who was pleased by his enjoyment and enthusiasm for the service, led him and Annie over to the Reverend Brown. A heavy-set, big man with a carefully coiffed afro, silver gray at his temples, his eyes wise and immense but rimmed, ever so slightly, by a pinkness, he towered over Ives, looked him over with great seriousness, and then extended his large and bony hands, and almost crushed Ives' fingers in his grip.

"We don't get too many folks from out of the community here, sir," he said to Ives. "Feel welcomed in this place, if it is to your liking."

And he looked at Ives again, and holding him by his arm, said, "There are some ladies who would like to meet you." They were sisters, Alice and Dorothea Harris, friends of the reverend and of Mrs. Towers, and after greeting Ives and Annie with great cordiality and without missing a beat, they began to talk about how the church needed money, local schools not always being so good. When Ives volunteered that he was an art director and that his wife was both an artist and an English teacher, the Harris sisters took Ives and Annie to see a church community center a few blocks away. It was on the second floor of a rundown building, with windows on the busy street, plain plaster walls, freshly painted and covered with poems and drawings on the themes of black pride.

During the next several months Ives sent the center several large boxes of art supplies and paper from the office, and every so often on a Sunday afternoon he would go up to run a workshop for the kids, work that Ives much enjoyed, as it got him outside of himself. He did this, either alone or with his daughter or Annie, on and off, for five years, and with those few hours of service, found an agreeable way of passing his time.

In those years he often remembered how he once took his son and daughter to see his father's grave in Brooklyn and how he always felt ashamed that he had no history about the Ives family to relate, except to explain how their grandfather's name had been chosen by a priest. Robert stood before his grandfather's grave, head bowed respectfully, Ives' mongrel blood in his veins. They both prayed for his father, whose soul, personality intact, perhaps awakened from death to rejoin the generations of ancestors whom he had never known in this existence, true identity restored in the afterlife.

And once a year, in the winter, usually a day or two after Christmas, he and Annie would visit their son's grave. Standing in the cemetery before his son's marker out in Long Island, as the years went by, Ives did not for a moment envision a seventeen-year-old in eternal repose, but a man the age his son would have been. And there were occasions when he viewed the grave as some kind of "stopover" his son had made on his way to another, more beautiful place. Sometimes Ives felt that a kind of trick had been played on him. Why else would he walk into a church and have the sensation that his son was *that* priest up by the altar, raising the Host and saying Mass? Why did he often think that he would see Robert again, his face serene and secure in his intimate knowledge of the Lord, the way Ives once used to see it?

ANOTHER LIFE

There was another life that years before Ives and his wife, Annie, had planned but somehow never realized: the life he had, upon occasion, glimpsed while visiting with friends up in Westchester and Connecticut, where there were oaks and maples in the yards and shady, tree-lined streets, fine houses with sun porches and patio barbecues and nearby lakes and parks, farms and antique shops and neighbors whom you never saw or heard. In the years after Robert died, he regretted that they had never made the change in the first place and then imagined his life that way: heading home from Grand Central Terminal and taking the train north; driving along a scenic country road from the station, up a slight hill toward a dream house, in whose cheery doorway his beloved children and wife would be awaiting him. Each night, they would come running down the path to greet him and then they would go inside to savor the wholesome and good life, the kind that seemed to exist somewhere.

In any case, when something happened in the neighborhood, when someone got slashed for no reason or when the cops found the head of a local activist who had been giving the drug dealers a hard time, wrapped in newspapers and left in a garbage can, Ives and Annie discussed moving, not so much out of the city but to a different neighborhood, to get a fresh start. But like it or not, they refused to, as they had made a life for themselves in the community; and for another reason, for a long time it would be difficult to separate themselves from the spirit of their son, who somehow lingered in their home.

A KIND OF COMPROMISE

In 1974, in a kind of compromise, they bought a modest ranch-style house with big picture windows set out at the edge of a field near Hudson, New York. During the summers on the weekends they would go up to the place upstate, and she would spend her mornings out in the yard gardening, in a big sun hat, white butterflies floating around her, or sit in the shade reading; or else out in the yard with an easel and watercolors, making paintings of the beautiful landscape, often saying little to Ives all day. In fact, it seemed they'd run out of things to say to each other a long time ago, their marriage, dense with love, having turned into a partnership; in his company she felt as if she were with a priest or a monk now, and a troubled one at that. She saw him off in his own world and thought that she was there mainly to attend to the outward details and appearances of their life: paying the rent, bills, insurance, and such, and seeing to it that his clothes were clean—in effect acting more as his mother or an old-fashioned wife, rather than a modern woman of the times: at least she could say, with a sigh, that her daughter had gotten it right.

And Ives? For his part, he did not like to be away from her and yet seemed to enjoy his excursions upstate alone, now and then, in the winter. The harshness and the monasterial nature of the place much appealing to his purgatorial side. The days would go by, Ives occupied by his work, the evenings desperately lonely. He would have a drink or two, put on some upstate public radio station that played 1940s music, the mellow voice of Roy Rogers crooning some cowpoke song; or there might be a Bach oratorio on another station and he would sit by the fireplace listening, the choruses rising, and suffer in the wondrous agony of memory.

There was something else. As the years passed, little things about life in the city that never used to bother him had him pacing the floor at night: loud Latin music, frying-food smells, voices chatting into the early-morning hours, the social life that he had previously found so quaint and familial—the men out on the sidewalks watching television in front of the stores, or playing cards or dominoes, or just talking. Even long after people had begun to forget, when his son's name was rarely mentioned at Christmas Mass, he still felt certain resentments toward his Spanish-speaking neighbors, his *amor* for the culture and language had cooled along with his heart. It was a side of himself that he did not like. He was still very close to Ramirez and his family, but in meeting or coming across someone *new* who spoke Spanish, he made a mental inventory of qualities over which he passed judgment, and he kept away.

Without saying it, Ramirez had long thought Ives, with his damaged heart and lofty ideals, the kind of person easily taken for a ride, so he had not been surprised when his friend suffered certain disappointments over the years. Ives' involvement with the blacks uptown was one thing, the kind of project that a mournful man with liberal ideals and a need to fill the time would undertake, but his attempts to con-vert—to *save*—the soul of Daniel Gomez, his son's murderer, was something that drove Ramirez to distraction. He knew about it because his own son, Pablo, first told him about it long ago. . . .

One Saturday morning, while leaving the George Bruce branch of the public library near Broadway and 125th Street, Pablo, then twenty-five or so—it was 1979—and still reading everything in sight, came across Ives as he went walking briskly along with an armful of letters and a parcel that he had addressed in thick Magic Marker to one Daniel Gomez at his residence in the Ossining, New York, Correctional Facility—Sing Sing. He heard from Caroline that Ives wrote the young man letters every so often, but he had not thought for an instant that Ives was open-hearted enough to send his son's murderer packages. Noticing the bulkiness of the package, Pablo Ramirez, or Cochise for his long and dark Indian-looking hair, as sarcastic neighborhood friends called him in those days (others called him *pellito* for "hairy head"), made a joke about it: "Gifts for anyone I know?"

Ives wanly smiled. "I'm sending some magazines and books off to that boy Danny Gomez. He's trying to learn how to read," Ives said matter-of-factly. Pablo nodded and he then asked: "That's really nice, Mr. Ives, but why are you going out of your way for this fellow?"

Ives sighed. "To tell you the truth, Paul, it's something that upsets my wife, but you know my thinking goes like this:

for a long time, I felt so bitter toward this young man that it was poisoning me inside, so I had to do something to get the poison out of myself."

Then, because Paul was quite fond of Ives and frankly a little worried about him, he decided to go along with him. They crossed the street, toward the north side of 125th, and walked east to the post office, where, finding long lines at the various windows, they waited together.

After the trial when the Gomez boy had served his first sentence as a juvenile and had been released, there was renewed pressure on Ives to exact some kind of revenge that meant something. Ramirez himself had known Cubans who would calmly find the boy on his street and "eliminate" him, and there was talk down in the bar again about hiring a Brooklyn punk, all of which Ives put a stop to. Someone had anonymously mailed him a .22 pistol, which resembled a toy, and twelve rounds, with a note urging Ives to do "right," but he threw the pistol into the river. Revenge was a subject that he did not care for, it would not bring his son back.

In those moments, he would pray for guidance, for wishing death upon another seemed so ugly that each time it occurred he felt a blackening of his soul.

The odd thing was that Ives was never certain as to how he should feel. Though the boy's mother had been dragged out of court, protesting her son's innocence, the day he had been convicted, his grandmother, with whom Ives had maintained something of a sympathetic correspondence, had felt deeply ashamed about her grandson. From time to time, when she felt particularly troubled, she would call him up to commiserate and to convey her own sorrow. Deep down, she would tell Ives, her grandson was a good boy who'd made a mistake. He was "heartily" sorry for his sins, even if he had seemed more smirkingly arrogant than contrite at the brief trial. About three years into his sentence she reported that he was a changed person, much matured and on the brink of overcoming his "moral illness." Wanting to believe her—and feeling truly sorry about her suffering—for the grandmother seemed to have taken things as badly as Ives and his wife, he began to feel a renewed faith in the system, hoping that, in the end, the young Mr. Gomez would be sent out into the world a changed person.

Unfortunately, eighteen months after he was released, in 1972, he got himself into trouble again, and killed two more people during a dance-hall robbery up on Third Avenue in the Bronx. This time, tried as an adult and charged with second-degree manslaughter, he was given twenty years to life. As for Ives, he began to wonder if, as Ramirez almost gloatingly told him, "This new nonsense would not have happened if someone had taken care of him three years ago."

Yet, as the years went by, Ives and the grandmother were getting along to the point where on several occasions, in the name of doing the "Christian" thing, he picked her up in a taxi, and took her to support-group meetings at a church on Ninety-sixth Street for victims of crimes and their families. These, as it turned out, were of great help to Ives. Occasionally he took Annie or Caroline along. Mr. Ives of the mystical experience, foundling beginning, and saintly demeanor heard, over the course of five or six years, hundreds of stories of heartache and tragedy, and concluded that the only way to deal with suffering was to trust in God and cling to the path of righteousness: and this he did, despite his doubts, approaching the whole notion of his faith as a matter of will and discipline.

As his hair had turned white, his features took on a compassionate power. On some of those evenings when people would get up and tearfully describe their tribulations, Mr. Ives would listen, his face reflecting the conviction of a man who may well have seen a Cross-of-light or an image of the Holy Mother in the sky.

In fact, he still had many doubts, but pushed onward with

the conviction that sooner or later there would be some kind of payoff, some sense that goodness, in and of itself, was its own reward; that events, even cruel ones, happened for reasons that, in one way or another, would benefit the community of man. Ives winced at some of the stories he heard, for underlying every tragedy was the question: Why? Yet he had to believe in something, otherwise he would have died, he loved his son so much.

So he and the elder Mrs. Gomez would sit together taking in the stories. On the second of those occasions, Mrs. Gomez, her face red with grief, told the group about her grandson and afterward wept inconsolably. Then she showed them clippings from newspapers that she had brought along in a Woolworth's shopping bag, the most recent showing a scowling but vaguely bewildered-looking young man being led away from court, handcuffed. She held up a photograph of Daniel when he was a young boy, posed beside her in the front yard of a cousin's house in Ponce, Puerto Rico, pretty blossoms and bushes behind them, the boy, beaming, happy and handsome, his future before him. "This is the same person: now, you want to know what happened?"

Then she answered: "The good part of him is asleep, that's all. He's still good inside; that part must be awakened."

And that had started Ives' interest in helping to rehabilitate her grandson, for in helping him, in doing the "Christian" thing, he would bring some kind of relief to his grandmother and perhaps to himself.

He began cautiously enough. A package and a short letter:

Dear Daniel Gomez,
    You would know me as the father of the boy whose life you took at Christmas in 1967. We have never met and I know that you are wondering why I would bother to write

*you, all these years later. Well, I will tell you, as best as I
can. It has to do with your abuela and what you mean to
her. I know that you have gone down a very bad road
twice, but I want you to know that it is not too late to
change. If you only knew how she suffered with worry
about you, then you would understand why you should do
your best to straighten yourself out. But I know it's not
easy, and, for my own reasons—to make something good
out of all this—I would like to help you. And that is why I
am sending you some pamphlets and a Bible. If you can
open your heart to certain good thoughts, then that will
change you, perhaps, or help you to change.*

    Please take this in a spirit of good intentions.

                    Sincerely,

                    Edward Ives

That was the beginning, he told Pablo; he had been sending the young man letters and occasional packages of inspirational religious magazines to make his life easier, so he would
not get involved with more "mischief," as Ives put it. He sent
him a box of food at Christmastime, comics, as per his
request, and the past year, a small radio.

"Does he write you?"

"He's written me a few times," Ives said. "Hardly knows
how to write. The thing I've been trying to do is get him to
read, and then to enroll in one of those high school equivalency courses, but it's rough."

He patted his shirt pockets, as if looking for a soft pack of
cigarettes, and pulled out a note, written in shaky, immature
script, with wild letters as if set down by a broken hand.

Pablo looked it over, his eye caught on one line, "Hope
one day weill get the chans to' meet. Like I'm change,
already. Thanks to you. Your man, Danny Gomez."

"Yes, he's got a way to go, but it's a start, you know. And
like I said, it can't hurt, can it?"

As word spread, few in the neighborhood understood why Ives would want to be so helpful to the man, least of all Ramirez. The first time Paul told him, he went to see Ives, and they had a big argument, but Ives did not change his mind. As a kind of proof that good deeds could make a difference in the world, he showed Ramirez the fruit of his labors: a short composition (150 words or so) entitled "Raising Pigeons in the City," by Daniel Gomez, which was printed in a prison newsletter in 1982, some six years after Ives had begun to send him books on how to read and write, cassettes of music, religious pamphlets, sausages and crackers and bars of chocolate and cigarettes.

It went as follows:

When I was a kid growing up in Manhattan, and we were poor, one of the things me and my brothers did to keep our heads together was to raise pigeons on our roof. Now there are two things you have to know. One, pigeons love to eat bread, even old bread, and two, pigeons love the color red. I don't know why, but when I learned about training them for the first time from an old man on my block, he said that the way to do it was to get a piece of red cloth and put it on the end of a broomstick, like a flag. Now a red flag catches their eye like crazy. When the pigeons see the red flag being waved around, they think it's their mother, or someone like that, and they'll just follow it around for hours. So, once you have their attention and you go one way with it, they follow. You want them to go in a circle you turn your flag and they will circle. In conclusion, it's a good hobby and you can eat them if you have to.

Ives never bothered to show Ramirez any of the letters he received from Daniel, because to Luis' skeptical eye, he was just being used. When Ives mentioned anything positive about Daniel Gomez, as in "He even sent us a Christmas card," Ramirez' face would gnarl up with disbelief and he would spit something back like, "And next you know, you'll be telling me that the kid is going to be canonized."

But he took Ramirez' attitude with a good-natured acceptance; indeed, to Ramirez and many another friend, Ives was the one who should have been canonized or put away; the former was certainly the opinion of Gomez' grandmother, who called the apartment several times a week to compare notes, as it were, on her grandson's progress. The tone of his letters was so newly genteel that Ives slowly began to feel that he had been correct in his beliefs—who knew, but maybe once this fellow Gomez got out he might have his high school equivalency diploma, go to college, and maybe with some breaks find a useful trade. In his letters to Ives over the years, he spoke of having learned much from his mistakes and wanting to help others. Said that he was interested in going into social work or getting a job in a halfway house, like they have down in Brooklyn or the Bronx for ex-cons.

As time progressed, there were more elements of piety in these letters, the occasional sentence like: "I hope the Good Lord is watching over you," or "In the joint, a belief in *El Señor* can be a comfort."

There was, however, one thing he often brought up that Ives was not sure he could deal with: in each letter, he'd invite Ives to come and visit him at the prison, so that they could meet and speak face-to-face; so that maybe he could be seen as someone human and, perhaps, as a little more like a friend, rather than an enemy who had done him harm. His grandmother had even suggested this to Ives, as she would sometimes take the train to Ossining with her daughter or get a ride with one of her son's old neighborhood friends. And yet, each time he got one of those letters and did not know how to react, he went for a long walk, usually through Sakura Park and along Riverside Drive, sometimes to the Soldiers and Sailors Monument and back, before the guilt about this familiarity began to fade.

On the evening Ramirez found a site for his restaurant, Ives conveyed as much to his old Cuban friend.

"You're kidding me, right? You're feeling guilty about hurting this swine's feelings?" And he looked off: "*Carajo,* I hope there's a God so that he can take me up there right now and put me in someplace where there are no crazy people." Then, taking Ives aside, he held him tightly by the arms, and said, "Eduardo, Eduardo, don't be stupid. I wouldn't trust that fellow if you paid me. How can you forget what he did?"

They went to look at a place on Columbus and Seventy-fifth Street that used to be a Chinese restaurant. Its interior had been gutted, arsonist style, fixtures, cables, charred wood and broken glass and foul smells everywhere, the scuttle of cats scavenging through the debris or looking for mice. Ives and Ramirez followed a rental agent shining a beam on the wreckage of the walls, the light cutting through the darkness, as Ives hoped goodness would cut through the ugliness of the world.

A CONFIDANT

Although Annie never talked about it, she had no use for Daniel Gomez and regarded her husband's interest in him as one of the stranger and less agreeable manifestations of his grief. She basically kept out of it, having enough concerns of her own. For her part, she had begun to question many of her own values: over the years, since the death of her son, she had become fearful—twice held up at knifepoint in different schools, once badly frightened in the South Bronx by a young man who would have raped her had it not been for the intervention of some other students. Having earned a master's degree in literature from Columbia, she was now working toward a doctorate in nineteenth-century English literature, though she figured it would take her forever. So she would teach once in a while in certain schools, even when she and Ives did not need the money, and rather than taking daily risks in the city schools, which, by her light, seemed to be getting worse and worse, she preferred to find ways to bring art and literature to the local community; she spent half her free time writing grants to the government, so that they could do something for the kids, meeting with their local congressional rep, and trying to get the State Arts Council to send visiting writers and artists to talk to the kids at schools like P.S. 125.

For all that, for all her principles, for all her open-mindedness and her belief in social progress, as she got older, whether she wanted to or not, she began to feel worn down by the daily grind of trying to help others. After so many years of fighting against a different kind of ignorance, she felt herself, in thought if not in deed, becoming more and more like her family. She began to almost feel nostalgic for that time when she really believed that concern would make a difference in the long run. She had learned, as her husband should have, that goodness and good intentions really didn't make much difference to a lot of people. There were always good kids who would get ahead, and bad kids who wouldn't, no matter how hard you tried to reach them.

She wasn't young. Once she had started to hit her fifties, not only had her resolve weakened but so had her body: limbs heavier, years of smoking catching up, and a kind of weariness aging her, Annie MacGuire slowly came to regret certain of her choices in life. On many a day, she would leave the apartment and go about her business, wishing she were a different kind of person. Her "goodness" was something of a curse. As a person of principle, who had put many years into her efforts, she could not turn her back on anything. And yet, at the same time, she had become caustic in her approach to teaching—it took her a long time but the old indifference of the system had caught up to her.

Still, she had made her life and, like marriage, had chosen to live with it. She had done so even as she and her husband drifted further apart. They slept in the same bed, made love, if rarely, shared many a meal, but their old congeniality had gradually died. She could understand a year's mourning, even five years, but with her husband the process had gone on and on. After a few years, even after she had suffered greatly and cried herself to sleep nightly, she was ready to put their son's death behind her, but for Ives, Robert's death had become the defining event of his middle-aged life.

What could she say? How could she persuade him that there was nothing wrong with moving on? Or keep him from comporting himself like a penitent on his way to a flagellation? How many times over the years had she rested naked next to him, and he had not moved? How many times had she suggested that they do something carefree, like booking passage on a seven-day wedding-anniversary Caribbean cruise, or, more conservatively, signing up for a two-week tour of the Holy Land through one of the Catholic societies, or just renting a car in the summer and driving off to Maine and parts unknown from there, only to have him find an excuse not to? She loved him, but it got tiring. It was not as if they could not afford to take a three-week vacation, but whenever she would stop by a travel agency to get some brochures about wonderful places like "France, the Gourmand's Delight," or "Tahiti, Dream Island in the Sun," he gave her a pitiful look, as if she were distracting him from something far more important. And how many hints did she have to drop about the nature of her desires? "You know if we don't get out of here, we'll go nuts after a while?"

She loved him enough to remain by his side, and yet there were days when certain memories of early love affairs made her melancholy too. She would remember a time in her life when dallying for hours in bed making love—as she and Ives used to—was more important than going to church; when the bohemian spirit, as she defined it in an artist like D. H. Lawrence, who lived for his work but also loved life dearly, seemed to thrive in her heart.

SECRETS ON THE TELEPHONE

When Caroline was in college Annie would spend hours with her on the telephone, and they would talk like sisters. They would often share secrets. She took an odd kind of pride in knowing that her daughter lost her virginity during a picnic at Bear Mountain Park in 1973 with Paul, whom she sometimes talked about marrying; and in return, her mother told about her circumstances: she was out on a high school senior-class boat trip to the Rye Beach amusement park when she met a handsome boy from Mount Saint Michael High School, named Johnny Crumm, in 1945. On that sunny day, she had worn a light blue dress with straps that were buttoned at the shoulders and a white frill-collared blouse, and was about to pay for a pistachio ice-cream cone when he interceded: later they went on nearly every ride in the park and then took a long walk on a nature trail, where they found a hidden place where she gave herself—"in love" but also disturbed by things that were going on at home. . . .

Annie and Caroline laughed and confided all kinds of things to each other in a way that made Annie feel young again. Later, having floated off on a cloud of sweet glory, Annie would catch herself in the mirror and begin to discern in her broadening figure, widened calves, and fleshier face the fact that she was changing into an image of her own mother, from whose fate she had once believed she could run away.

A Beautiful Man and Other Tales

HIS LAST DAY AT THE AGENCY

On December 29, 1982, there had been a big party in the boardroom, and it was attended by many of the old-timers like Ives himself—Crane, Silverman, Schamberg—and Mr. Mannis, having survived his third open-heart operation, made a speech. They had given Ives a watch—a gold Swiss pocket watch from the 1920s, engraved with his name on the back (to go into a drawer along with the watch he had intended to give to his son long ago at Christmas)—and a plaque.

A good pension and many years of savings left Ives and Annie in good shape, even after having paid for Caroline's college tuition. He hadn't realized, however, that being home in the old apartment on Claremont, largely unchanged in the years since *that Christmas,* could make him feel so restless. For that reason he got Rex and Alice, two high-strung, sniffy collies, so he had an excuse to go outside several times a day. And at first it had not bothered Ives to continue living there. He liked the apartment, enjoyed the company of the dogs, who slept like guardians by his feet while he drew. He purchased new lamps, a tropical fish tank, and several new bookcases, where Annie kept her collection of literature and books on art. All was well, until they came home from the country one weekend to find the place ransacked, everything smashed, and, most sadly of all, his "heirlooms"—his first-edition books by Dickens—were missing. He did not care about the watches, cuff links, or necklaces that were taken, but when he learned that his Dickens volumes had been stolen he could not believe it and sat dumbfounded in the living room, among the debris, stricken, for a long time.

Then, too, there had been what he could not perceive: his lingering sadness. That next year, in 1983, they finally decided to move and took a place on Ninety-third Street, near the park.

Several years into his retirement, Ives invested a little money in Ramirez' restaurant, the Arena Colón Café, its name coming from the Havana stadium where Ramirez had once gloriously fought. The restaurant was situated on Columbus Avenue, its decorative motif historic Cuban sports figures. During the months before the restaurant opened its doors, Ives spent nearly every afternoon helping to get the place into order. As per Ramirez' instructions, he painted two large murals that depicted baseball and boxing in Havana, over the years, and a third, smaller mural near the bar, of a white-bearded Ernest Hemingway and several Cuban friends drinking at the famous Floridita bar in Havana. (For that matter, Ives had painted murals of a religious theme for two local Catholic schools, gratis, and had enjoyed the status of becoming a community artist of a sort.)

And Ramirez put up the memorabilia he had brought along with him from the Biltmore Bar, when the hotel had closed down for good in the late 1970s. Ives also invested seven thousand dollars for the restaurant flatware and utensils, designed the menus, and arranged, through old connections, a number of free radio spots and bus cards that appeared here and there in certain ethnic neighborhoods in the city, proclaiming: THE BEST CUBAN FOOD IN THE WORLD!

There were other partners, a large and sweet-natured Puerto Rican fellow named Hector Sanchez, a former cook at the Biltmore, who wore a high white toque, and ran the sparkling kitchen with a firm but gentle hand, and two brothers, roly-poly clothing entrepreneurs from Elizabeth, New Jersey, Cubans who had come to the States in the early 1960s, and, prospering, had money to throw around. It was the first time Ives and Ramirez had spent so many hours together, day in and day out. That's when they made the pleasant discovery that, in a way, they were like brothers. Ramirez never had to explain away the gruffness of his moods, nor Ives, his sad heart.

For the restaurant's opening they had a party, whose luminaries included the Panamanian boxer Roberto Duran, the movie actress Shelley Winters, who lived nearby, and a number of well-known musicians, among them the dapper and gentlemanly Johnny Pacheco. For music, the orchestra leader Mario Bauza, one of the nicest people Ramirez or Ives ever met, came down from his place on 106th with a retinue of young musicians, the maestro setting up an electric keyboard in a corner and cheerfully conducting an impromptu ensemble of Afro-Cuban, bebop musicians, the place, with its free inaugural buffet and one-dollar margaritas and cuba libres, so crowded that people were spilling out onto the sidewalk.

The party, Ives would remember, was particularly memorable because he had never seen his friend Ramirez so happy: he even saw the man hugging his son a number of times. He was also pleased to see that the portrait he had painted of his friends Luis and Carmen, years before, had earned a prominent spot on one of the light-lavender-and-pink walls.

Nor had he ever watched Ramirez so openly affectionate with his wife, often kissing her while posing for photographs and rarely leaving her side.

Clearly, after so many years of servitude, Ramirez could not have been more content about operating his own place; the others were to be silent partners, their main concern eventually to make money on their investment. In a white tuxedo, and smoking a Cuban-seed Jamaica-grown cigar, with a carnation in his lapel, Ramirez was proud of his accomplishment and looked forward to a prosperous and respect-filled future.

The business would last six years before closing, and then Ramirez would try to open another restaurant up on 138th Street. And yet for the first several years the restaurant did good business, having gotten a favorable writeup in *New York* magazine, which made it, after Victor's Café on Seventy-second Street, a local bourgeois attraction.

Money seemed to pour in—Ives was paid back within the year and emerged as one of the patrons who always received special treatment: now and then he would turn up with troops of poor kids that he met through the Parish Student Exchange program, when the scruffier public school kids would come over to Corpus to study with the nuns once a week; and sometimes he came in with priests, like his old friend Father Tom or simply priests from the local parishes, with whom Ives had maintained cordial relations over the past several years.

But Ives would mainly recall that restaurant for the night when Ramirez, who was not given to a show of his emotions, particularly around men, had celebrated the third anniversary with his family and best friends. After drinking much champagne Ramirez had made a series of toasts, one of them to his friend Ives: "For my best American friend with the kindest heart—an honorary Cuban—Eduardo!" And he'd embraced Ives as if he were his dead father, or the loving brother he never had. Then as he stood before the crowd, packed with many of his Cuban and Puerto Rican friends from the neighborhood and from the hotels downtown, Ramirez produced a large jeweled diamond ring, which he presented to Carmen, who had aged elegantly, thanking her "for all that she had done for him."

It turned out the ring was part of a deception. Among his employees was a young Cuban woman, by the name of Anita Flores, whose attractive body, lovely Andalusian face, and sexual air had distracted Ramirez from his husbandly concerns. His interest in her surprised him, because while he believed in fidelity she had come into his life just when he, in his sixties, had begun to experience the trepidations and fears of a man approaching old age; and while he could always take a drive out to Elizabeth, New Jersey, or uptown to Washington Heights, where there were several quite well-established cat houses, Ramirez wanted to prove his virility on his own merits. She was the kind of woman to wear nearly weightless brassieres, of sheer fabric, to show off her breasts, and when they went to bed for the first time, she elevated both his blood pressure and ego. He, in turn, gave her money and gifts and could not care less if she was taking advantage of him. Spending more and more time with this woman, in a second-floor studio apartment near the Museum of Natural History, he began to detach himself from his friends to the point where everyone, even the naive-seeming Ives, noticed a change.

Carmen soon enough found out. She was used to his habits. Hard-working for many years, he never failed to come home to her, to sit watching television for an hour or so before dozing off; and yet, in recent months, on many a night, he had not shown up, claiming that he was just sleeping on a cot in the office in the back of the restaurant. Sitting in Ives' living room on Ninety-third Street, one evening, she wept unashamedly, Ives and Annie MacGuire trying to reassure her—"You know your husband lives for his work."

She shook her head, producing from a bag several frilly pairs of naughty-looking panties, a brochure from a hair-replacement company, and a woman's compact: "Look at what I've found; he doesn't even try to hide anything."

"Have you said anything to him?"

"Yes." And she started to cry anew. "He told me that he's spent his whole life working for me; that he brought me and my family here, supported us for many years, and should have the right to do as he wants to do. And when I told him, 'Okay, *vayate*—go!' He said, 'Okay, I'm going.'"

It was a pity because they were both fond of her and, furthermore, one of those days she would become directly related to them through marriage, for Pablo and Caroline had always gotten along and were, by their own admission, intent upon one day marrying. Personally Ives found the whole business disheartening—wasn't there enough trouble in the world already?

"He'll come back, I promise you that," they told her.

But that only made her talk about how he had lost his head and said many cruel things to her, which she would not repeat in front of them, and so the damage had been done, even if he were to return.

And eventually, after three months, he did come back home remorsefully, with hat, suitcase, and a bouquet of two dozen long-stemmed roses, whose thorns he carefully picked off one by one. Bored with his aging sex and his possessiveness, his mistress took up with a Jewish-American entrepreneur from South Beach in Miami. Humbled, with a number of new lines added to his guilty brow, and the crevices of his natural scowl deepened, he begged her forgiveness. She, loving him, took him back. Still, his credibility as a gentleman, and his sense of self-respect had suffered. And although the subject was hardly ever mentioned again and things had gone more or less back to normal, there was an air of sadness about the couple, as if something had violated their love.

Old age, too, had rapidly descended upon them. Humiliation had thinned their eyelids, and the skin under their chins began to sag. Absent-mindedly on her way to a bakery to deliver a piñata that she made for extra money, Carmen slipped down the stairs and broke her hip, thereafter requiring a cane and taking on the slightly stooped posture of an older woman.

Carmen never talked about her husband's infidelity or her solitude, even when Ives and Annie might encounter her alone on the street; but one night, a few months after that love affair had ended, and at an hour when the place was empty and about to close, Ives had stopped off late, wanting to get a fast bite—the *paella* and *tostones* excellent. Afterward, he had sipped a double scotch and asked, "How's Carmen?"

And Ramirez had snapped back: "Come on, you know how she is." Then, he threw down a rag from behind a counter and said: "Look, the reason I did it was because that young woman made me feel like I was the king of kings in bed. You see this hand?" And he held up his right hand, the one that had been crushed by a mallet years ago in Cuba, and was gnarled and scarred: "She would take this hand and rub it slowly across her skin, and I'll tell you something, Eduardo, she had the softest and firmest skin you can ever imagine: and sometimes when she felt like it, she would take my fingers in her mouth, sucking them like candy, kiss my palms and tell me, 'You are a *beautiful man.*' And about my baldness, she'd say: 'Your bald head makes me horny.' You can laugh, but that was part of it, *coño.*" And he turned on some water, and was so angry about the very idea that he may have lowered his standing before his friend, Mr. Ives: he nearly smashed some glasses in a bar sink, he put them down so hard.

Suddenly despondent, Ramirez leaned against the bar and said, "It's Carmen, her health. She's not doing so well. Something with her *pecho*," and he tapped his chest.

Ives did not pursue it then, but would find out later that Carmen, a figure of grace and personality, who was pure *dulcería*, would have one and then another and then a third debilitating operation, not upon her heart, as Ives had first thought, but upon her breasts and the surrounding lymph nodes.

"Eduardo, my friend, all I can tell you," Luis said, "I can't believe it's going on."

And as he looked sadly toward Ives, the smooth skin of his face glaring in the pink neon bar light, as he was about to say, "*Ay,* but what is it to anyone?" two police officers appeared in the door. And because the place was closed up for the night, they tapped on the glass.

Cops had been making Ives anxious since 1967; for Ramirez they usually meant two free meals to go, thank you. He went to the door, referring to their presence as *la mordida* because he did not know these cops, and thought they might want money. One was black, one white—the latter resembled the actor Steve McQueen—both were tall and sturdy-looking young men. Above their badges their names were sewn on patches: "Wiggins" and "Palmer." The white cop looked around and asked, "Slow tonight?"

"In fact, it was pretty busy earlier," Ramirez told them.

And the white cop smiled and then, approaching the register, pulled out his revolver and stuck it in Ramirez' belly, "You know the score, pal," he said. Then in Spanish, *"Dámelo."*

The other one forced Ives to lie down on the floor behind the bar, and while Ives awaited, his body in knots, the white cop pushed Ramirez into the back and, with the revolver's muzzle at his temple, ordered him to open up the safe. Ives heard a brief scuffle, then the words "Open the safe," again. By that time, Ives had started to whisper Hail Marys and Our Fathers for Ramirez first, and then for himself, and he thought they would both be shot, but then the black man leaned over the bar and said: "Would you be cool with that, I'm not gonna shoot you, all right? But please cut the prayers? You're making me nervous." And then, when his friend came calmly out with a bagful of money, they were shortly gone.

YEARS LATER, THE PHONE RANG ONE DAY

Then the phone rang one day. Annie was in the kitchen of the apartment on Ninety-third, sitting with her two granddaughters, Carmencita and Mary-Ellen, and grandson, Bobby, whom Caroline and Paul had named in honor of Caroline's late brother. (In the mid-eighties Paul, or Pablo, had published an autobiographical first novel, which had gotten him in trouble with a lot of Cubans—and especially with his father, who didn't want to hear about his particular experience. It was called *A History of Cuban Hippiness,* and chronicled the exploits of a troubled young Cuban-American during the midseventies and his travels around the United States as the bass player of a band called the Savages, its underlying theme a meditation on just what being a homegrown Cuban-American was all about.) Paul was downtown at his office job, in the Time & Life building, but Caroline had come over earlier to help decorate the tree and to cook a Christmas stew. The call was from a Father Jimenez.

"Pop, it's for you," Caroline had said.

"This is Father Jimenez of Saint Maria's, uptown. I've called to let you know that Daniel Gomez was released from prison; and he has asked me to speak with you."

"Where is he?"

"Well, his family lives in the Bronx now, but he's staying upstate. He would like to set up a meeting with you. In the name of goodwill."

Ives cleared his throat.

"I . . . don't really know, father," Ives told him.

But the priest continued, "Look, Señor Ives, I understand that over the years, even after what happened, you tried to help the boy out. . . . He's not a saint, no doubt about that, but this is a crucial time for him; you know if he messes up again, they lock him up and throw away the key. Just in terms of psychology—you're an educated man—you must see that if you can open up a little to him it would make a world of difference. Look, sir, I know it's a lot to ask, but we of the *comunidad* have to do something to make it better for people like him, the government won't." Then: "What it's about is compassion, sir. I beseech you to think about what Our Lord would have done. Will you think about this? I know it would make a difference."

Leaning against the wall, he had kept his eye on his new little granddaughter, her body so fresh, eyes large and liquid upon the world, and somehow the very mention of Gomez had the effect of spilling a poisonous gas into the room. Ives had listened, and although his face still had a pious cast, the years of longing and of missing his son, without being able to forget or forgive, had taken their toll on him. He'd turned into stone. It had been difficult to show affection to his own wife, but to open himself to the man who had killed his son?

"I have to think about it, father."

He knew how to hold a baby, to cuddle her, to smile and

to tickle the curling toes, to clean the snorting nose, the damp rump, how to heat the bottles, change the Pampers, heat up a little baby food in a pan, as he used to for his kids, but inside . . . ? He had nothing left; his heart, in a sense, had died, years ago. The crazy part of it was that Ives hadn't realized it until his grandchildren were born. Yes, he said, I love you, yes, he rocked each one of them, but it was more a pretense—would the kids, he often wondered, grow up wondering about why their grandfather was so stricken-looking, so cold?

As for compassion? He didn't have that for anyone else— that was a saint's or a young, naive person's emotion, he'd decided.

"Can I ask you to take my number, sir, and to think about it?" the priest asked. Ives wrote his telephone number down on an old Mannis Advertising Agency while-you-were-out note, and stuck it up on the refrigerator door, under a banana magnet. And when Annie asked what the call had been about, he told her, "Just a priest asking about something." Then he made himself a drink and went into the living room, where he sat listening to music and watching the blinking, prettily decorated tree.

DOES IT PAY?

One part of him sincerely hoped that Gomez had changed for the better. Gomez did get his high school equivalency (so he said) and apparently some credits toward college. And a few years before, Ives had received an odd letter, from a young woman who lived in Albany, New York, a certain Shari Hagan. In the letter she related that she had been maintaining a correspondence with "Danny." He had first written to her after she had put an advertisement in a lonely-hearts magazine. After a year, they had met, and fallen in love. And now she looked forward to his day of release. She was writing to Ives because she wanted to "touch base," with him, as if they were all going to be friends. "He told me that you were in an advertising business of some kind. I had an uncle who did that, out in Chicago."

Her casual tone and her familiarity with Ives and her use of the word *love* while describing her feelings for a man who once upon a time had killed three people, made him feel vaguely distressed. She enclosed a color photograph. She was a heavy-set woman with long, frost-tipped blond hair and large blue eyes. She wore too much rouge and had an apple-shaped face that would have been funny and charming in a lady comedian's way, if it were not for the general sadness of her expression. Another letter, which came in October of 1992, advised Ives that they would be married when he got out, and would he and his wife come to the ceremony?

He ignored her as he had come to ignore Gomez. In fact, the last time he had pursued a correspondence with Daniel Gomez was five years before, his last letter, a letter of condolence over the death of his grandmother, who had died of a stroke. Now it amazed Ives how long he had kept writing Gomez, nearly ten years, mainly to comfort his grandmother. He had not entirely turned his back on him, however. For the last several years he had written the parole board on his behalf:

> . . . Even though I was a victim of this man's earlier crime, I believe that he has overcome that evil part of himself. . . .
>
> . . . Even though I have not met him, I have been encouraged by his apparent change of heart and spirit; I would find it hard to believe that he had not overcome the obstacles to approaching a normal and productive life. . . .
>
> . . . I am writing on behalf of Daniel Gomez and wish to express my strong belief in his worthiness for parole. . . . I can only urge you . . .

Crumpling false start after false start, he had felt sick, halfway dishonest: deep down he thought there was evil in that man, and yet could not admit it to himself. Or was it that, after receiving those letters from Gomez' prospective bride, he could not bear the idea that while his son remained in a lead-lined coffin under the ground, in the interminable darkness, this young man could look forward to an amorous rendezvous and marriage with a woman who said that she loved him.

As the years had passed, as Gomez approached the year of his release, Ives began to feel less compassionate.

THINGS CHANGED

On another day, while heading downtown to get in a little shopping and to meet his friend Father Tom, he could not help but wonder how life could go so badly for some, and so splendidly for others. "Who inherited the earth?" had become a question he often asked himself; who deserved to prosper, who deserved to suffer? On the train coming down he had counted seven beggars, who came in through the cars asking for money, one of them, a large black man, his lumberjack shirt open, with purple splotches all over his body, black-and-blue marks on his arms, and with a piece of filthy catheter jammed into his stomach just above his navel. Ives gave something to every single one of them.

He watched the column lights passing rapidly in the tunnel, tried to read the newspaper, felt a little despair. Earlier, getting on the train at Ninety-sixth Street, he was amazed to think that he used to ride the subways at least twice a day during the week for years, and he used to stand in the middle of the car, lost in the newspaper, his portfolio by his side, fairly oblivious of people, and now? He kept to himself, preferring to sit in a corner like everyone else, except the wide-eyed tourists.

. . . So then the subway pulled into Times Square, his reverie ended, and Ives waded through the dense crowds and caught the shuttle east over to Lexington. In past years he might have had an afternoon visiting different offices, dropping by to see certain of his friends from the business, too, but with each passing year, there were fewer of his friends to visit. Many had retired, or fallen out of touch—each year he would go through his old office Rolodex, which he'd brought home for good when he'd retired—and spend an evening, sometime around Christmas, on the telephone saying hello to as many people as he could reach; and each year he'd find that people had moved or numbers had become obselete or that someone like Tilly had passed on. Every so often Ives would find himself attending a funeral out in Queens or Jersey: an old supplier he'd known, one of the chain-smoking women from accounting, an alcoholic exec.

Then there had been Mr. Mannis, from whom he would receive a card, a package of very expensive chocolates, and a phone call on Christmas Eve, their brief but cordial conversations always starting, "Eugene Mannis here." When he was dying, a few years ago, Ives had gone over to the Flower Fifth Avenue Hospital to see him. He had been a tall, handsome man; fancied himself a George Sanders type, sharp-featured, with a powerful-looking head and perpetually tanned skin—and yet as he lay there, his thick head of hair was now sparse and gray, his eyes, once impenetrably black, were watery, his heavy lids nearly transparent and pink. And so was his skin: and he was skeletal and seemed embarrassed and wan and lost. But Ives had gone there with Annie, and sat beside his boss for half an hour, talking to him about normal things, and reminiscing about the old days when they had to figure out inventive methods to present products like Murphy beds and laxatives and my, my, how the time had passed.

Ives himself was seventy, Mannis nearly eighty—not a bad run—but all the same he seemed to have gotten rather attached to the good life, and, trembling, he had coughed and asked Ives to lean close, and when Ives' head almost touched his own, Mr. Mannis sighed and tried to find within himelf strength for what he was about to say. Yet he whispered to Ives: "Pray for me."

Ives nodded and Mannis seemed to drift off into sleep, and so Ives and Annie got up to leave. But as they were on their way out the door, Mannis opened his eyes again and said, in a raspy voice, "I'll see you," and he'd thought to add, as Ives turned, nodding again: "Won't I?"

Coming off the shuttle and into the late-morning clamor of the terminal, murmuring voices and booming loudspeakers, high heels and taps clicking on the marble floors, life and bustling humanity echoing in the cavernous hall. Perfume and electrically charged train-tunnel air, the strong smell of buttered rolls, coffee-with-cream-but-with-only-one-sugar, rancid gutter smells, pizza and cigar and cigarette smoke, fast food and vomit, all mixed up and circulating around him.

Making his way through crowds and vendors, several new generations of office workers swarmed around him: swami-looking fellows manning the newsstands, an endless procession of Asian businessmen zipping in and out of the revolving doors. And the feverish tangle of office workers, female executives represented in abundant numbers, weary, snooty, pissed, perfumey and vaguely depressed—trudging over trash-covered mica-specked sidewalks on their way to work on bleak Monday mornings.

MERRY CHRISTMAS, MODERN WORLD

Frost from the mouth, Santas wearily taking up their cause, voices raspy, expressions unconvincing, office boys smoking marijuana cigarettes, many a businessman smugly hiding away inside their muff-style headphones. Young ladies, somehow gangly, in jogging sneakers or shoes—Ives did not know what to call them. Ginseng from Korea and vials of love lotion in petite amber hourglass-shaped vials—he found them quite attractively displayed alongside; twenty different incenses set out and sold on tables by some quite proud African fellows, God bless them. Tucked in the corner of an appliance-store window, framed by silver-green-and-purple stapled garlands, six different varieties of "personal vibrators," package copy showing women pressing these phalluses against their ankles and necks, as if that's what they're intended for.

And in the corner of that same window, gaily decorated with silver-green tinsel, five bright red "adult" videos stacked in a pyramid—each box covered with many explicitly sexual photographs. (A funny thing, Ives, in a flash, thinking about a bachelor party for one of the executives in 1953; there had been a rented bar off Lex somewhere in the Thirties, dancers, lots of booze, and a buffet, the perfunctory stripper hopping out of a hollow cake, and at one point someone had said, "Show time!" Someone turned up with a carton of film spools and unveiled a projector. Lights off, a switch on, a beam of light shot out and hit a screen. No sound track, just the ticking of the turning mechanism. In a wavy rectangle of light appeared a grainy depiction of a darkly lit man whose eyes never faced the camera, as he manipulated the rubbery femininity of a chubby middle-aged brunette, whose visible ecstasies—she had a pretty face and tender eyes, which opened wide when she seemed to be coming—seemed otherworldly.)

He moved on, stood before yet another demolition site. Seemed that for years and years, for as long as Ives had worked downtown, every other street was wildly noisy with construction or demolition. Remembered whistles, followed by muffled blasts, coming every half hour or so for months and months, vast scaffolding and chaos. Even now, as he walked along, Ives found himself entering yet another construction tunnel, one more zigzaggy makeshift board-and-pipe passageway, walls covered with posters, and so congested with people that it seemed nearly impassable at points, Ives moving along.

A pneumatic drill in the distance. A piling of new green rope by an entrance to one site, no one around, Ives wandering in. Architecture. The building, a skyscraper—maybe a new Chrysler or Graybar or French building—going up.

The old Pan Am building: Ives remembered walking up Madison and over to Fifth toward the Scribner's bookstore early one evening after work, a few months before he retired from the agency, when a commuter helicopter clipped the top of the Pan Am Building, everyone stopping in their tracks: in its falling debris a heavy shard of glass that just happened to kill one of the sweeter girls in the office, Marlene. Secretary by day, student at a community college by night, she'd spend her lunch hours studying accounting books, and, among the girls in the office, struck Ives as the least frivolous, someone who would always land on her feet in life. A young girl living with her elderly grandmother in Queens, so guileless she had never thought twice about walking into his office one Christmas and asking Ives for a little favor, that he, an important art director, knock out a drawing of two angels kissing on a card for her boyfriend, "Ronnie, with two n's." The image of Marlene happily planting a kiss of gratitude on Ives' lonely cheek, colliding with the image of a single shard of glass coming down out of nowhere, as it were from heaven, cleaving open the top of her head, haunted Ives for months, back then.

Remembered her mother, beside herself with grief at the funeral, repeating, "Why, why, why?" And the priest in her company, holding her hand, kept whispering something to her. Ives standing nearby, trying to hear, and making out three words: "He called her. . . ." (The sweet summons, was it?)

Remembered how Robert, coming home in tears after John F. Kennedy was assassinated, had asked him, "Did God *will* that?"

So the Biltmore closed up and so did the Horn & Hardart's. Gimbels closed, and B. Altman's, where Ives had especially liked to go shopping during the 1970s, when the other major department stores in the area seemed in deep decline, when service in Macy's was terrible, B. Altman's, ever classy, forever closed.

And the two-thousand-square-foot D & L animated sign

overlooking Times Square had been replaced by a fantastic computer-generated display that could flash a new advertisement or message in a matter of seconds.

LUNCH

When he met with Father Tom in a French restaurant up on Fifty-third Street, they greeted each other, embracing, the priest as amused by Ives' white hair as Ives was by his own—it seemed like yesterday when Father Tom would hurry into the studios at the Art Students League, his collar stuck away in a drawer while, his face burning red, he would sketch beautiful young women. That he'd stayed in the order so long had amazed Ives, considering how he seemed to like women, but for the most part the priest had lived the "hard life" in Rome, and his letters over the years had been filled with more good news than bad and the names of many interesting and holy places. About once a year, usually around Christmas, he came back to the States to visit with his family in the northeast Bronx, and he and Ives would get together and get drunk and talk about the existence of God and the Bible and death and the soul to their hearts' contentment.

But this year Ives seemed especially preoccupied, and so his priestly friend had asked him, "Is it your health?"

"No, it's Annie. We've had our ups and downs. For a long time—too long really—we've been living under the same roof but going our separate ways. I mean, we're happy, Tom, but the . . . passion has been gone now, for years."

"My God, Eddie, but you're seventy, aren't you?"

"It's not that," Ives said. "If only it were. I've just been shut off, for a long time, since Robert's passing, and it's worn her out. I mean I've held her at bay. I mean," and Ives' face was shaking from shame, "I don't know what I mean." Then: "I've always done my best to be a good man, it's just that it's gotten to the point where we hardly talk to one another, except about superficial things, and it's killing me."

Then he shocked the priest, rolling up the sleeve of his bright red cashmere sweater, which he wore that day with a white shirt and a red bow tie, to expose his arm: his skin was covered with deep cuts and scabs from tossing and turning and scratching himself at night until he bled.

"My God, Eddie, what have you been doing to yourself?"

"It's a nervous condition I've had for a long time; it comes and goes. I've even gotten used to it, but lately it's been doing a number on me, worse than ever. Hasn't allowed me to sleep much and hasn't done much for my moods." And he sipped some wine. "And there's something else. You know that man Daniel Gomez? He's gotten out of prison."

"When?"

"About six months ago. He got married this past September and lives in Troy, New York, works in a restaurant with his wife. She's got two kids from an earlier marriage, and he's happy. And Tom, even though I may sound like a hypocrite, all of that is killing me too."

Then from an envelope folded in his pocket he took out a letter and handed it to the priest.

In the clamor of the restaurant, and with bifocals resting low upon his nose, Father Tom read the note. It was dated November 20, 1992, and written in carefully rendered script, if not spelling.

Dear Mr. Ives,

I spoked with my wife, and she told me that you haven't responted to any of her letters about us gettin together. I cannot tell you the pain it causes me. I know you think that I am as bad as the devil, but you must remember that what I did happened a lone lone time ago, when I was a punk kid. Now I am changed, and would like to have a friendship with you. Not 'cause I expect anything from you or your world, but because I want you to see that I'm not as bad as you think I am. One thing you did helping me I'll never forget, and I don't think you

would either if you was in my shoes. Lot of people who do
time compare up in the joint as it being worst than going
to Viet-Nam. You are hassled to death every single
moment of your life. People are loud, the blacks hated the
whiteys, the whiteys are on top of the Spanish, the Spanish
are on top of the Chinese and it goes on and on and on.
That I kept my nose clean and found a little salvation, I
feel that I owe to you. I didn't mean to kill your son, but
no matter how many times I tell myself that or tell you, I
know that he can't be brought back. And in any case, I've
paid: you know when I got 'rested first time, they sent me
to the Spofford Detention Center in the Bronx, and then I
did time in Elmira, upstate.

But that was nothing compared to my time up in
Ossining. I'm just saying that to let you know, that I've
paid my debt to society, and now I'm trying to keep my
self on the straight and narrow path. Now and then, I
am in the city, but things being what they are, with people
remembering me and stuff, I've got to be careful; other-
wise I would have come down to Manhattan to visit where
you live.

I'm working now six days a week in a restaurant,
Lily's Hideaway. If you don't ever want me to go down
there, then please bring your family up here and I will
make them feel at home. Hope you answer this.

And he wrote down an address and a phone number,
and signed it, "With God's Blessings to you, Daniel Gomez
Morales."

"What do you think?"
"Do you believe he's being sincere?"
"I don't know what to think. When I try to give him the
benefit of the doubt and tell myself that he is being sincere, as
soon as I go a step further, I try to figure out what Annie or I

would get out of it. Obviously, he's feeling guilty and wants us to let him off the hook. Forgive him."

"Well, maybe if you did, *you would* feel better. Ever think of that?"

Ives did not answer him because he did not know.

TWO YOUNG LADIES

He had wanted to go on with Father Tom about how he really felt. That forgiveness was something he had struggled with for years. That he spent thousands of hours in church kneeling until his legs went numb, waiting for his burdens to be lifted. That he had started to calcify inside and, if anything, grown more rigid with time. That for all his prayers he had somehow felt cheated, especially when he thought about how he had allowed himself to become so indifferent to his wife's feelings. That nothing had come *from without* and he resented that.

But it was Christmas, and so to restore a mood of holiday congeniality, Ives made a toast and declared, "To heck with our troubles, Tom. To our friendship. And as the Spaniards say, ¡Salud! ¡Que Dios te bendiga! May God bless you!"

"To all of us!"

As they ate their lunch, two young ladies in their mid-twenties came into the restaurant—both apparently worked for television stations and talked about the pains of Christmas shopping, job hunting, and by and by their love life. Later, when Father Tom got up to use the restroom, Ives heard them talking about sex and what they most enjoyed during the act of love, and their lovers' anatomies. They were a little drunk and their voices loud enough to turn heads, but they didn't seem to care. They toasted and laughed, celebrating youth. Even when heads turned, they kept on laughing and laughing, and Ives sitting back, tightly wound, could not help noticing the loveliness and smoothness of their skin.

During a More Recent Christmas

He and Father Tom went their separate ways, Ives watching the priest get into a taxi. Nicely invigorated by the chilly air, he stood looking into a travel-agency window near Rockefeller Center. Up on the walls were placards about places he had never seen and probably would never see in his life, from Singapore to Lima, Peru. He thought about the family trip to Italy back when they had returned in a celebratory frame of mind and how he and Annie had once talked about spending their retirement traveling. Some places he still wanted to visit: Egypt and Israel, for the old ruins and for the Holy Land; he had even found out about Catholic group tours to the latter, sent away for their brochures, but, as much as he had wanted to go, he was afraid of going to Jerusalem or to the Church of the Nativity and being disappointed. When he shut his eyes, having just looked at the image of the bright Egyptian sun, he remembered back to when he was a child and would look through books about Egypt, with their endless pages of sarcophagi and temples, and depictions of bright orange Egyptian suns, and he would think that Egypt was a land of God and eternal things. He had once thought he would go there, to see the pyramids, that he would then travel to the Holy Land and rest his eyes on the Sea of Galilee one day— and now?

During their lunch, Father Tom had asked Ives if he and Annie had ever planned on going back to Europe, and Ives had related how they "just never got around to it." But if they hadn't gone anywhere, it was no one's fault but his own.

Many times over the years he had received invitations to visit Latin America from executives he had gotten to know. A Señor Miguel Alvarado, a certain Señor Barrancas, Señor Oliver. Friendly men who had simply extended a bit of hospitality, which Ives had declined again and again, until the invitations stopped coming. There had been an invitation to give lectures on the advertising business in Japan. He and Annie were going to combine that trip with a cruise of the South Pacific on the old Holland-America line, one of his agency's clients, but Ives, in a fit of depression, canceled that. Every year, too, his wife had suggested the British Isles, as he told Father Tom, and every year he had been held back by his own doubts, making untruthful excuses about one job or the other. His anxiety about flying, which he had never liked, his tendency in his advancing years to become more and more staid, was closer to the truth.

He thought about the last time she had come home with one of her pep talks in mind, clutching a *New York Times:* "Just look at this, Ed. Look here," and she showed him a page. A sleek jetliner was pictured flying over the skyline of London, Big Ben and Buckingham Palace prominent, the advertisement declaring: "It's Never Been Easier. Or Cheaper!" And he looked it over and handed it back to her.

"Well, what about it?" he'd asked.

"Don't you think it would be nice for us to go?"

"Yes, yes . . ."

Then, slapping a book down on the table, a chronic weariness of mind and body hit him.

"Yes, we'll go. I'll pay for it, and then you tell me who'll pay the bills a year from now if something should happen to me."

"But Ed, we're not badly off."

"That's not the point. You don't understand, do you?" and he went down the hall into the bathroom, slamming the door. Then he stood before the mirror, pouring cold water over his face, already regretting his outburst. Later, when he came out, he found a note. She had gone off to the movies with a friend.

As he started walking west, he promised himself that he would go through with the trip this time, overcome the paralysis that sometimes seized him. Headed toward the subway, he decided to be more upbeat about things. Annie was in her early sixties, and even though he looked about fifteen years older than she, with the exception of his troubled skin they were both in good health. God willing, they'd have another ten or fifteen years together, and even though it would become progressively harder to get around, maybe they'd even make that trip to see the pyramids. They'd go on tours of the Greek Isles, maybe return to Italy, maybe rent a car in Portugal and drive into the Algarve, and then hop a ferry for Spain. Or simply remain in North America, drive out west and perhaps head down to Mexico and search for the Plumed Serpent. He felt exhilarated by the whole notion, and yet by the time he had gone down into the crowded subway, smothered and pushed aside, and asked for money a half-dozen times between the Fiftieth Street and Ninety-sixth Street stops, by the time he had gone into a D'Agostino's to buy some groceries, and waited in the interminable line, finally getting home, he was so exhausted that he could not keep his eyes open for the six-thirty news; and by that time, feeling the wine and his age, all these other trips had become fantasies, and he'd decided that it would be enough for them to go to London.

HIS GREATEST HAPPINESS

Another Christmas was approaching, and although the holiday did not mean as much to Ives as it once did, Ives took a deep joy in his grandchildren. And he was happy to see that despite some rough times his daughter and Paul had a good marriage. They lived in the old neighborhood, in a rent-controlled apartment that Paul had found years before. Their domestic happiness was something he could not have predicted, because, way back when, Ives, deep down inside, never thought Paul would make it, so many different things pulling on him at the same time.

They were a nice enough couple as teenagers. Then came those years when Caroline went off to college and he had remained in the city, suffering from afar over their separation, the poor kid hitching out to see her every so often. He remembered that when she had first gone off to Antioch she had been a well-behaved, if somewhat exacting, individual, a self-confident young woman (thank God), who played her Liszt and Mozart on the piano and was a good student, starved for the world. Even though Paul, it seemed to Ives, had gone off the deep end, possibly to irritate his Cuban father, she had remained fairly level-headed. And yet slowly she started to change. Around her junior year she broke up with Paul, started dating a Danish exchange student. Nothing came of that, but it left Paul so unhappy that he dropped out of college and hit the road with a rock 'n' roll band and made a couple of well-received, but modestly selling record albums—his great "moment" an extended tour through the mid and far west, during the last lingering days of the hippy phenomenon. He was considerate enough to write the occasional letter to Ives and his wife, from Boulder, Colorado Springs, Tucson, or Sante Fe. Every one of his notes ended with some sad summation involving Caroline: "When you talk to her, tell her I miss her very much." "Would you ask her why she hasn't written me?" "Do me a favor, please use that ten dollars to buy her some flowers, next time she's home." And, sometimes: "As for your daughter, I wish it had worked out."

Ives could not imagine what went wrong—he and Ramirez were counting on becoming in-laws. On this matter, Ramirez would say to Ives, "The one good thing my son had going was with your daughter, and he fucked that up." He had made this kind of statement without realizing, as Ives later found out, that Caroline had broken up with Paul because of the way he dealt with his father. She couldn't bear to be with someone who would take so much abuse. Their fights and loud arguments were legendary in the neighborhood. Once at two in the morning, when Paul had come in stoned with a Christmas tree, which he'd set up in the living room, the half silence of the noisy city, even at that time of the night, was split open by the crash of shattering glass. Noticing his son's glazed eyes, pinched like Spanish olives, Luis had it out with him, shouting things in Spanish like, *"¡Yo soy el dueño de la casa, y lo que quiero hacer, lo hago!"*—"I am the master of this house and what I want to do, I do!" and Pablo answering him in English, because Spanish sounded to him like the language of terror, "Would you . . . would you please leave me alone!" "What have I done to you?" And: "No! Don't, Poppy!" all of that resounding in the courtyards, and so loudly, that people, like Caroline, awake and sitting up in bed, could hear his shouts and sobs.

So that night they fought—that is, his son who would not hurt a fly, covered up, took his blows with belt and fist, in the name of "love and peace," which was how Pablo greeted his friends on the street—and it got to a point where Luis took the Christmas tree and tossed it, stand and all, out *through* one of their front windows. When the cops came, Ramirez told them to arrest his son for drugs, but Paul had climbed down the fire escape, spent the night riding the subway trains. Through it all, Carmen had stood in a corner of the living room, pleading and praying that they stop.

There were other incidents: his father found everything about his Americanized son exasperating. Politics particularly killed him, because Paul, even knowing about the experiences of his cousins who'd left Cuba, reluctantly, dejectedly, angrily, had a strong sympathy for the leftist Cubans. It was not even an issue of whether his father might have been correct in his beliefs, but that he didn't leave any room for discussion. Reading all kinds of books, and having studied political science in school, Paul could say with some authority that, no matter what one's feelings were, revolutions happened for real reasons—and in Cuba, before Castro, there had been a widespread underclass that suffered great privation. That was all he wanted his father to admit, but even that was too much. Why he felt so compelled to put his own son down no one knew. But there were occasions when even Ives was taken aback as Ramirez had told him about fathers having to set their sons straight sometimes or else they might have it too easy: "What's a little argument or slap in the face," he used to say.

The craziest thing about it, and what had exasperated Caroline, was that Paul remained so good-hearted about the whole thing. Every time something like that happened, he wanted to move out, and his mother, her two daughters married and living on their own, would beg him to stay. And she would needle her husband until he apologized. He probably felt genuinely sorry, but, in Caroline's eyes, what he said made the situation even more pathetic. "You know, son, no matter what I say to you, or if I hit you now and then, you know that, underneath, I really love you." Or: "A fight is a fight, and passes, but our blood will bind us together forever." And Paul would think: Okay, cool *esta bien, hombre,* and that would be it, until the next time, and Caroline would go out with him, and they would sit in the park, and this cool Cochise-looking hippy would start crying with frustration, and she would kiss and hold him, in the way that he had held her, with great tenderness and compassion, when Robert had been killed, and she was beside herself with confusion and grief.

Then she would tell him, "You've got to get away from him. He may love you, but that's not the way people are supposed to show it."

"I know, but really, Caroline, he's a good guy, deep down."

And she'd say to him: "My God, what's he got to do, kill you?"

Over time Antioch changed her. With each year she felt herself more mature, declared that she saw things with more clarity. Like her mother she was attracted to the arts, and had studied languages—Spanish, to her father's amusement, Italian, and a smattering of French. After two years of study, after several intensive "saturation" courses in Spanish, she could have a good conversation with Luis and Carmen if she liked, and so impressed her future father-in-law, Luis, that he commented in front of his son, "My goodness, she speaks better than you do."

After her third year in college, when she felt that she needed time to think about their relationship, he felt like killing someone, but didn't; he felt like throwing a Molotov cocktail into the church basement, but didn't; he felt like shoving his father out the window, but didn't.

(Curiously, everybody who later read his book *A History of Cuban Hippiness*, 1990, was surprised by his candor, for in that "novel" he described the pure agony of that rejection—accustomed as he had become to bedding her down within the very first day of her visit home, and suddenly finding himself alone in the world, in a sense. In any case, one of the things that would impress Ives was how, despite such mangled, horrible feelings of confusion and pain, Paul Ramirez had managed to keep himself out of trouble. In that book, there were hints about how certain people in the neighborhood had helped the protagonist, how reading different books early on, which he borrowed from a family whose father, Mr. Currier, worked in advertising, had exposed him to ideas and possibilities that he might not have had otherwise: certainly he would not have found them in his own home, and so he cited that kind of exposure to literature as an important, life-saving influence. There were other influences: being around the work ethic, and people who bought all that hokey stuff in the Bible, made a difference too. And although Ives did not care for certain of the graphic sex scenes, which he suspected might have been about relations with his own daughter, even when he was told that it had been "made up," so much love and good feelings came through in the book that all was forgiven. And reading, he could not help but wonder how years ago that other troubled young man, Daniel Gomez, might have fared given just a few better breaks; perhaps his son would still be alive and saying 9 A.M. Mass that coming Sunday somewhere in the city.)

Hitting the road with the Savages, Paul Ramirez experienced fleeting comforts and amusing interludes; a few years later found him finishing school at City College and moving out to San Francisco, coming back and finally beginning to reconcile with his father.

For her part, in the spirit of the times and not wanting the life of her mother, Caroline thought she should see something of the world and signed up for the Peace Corps, which sent her off to Nepal. One of Ives' happier times took place during a four-month period before she left for the Peace Corps, when she came to work at the agency, in the "international" division (one executive and a clerk). Regarding his smart daughter with great pride every time he ran into her, which was daily, he would eavesdrop on her speaking her Italian or French or Spanish on the telephone. . . . And he loved the fact that Mannis had come into his office one day to say, "Nice job you did raising your daughter, Ives." He'd gotten so used to riding the subway with her in the mornings and seeing her on a regular basis that when she gave notice he fell into a deep funk again.

Traveling to Nepal, and for a period of time so much longer than Ives, loving her so, would have wanted, she spent two years in mystic Kathmandu and in the foothills of the Himalayas, teaching English and modern hygienic practices to the good-natured people who lived there. Then she passed another year in independent travel through that region, at the edge of the world.

HER MYSTICAL EXPERIENCE EXPLAINED

There was the autumnal day when the first of several crates began to arrive at the apartment. They contained, Ives would later observe, rubbings made of rice paper and chalk, taken from many a Brahman temple wall, a number of them images of men and women, limbs entangled, sexual organs engaged in amorous sport—the prankish, juvenile Krishna or Bala Gopola, "the cowherd lad," with various women, most prominently his mistress, Radha, at play in their gardens of love. And there were representations of Vishnu and Siva, Lords of the Universe, and a box filled with what seemed to Ives like ordinary stones, in fact *s'alagram* stones, symbolic of Siva.

Much was there that baffled Ives, and intrigued him—numerous representations of Hindu deities, some of which Ives could not identify and some which he could, and many representations of mandalas and other such mystic symbols. Some cloth paintings were representations of the All-Seeing Eye, the eye of the Buddha. And with them were all kinds of craftswork, many samples of Tibetan textiles, such as one might find in Kathmandu, items that she'd hoped to sell in New York for a little money, while settling down again.

She had discovered, it seemed, the mystical.

She had left in '77, returned in early '81, face weathered, expression transcendent, twenty-seven years old. One of the first things she did when they met her at the airport was to kiss and hug them for a long time. One of the first things she had asked for, when she got home, in an accent slightly tinged with Nepalese: a Skippy peanut butter and Welch's jelly sandwich on soft Wonder Bread. Then she took a bath for two hours, reading foolish magazines in the tub. Later she stood for long periods of time at the window just watching life on the street. Then she seemed to revert to a neighborhood teenager again, listening to the Shirelles and Beatles on her phonograph, calling a few friends. She had just walked into the living room eating a Hershey bar—she'd lost a lot of weight—to join her father as he watched television, when she asked, "You hear anything from Paul?"

Ives told her: "You know he's in California writing for a newspaper or something. You wouldn't recognize him." And he made a snip-snip haircut motion with his index and forefinger around his ear.

That night "Uncle" Luis and "Aunt" Carmen came by—a happy reunion, after so long; Caroline was even glad to see him. They had dinner—a pot roast, though she could not remember eating very much meat, and contented herself on vegetables and rice. She was starting to eat, when Ives, still upholding his tradition of saying grace, led the family in a brief prayer. That had struck her as something far and remote from her life—after a while the image of Jesus had reformed in her mind as some kind of swami—and then she brought things out to show them, and gifts—beautiful scarves and bracelets for Carmen, and for Luis a prayer stone, which he thought a paperweight, even when she explained its mystical import—"On it is written in Tibetan the words *Om Mani Padme Hum,* a chant to the lotus that is the center of the universe."

"Muchas gracias," he told her, meaning it.

And then there were the questions. What did you do? How were the people? Were you treated right? And they were happy enough, and interested by her responses. Then the subject of Paul came up. Carmen, who'd always been fond of Caroline, asked, "And did you keep in touch with him?"

"Sometimes, but the mail can be very very bad. And I don't think I've talked to him on the phone since I left."

Excited as a child, and reading correctly a bit of longing in Caroline's face, Carmen sprang up, saying in rather agitated Spanish, "I'm going to call him right now, why, he'll be so happy to hear from you."

She did so, but when Caroline got on the phone, their voices sounded strange to one another, and his tone was cooler than she had ever remembered: and he was a little evasive.

"I can't really talk now, but can I call you tomorrow?" he asked. "Then we can catch up, okay?" And shortly they'd hung up.

Later, holding forth with an elated madness in her eyes, she talked about her "most interesting experience."

"Imagine an avenue of incredible temples, and crowds and crowds of Hindus, many of them naked, gathered to cremate their dead. Imagine spending one day and then the next and then the next watching the pyres burning along the Ganges. And at sunset the bodies burn; you see pyres everywhere along the banks. Bodies crackling, the fat spitting, and from time to time you see a bird swooping down to take a piece of something, or you see a wild dog, and there are packs of them, carrying away bones in their mouths. You sit and stare until you begin to feel the souls of these dead people so thickly in the air around you. You inhale and you think, my God, you're breathing in the essence of a human being's spirit. And even though it all reminds you of death and of how useless and fragile we are, you somehow get a kind of faith. You feel good inside, you feel as if whatever happens to the body the soul will go gushing out, to become a part of something unimaginably serene.

". . . Well, I was there with a friend one evening, and we were watching the water, shimmering wildly with sunlight. There were squiggles of light moving about, agitated, and as we stared at them, they clearly became the letters of some kind of alphabet, nothing we could read, but ancient sorts of letters—like Sanskrit, or hieroglyphics. And yet, even though I couldn't make out their meaning, I felt that I was being told something. . . .

"Then, what happened was this, I was staring at this writing when it began to rise up out of the water, that odd script floating in the air for a few moments before us, each of these letters, and there were about five or six of them, flattening out like banners. And suddenly . . ." And she shut her eyes even while touching the fluted stem of a wine glass, searching for the right words. "Suddenly these banners coiled up into something of a cylinder and began to roll and pitch forward toward us."

"Goodness," said Carmen. "Were you scared? Did your friend see it, too?"

"Yes, that's why I know it wasn't a hallucination or mirage, if that's what you were thinking. In fact, my friend asked, 'Can you see it too?' And I could, something very real, though I have no idea what it might have been. Anyway, it happened very quickly, in a few seconds. Was it a sign? I don't think so, but it was something out of the ordinary, supernatural. . . . So we left that place, feeling divine, and we told a few people. The word is that our karma was good and that we engendered the appearance of this miracle, if one could call it that. And it was wonderful, until it occurred to me that this apparition had nothing to do with us—and that vanity had led us to believe that it had." She shrugged, sadly.

"A mystical experience? Would you call it that?" asked Ives.

"I don't know, Pop. Maybe. That happened over a year ago and I still don't know what it was supposed to be about. Just that it left me with a humbled kind of feeling. I mean unless you've gone through that kind of thing it's quite impossible to convey, do you know what I mean?"

"I can imagine it would be that way," Ives told her, remembering his own experience from long ago.

And Ramirez nodded, and then said, "The only kind of spirits I care about are these," and he raised a glass in a toast to her return.

There was something else that she'd only tell her husband, after they'd been married in 1988. By then they could look back at seven years of renewed courtship and love, the two joined by mutual interests—literature, sex, religion—and concern for their parents, no matter what their difficulties. She taught literature in college, he wrote and struggled along, integrity intact. They would have two little girls and a boy. Now and then, when they wanted to get away and have "fun," they would rent a car and drive up to the house near Hudson and move in for the weekend, holing up as Ives and Annie did, reading and passing their time tranquilly. One late autumn night, around '92, they were talking about that first phone call together when she had gotten back from her stint in the Peace Corps and how she figured he already had a girlfriend, or someone in bed with him at the time. And the story she had recounted for her mother and father, and for Carmen and Ramirez, about the hieroglyphic letters, now nothing more than a distant memory, that had risen out of the Ganges. . . . They were in bed when she told Paul, whom she now called Pablo, that there had been more to that story: she swore that "he," Robert, was present that day in the soul-thickened atmosphere—and his apparition, her imagining of his presence, followed her around for days, but that no matter in what direction she turned, she did not find him.

THEIR JOURNEY

It was fortuitous: just when his wife began to have less patience with him, Ives went ahead and planned a trip to the British Isles, as he had promised that previous Christmas. She could not have been happier. It came just in time. After Ives had placed limits on the things he considered worth doing with Annie, she began to construct a life separate from him. She went to lectures with brainy university friends, on "literary" themes that would have put him to sleep, and she took special exercise classes. She would sometimes sit quietly in the back of a jazz bar with a book, liked to see arty films, and spent more and more time, when she was not working with kids, in libraries, accumulating notes on Lawrence and Dickens. Sometimes they would go out to dinner and pass their time together in silence. For the past few years it seemed that their three grandchildren gave them the greatest reason, aside from love and morality, for staying together.

There used to be occasions when Annie still got admiring looks from men, but those had passed: if she had stripped down under the lights of the Art Students League, she would have been one of those older women who somehow conveyed that she had once been spectacularly attractive and athletic. Her flesh wilting and riddled by hairline wrinkles, breasts that were still large but that had flattened out, a few telltale veins up her thighs, saddling buttocks, a pubic mound of gray hair still dark at its roots. Even so, with her still lovely and youthful face and interesting body she would have been a joy to draw. Sometimes when she sat across from Ives she would have feelings of hatred for Gomez, for having ruined her marriage. She would reach over and tenderly touch her husband's chin, while he was eating his soup, and touch his ankle with her toe. Sometimes she would not have minded risking the embarrassment of disrobing at the Art Students League, just to be reminded what it was like to have a man look at her body again. She could stand naked in the same room as Ives and he somehow averted his eyes. . . .

The worst time had been during her menopause, when the hormonal changes going on inside of her began sending tongues of fire through her belly and her chest and up through her head. She felt so restless and impatient with others that she would take the subway to Fiftieth Street and wander around that part of Manhattan for the whole day. One afternoon, fresh from buying several new dresses at Saks, where she usually never shopped, she came out through the revolving doors and for a few moments had the impression that it was 1948 again and that she was on her way to the Art Students League. On that day she fantasized that men were looking at her again, and she began to accentuate her walk, as if on a tightrope, her spreading hips going up and down. She entertained the thought of their excitement, and grew wet fantasizing about it. Then she stopped before a window mirror to fix herself up, and her crow's feet, emanating from her lovely blue eyes, and the width of her face and figure reminded her that she was no longer twenty-two.

Another day, she went down to the Village and hung around in bars drinking mugs of beer and chain-smoking cigarettes and, though she knew she would never have an affair, she had several hopeful conversations with much younger dashing-looking artists, who would have tried to jump her in her youth, but who now must have thought she was waiting for her son. She took a taxi home and wept, thinking about how to an older person youth seemed smug and aloof and exclusive.

As far as Ives was concerned, all was well with her, so out of touch had he become with her feelings. She remembered a time when, without saying a word, she would have a sad thought and he, sitting by an easel or by his drawing board, would somehow know. Putting aside his brushes or pen, he would throw on a jacket and step out to hunt down some chocolates, which she loved, and a bouquet of flowers. Or he'd say, "To heck with this work, let's catch a movie, huh?" Now he sometimes seemed deaf and blind when it came to her feelings.

Still, she loved him.

When he was younger and they used to go out with Carmen and Luis, she did her best to pick up the Latin dance steps, but he, having no sense of rhythm, and feeling vaguely foolish, just trudged along: but at least he tried. Now as an older man, Ives found those efforts at gaiety undignified. The last time they'd all gone out together, before Carmen's health began to decline—a party for Ramirez' sixty-fifth birthday, held in a rented Knights of Columbus Hall in Astoria, Queens—Ives sat off in the corner, wearing dark glasses and watching life pass him by. Now and then, he would chat in Spanish, for years later he was still famous, in a limited sense, as the father of that poor, unfortunate boy. So people who knew this went out of their way to befriend him; some insensitive few, drunk and carried away by the memory of that tragedy, foisted their outrage and sympathy upon Ives, who, even after so many years, did not like to hear about it. After a while he sat at Ramirez' table, picking at his food and wanly waving hello to passersby. Annie in a low-cut black velvet dress, which Caroline had made for her, passed her time dancing, occasionally with men, but her partners most often being a cluster of fun-loving Cuban women, who remained in front of the bandstand. To his credit Ives did dance two slow boleros, but he was so self-conscious that it was impossible for her to get lost in the music; enough was enough, she sometimes thought.

In recent days, on their once-a-week outings, they would head uptown to visit Ramirez and his wife, poor Carmen on the downside of her illness, cancer, yet ever faithful and sweet-tempered, a friend to them as ever. No doubt about it, after years of a seemingly endless ordeal, Carmen herself, whom Annie often accompanied to the hospital for her chemotherapy, knew that she was on her way out, and yet the only thing she could ever talk about was the love she felt for her husband, despite his harshness, for her children and grandchildren and for Ives and Annie, insisting when they came over that one sit on each side of her on the couch, so that she could hold their hands. She was impressive in her resolve and her lack of fear, and she cried only when she would have a reminiscence about her children when they were young, or about some incident involving Robert, like taking him to the movie *Three Coins in the Fountain* with her kids, and how well behaved and gentlemanly he had been. She spoke often of God, and carried a rosary, a crucifix, and a pendant with her mother's picture in it. At times they would find her in the company of her cousins, long settled and prospering for the most part in the States—though some were barely surviving. Sometimes she was well enough to dance a few steps of a cha-cha-cha, but most often she would be in bed, staring at the ceiling and barely aware of anyone else in the room.

As to her husband's infidelity, she seemed to have forgiven him, and encouraged him to find a mistress, not a wife, after she was gone, as they would be reunited forever as man and wife in eternity, "as beautiful young people." She even joked, saying to Luis, "Now I'll finally get to see what you look like with hair." And she touched his face and then fell asleep, and he and Ives and Annie would sit around for hours, Ramirez having nothing new to report.

With several ventures behind him, a union pension, social security, and some savings, though not a lot, after so many years of hard work, Ramirez had finally retired himself, just in time to spend most of his days, good or bad, in that apartment, doing the same things over and over again, or else taking his wife out in a wheelchair, which she hated, as it made her feel old and helpless.

It all cut to the bone. Ives was unable to imagine Ramirez without her, as she had always been able to bring out his most tender side. He could see Ramirez sinking into total irascibility and solitude: with many acquaintances, he, because of his rough nature, had few close friends outside of Ives. Over those years Ives sometimes had the impression that Luis had simply tolerated him, though Paul had told him, "No, he respects you and loves you like a brother." And Annie would miss Carmen's visits, their Chinese meals, their outings to church, to Mass, or to play Bingo on certain nights, or to participate in a clothing drive or bake sale or raffle; and Annie would take her to browse in bookstores and to lectures, here and there in town, and to movies and senior citizens' exercise classes. In more than thirty years, Annie and Carmen never had one argument, nor any unpleasantness, nor misunderstandings that did not involve Carmen's sometimes shaky English. She exuded so much *goodness* and was so lacking in malice toward others that she may well have been a saint; and for that reason it almost made sense that she had such bad martyr's luck.

MR. CHARLES DICKENS?

Surprising himself—surprising everybody—Ives had, as he promised, booked the tickets. All arranged, it seemed a dream, their journey to begin and end in London, and taking them to Ireland, Scotland, and other parts. They went by rail and by car in September, when the weather was mild. Interested in the literary ambience, she planned to soak up the atmosphere and allow it to influence her readings of Fielding, Smollett, and Dickens, whose books she brought along. And she had been working on a children's biography of Dickens, which she hoped Ives might illustrate, so part of their plan was to make like tourists, and the other to go about with sketchbooks and diary, and to absorb the spirit of those places like young students. They were happy, buoyant—"ghosts," as it were, finally, it seemed, to be left behind them.

If they had a worry, it was about Carmen, who seemed not long for the world, but she felt insulted at the notion that she would "suddenly" die after having coped with one thing or the other for the past seven years and had practically gotten out of bed to run out around the block to make sure that her American friends had some happiness, by way of their late-life journey. And they left sadly, reluctantly, feeling as if they might never see her alive again.

A week or so after their departure, Ramirez received the first of three postcards—one from London, one from Edinburgh, one from an inn in the Burren in Ireland, for they would be away for a month. He was glad to have received these cards, and instead of throwing them in the trash he put them in the top drawer of a Chinese lacquered table, usually reserved for bills. But before stashing them, he read them aloud to his wife, as he had read her *El Diario* and *People*, which she liked very much. It was tough going sometimes, given her physical suffering and the fact that, because of all the drug treatments and pain, she had gotten to a stage where she would have waking dreams: she had wanted to be a dancer when she was a girl in Cuba and so he would sometimes find her in bed, eyes shut, yet with one arm raised above her, her hand, a lovely ballerina's hand, making curving motions, and he would hear her humming—melodies that only she could identify. At other times, he leaned close to her and whispered, "Carmen? Carmen?" and she answered, "No, no, you're mistaken, my good man," in an aristocratically inflected, Spanish-accented version of English. "I'm not she, I'm Grace Kelly. Don't you recognize me from my movies?"

Then she cried out with pain, and jolted back to reality, tears rolling down her face. That's what offended him more than anything else: that he couldn't help her. There were times when he entertained some rather dark thoughts, like taking a pistol, such as that which he also kept in the lacquered Chinese table, wrapped in a rag and held tight by three tightly wound rubber bands, and shooting her outright. But he couldn't, and yet, because he knew what she was going through, he felt a different kind of rage. Why her pain? When some others like that phony son of a bitch upstate, whom his dear, naive friend Ives had started to believe, was now living the good life?

Lord, how he sometimes felt like getting his car and driving up to Lily's, where Gomez worked, and bringing about a few moments of justice in this world. . . .

On the afternoon he received the first postcard, he read it to her. In that first postcard Ives and Annie mentioned that London was a revelation, "nothing like Harlem . . . or Brooklyn." The black men spoke like English lords and everything was storybook tidy. And they had gone to the Dickens House museum, 48 Doughty Street, to see where Charles Dickens had once lived and worked, and Carmen, coming around momentarily, said, *"Ay que nice?"* But then she said, perhaps remembering one of the lectures Annie had taken her to, "Ah, Charles Dickens, *el gran escritor.* "

Luis smiled and flipped the card over to look at its photograph of the restored Dickens House, and he seemed perplexed, because for a long time whenever he had heard that name Charles Dickens he would think that he was an English actor. (On the other hand, in his fantasies of England, he thought the men all wore brushed derbies, carried umbrellas, and hid teacups in their coat pockets.) A writer? Charles Dickens. Yes, now he could add it to his list of writers he knew something about: José Martí, for there wasn't a Cuban, left or right, who hadn't known him; Raymond Chandler; and of course the famous Ernest Hemingway, who used to come visit him at the Biltmore, in the years before he shot himself.

He sat with the card, examining it, and finally he asked, "And what did Mr. Dickens write?"

Halfway to some other world, she started to say *War and Peace,* but then she changed her mind, and blurted out, "I can't remember, but they were good books, my love."

HE WEPT

It had been a lovely trip, London everything they had wanted and imagined—for Annie, reading selections from several Dickens novels at the time, it was an enchantment; they took strolls through the Queen's gardens, fed the swans in Regents Park; tried to envision the shantytowns that Dickens had once written about, along the Thames, the city's architecture sometimes suspending their notion of modern time. In fact, out of their usual context for a glorious period of several weeks, the veil of grief had somehow lifted from their hearts, Ives regaining a sense of childhood wonderment about many things. Walking about the city with a black-bound sketchbook, Ives drew madly, as he once had as a kid; for several hours he sat in the Assyrian room at the British Museum sketching griffin-kings, and among their greatest joys were their visits to the fifth-floor archives room of the Victoria and Albert Museum, where they looked through cartons of original artwork. There Ives and Annie spent hours going over the drawings of Sir John Tenniel of *Alice in Wonderland* and *Punch* magazine fame, those of Shepard, who illustrated Milne's Winnie-the-Pooh series, and among so many others, the drawings of Seymour and Cruikshank, the venerable illustrators of the works of Charles Dickens himself. There was a true joy in studying the erasures, the paste-ups, the blotched samples of work, which, once repaired, appeared in a refined state for the pleasure and admiration of the public.

They flew to Ireland for a week and then traveled to Scotland, meeting people here and there. Ives would not leave Annie's side, and for an older couple they seemed still deeply in love. It was invigorating to be away: liberal as he had always been and more or less remained, he felt nearly envious of the tribal peace he sensed in the small towns they passed through; he imagined what would happen if one were to transport the people who lived on a single New York City street "uptown" to one of those towns.

Mainly, it was an emotional experience. Annie posing for photographs on one of the Highland passes, Ives taking her picture and feeling as if he were floating high and free above the tenements, and wishing that his adoptive father and his son, Robert, could also take in that beautiful and worldly splendor. He wept, at one point, with happiness, and realized that he had not openly wept in years. Among the passing clouds and falcons, overwhelmed by the sun's grandeur, he looked in four directions, the Highlands seemingly going on forever, and he found himself pinching the bridge of his nose, unable to stop his eyes from tearing.

CARMEN

For several weeks after the funeral, Ramirez holed up in his apartment, keeping to himself: he did not answer the doorbell when it rang nor his old metal-case telephone. But then one Sunday in mid-December he decided to see Ives, and called him. He'd been in bad shape, but Ives had left him alone, knowing what it was like to lose someone you loved so much. Part of it was the shock: Ramirez had no idea of just how deeply he had loved his wife, no idea at all, and even though he had fooled around a little over the years, he had been surprised at his grief when he watched her coffin lowered into the opened ground.

When she'd finally died, and he and his son, Pablo, and two daughters attended the funeral, it seemed as if it were happening to someone else; that he hadn't given her a bad time and created so many scenes at home about his son; that he hadn't said some of the things that had frightened her so or threatened to throw her out of the apartment and divorce her if she made a fuss. Then it hit him that he was dreaming and that she was gone and he started to wish he had told her the kind of corny things one heard in movies and songs and on Valentine's, the very syrup that used to turn his stomach and make him think that only a sucker or a fool would talk that way. He wished that he had brought her more flowers and less heartbreak, that he hadn't dominated and ordered her around so much, hadn't acted like what his own son called, in that piece-of- shit book he wrote, a "well-intended but sometimes unfeeling, overly impulsive, hot-headed macho bully." (Offended, Ramirez had never gotten further than that phrase, on page 67 of *A History of Cuban Hippiness*.) And he wished he had paid more attention to her when she really started to get sick, instead of thinking that it was some kind of scam to get his attention. That once he knew for sure that she was bound to go sooner or later he hadn't begun to lose his temper with her because it was taking so long. Wished he hadn't acted as if he wanted it to be over with, conveying that feeling with his short fuse and the way he looked at her when the treatments made her hair fall out and she lost her late-middle-aged beauty, resenting her as if she had just dropped a baby out a window. And on the days when she felt better and sat up in bed like a child home from school on a rainy autumn day, and called out to him playfully, *"¿Quiero saber, Luis, si tú me quieres?"*—"Luis, do you love me?" he wished that he had said "Yes" with some kind of conviction rather than with the sequence of grunts and annoyed yeses that made her feel as if she had done something wrong. And he wished that he had been able to convey with greater sincerity a measure of faith when she would call him over and ask him to pray by her side, and he tried, mumbling prayers whose words he did not even know anymore, but he was a lousy actor. He regretted all that.

What really fucked him up was that, even though he wore a thin gold crucifix around his neck, he really hadn't believed in God. To him He was one of the greater inventions of man. But toward the end, when his wife had to be taken to the hospital "for good," and seemed, after so many years of devotion, to have lost her faith, entering a state of fear and panic and bedevilment that lasted for days, he wondered how much of his attitude, and indifference, had rubbed off on her. Because toward the end she started to have a vision of an emptiness before her, something that would swallow her forever, oblivion, and had started to scream and cry and shake, sometimes in her sleep. They tried everything to soothe and reassure her, brought in priests, turned up the *telenovelas*—the Spanish-language soap operas—kept her room filled with flowers. It was bad: one morning she started swearing that there were devils roaming the ward. When her own husband sat by her on the bed, to assure her that there were no such things, delicately taking her hand and gazing upon her with all the sweetness in the world, she started to cry, "Begone, *espíritu malo*! *¡Váyate!*" And when he took her hand again, she sat up and imagined herself at the head of a Good Friday procession, winding through the streets of their neighborhood. She could see a man carrying a cross and hundreds of believers following behind him, hands folded in prayer. And she saw herself addressing them in a tormented, hoarse, and mysterious voice that could be heard above the sorrowful Spanish chants, which echoed eerily for blocks and blocks around; it was with that ferocity that tender Carmen, eyes wide and head held high, shouted a message as if to a congregation: "Listen, my children, listen to the truth: Satan is denial and blindness; he is the deceiver of men; he is the curtain that has hidden God from us and has brought us grief and suffering; he is the negative; he is doubt! He is death; he is against goodness; he is the destroyer of men; he is hopelessness. Listen and pray and cry out 'Hallelujah!' Raise your arms and beg God to have mercy on our souls. . . ." And she went on with such effect that even those people who did not understand Spanish trembled; and the nurses had to sedate her.

When she came out of that delirium the next day no one could console her about the bleakness of her visions, nor did she recognize anyone, nor could she stop her anguished prayers, nor could she control her fear; and because she was close to the end, they brought her grandchildren in to say their farewells to their *abuela*. That's when they found out that the youngest, three-year-old Carmencita, after her grandmother, easily calmed her, the panic ending when the girl, fresh and sweet-smelling from a strawberry bubble bath, leaned over the bed, placed a rose in her hands and planted a kiss upon her tearful face. With that her sobbing stopped and panic left her and her expression changed, as if in a fairy tale; her fear of death and the devil lifted, and for a moment she became aware of who was in the room, and, seeing her husband, said, *"Ay, Luis,"* and then she was dead.

There had been the funeral . . . and for weeks Ramirez remained alone. What he did was to sit in his living room, curtains drawn, window gates locked, to shut out the world. With the television and old boleros playing on the stereo at the same time, he thought about what he had seen over several nights. He did not know what to do, but after the third week he had to tell someone and called Ives. He left the apartment on Claremont at about four in the afternoon and shortly he was sitting in Ives' living room on Ninety-third Street—Lord, he looked a mess—with a drink in hand, and could barely speak, his exhaustion being great.

There had been greetings and then a long silence.

"What is it, Luis? Are you okay?"

"Eduardo," he said in a low voice, "I'm scared."

"Of what?"

"*La muerte.*"

"What? Is something wrong with you?" And more reassuringly: "Look everyone's afraid."

"Yes, yes. Eddie, Eddie, but it's not that. I'm not afraid of death, but of what happens after that. . . . To the contrary I'm afraid that *something is there. ¡Carajo!*" And his tone changed, his face began to quiver, and he almost cracked the glass on Ives' coffee table, pounding it with his fist. "The goddamned thing of it, Ives, is that I didn't give a shit before: I didn't believe in any of that, but now, fucking now, I'm afraid."

Ives leaned closer.

"Of taking all my *verguenzas*—my shames—with me, and I'm not talking about taking them to heaven or hell, but taking them with *me.*"

He sounded crazy and agitated, and for that reason Ives poured him another drink. *"Cálmate,"* he told his friend.

Sighing deeply, Luis went on: ". . . She, my Carmen, came to see me for three nights in a row, after the burial. I swear on it. She did not come in rattling pots or any of that nonsense or going *ooooohh* like what happens in the movies. No, the first night I had gotten so drunk that I was asleep on the bed in my clothes, and at about three in the morning I felt someone in the room and opened my eyes and saw her, but only for a split second, standing by the door, and she was trying to say something to me. And I thought that I was dreaming, but the next night, about the same time, she came back, but stood a few feet closer to my bed. I could see her standing there and trying to walk ever so painfully toward me. . . trying to say something. . . . And that only lasted a moment. By the third night, I was a wreck, and could not sleep: I sat up until about five in the morning with my lamp on, and only then did I begin to doze: and that's when she stood before the bed. You believe me, yes?"

"Of course, I do."

"I don't know what happens when you die, but, I can tell you, whatever goes on is painful, because her face was all twisted and contorted: it was if she had to pay dearly to come to me, even for a few moments, as if it were a tremendous burden; as if she was violating something or breaking a law." And then his voice changed and frightened Ives: "Can you imagine what it was for Christ to come back for so long a period of time when He rose from the dead and went to visit His apostles? . . .

"And what she did was to hold out her hands and say in a whisper, *'Te amo, marido,'* and then she managed a smile and she was gone."

"And you're sure it was Carmen?"

He sighed.

"I'm a moody man, Eduardo, but I'm not crazy. And I don't imagine things. And I'll tell you, after that I never saw her again. Now I want to ask you, as my long-time friend who is a real believer, what do I do with it? I still don't feel like becoming one of those sentimental men with tears in his eyes about religion. I'll never change. I'm the same Luis Ramirez," and he tapped his own chest. "Only now I'm scared of death."

And they sat for a time trying to evaluate what had happened.

THE MIRACLE OF HIS SKIN

After telling Ives his story, Ramirez hung around the apartment, and when Annie came home from running some errands, they had dinner. To his surprise it was enjoyable to be with friends, and particularly so in this instance, because even through his pain he could see that Ives seemed much happier since their return from England in early October. Ives seemed less troubled, though he had moments of melancholy. Still, he had the air of a man who had found something he had been looking for. And to a certain extent Ives had, but because of Carmen's illness, he'd never gotten around to telling Ramirez about it. One night, after dinner, he and Ramirez walked over to Central Park with his dogs, Rex and Alice, and Ives explained the miracle of his skin.

Driving down from the Isle of Skye along the winding roads that took forever, they reentered England, and on the advice of a friendly elderly woman from Manchester, a certain Mrs. Madelaine Powers, whom they had met earlier in a pub, they decided to rest up in an inn not far from Nottingham, in the Midlands, which to their delight happened to be near Sherwood Forest. A lovely but rustic inn, its walls of local oak, a smell of stone and brook water about its grounds. "Old and tranquil" was how Ives put it. A high stone fireplace sending crackly pops of smoke into the air; and in the old, well-furnished rooms, things to pick up and look at, like the pictures that Ives happily examined, hanging in the long hallway between the dining room and a sitting area, among them a nicely done children's book illustration of Robin Hood, signed by the artist "Howard Pyle" for the owner of the inn; a framed handwritten dinner invitation, dated October 27, 1712, from one Daniel Finch, Second Earl of Nottingham, to the local curate; and a photograph of the writer D. H. Lawrence, who had been born and raised in the little mining town of Eastwood nearby.

To be sure it was not a place for luxury, in the sense of modern conveniences: old lighting fixtures appointed to illuminate the rooms, no radio or fans; a cold-storage room stood off the kitchen; water came out of hand-pumped spigots in the kitchen and washrooms (a main pump drawing well water in the front yard); the water closets, one marked with the moon, the other with the sun, at the end of yet another long, musty-smelling hall on the first floor. It was, however, despite the lack of certain amenities, quaintly nineteenth century and serene.

Their bedroom was on the second floor, a little cubbyhole

really, attained at a special price, thanks to the Mrs. from the pub, a cousin of the owner, Mrs. Gwendolyn Parsons, its window looking out beyond some rosebushes into the forest, thick with elms and oaks and hedgerows, a brook's rushing waters and bird song waking them in the morning. With the early light flowing into the room, they entangled themselves pleasurably on the bed's crisp sheets, without making love or attempting to, yet with renewed affection for each other, it did not matter.

They stayed for three nights, got up, ate breakfast, headed out to the fields with a watercolor kit and a sketch pad, as they might have when they were younger. Touched by their reflective natures, Mrs. Parsons, in her eighties and still going strong, took quite a liking to Ives and, especially, to Annie, who had struck her as an independent kind of woman. On several occasions, they went on walks together, and would sit quietly in the woods, talking. She knew quite a bit about birds and, it seemed, was quite deeply religious: a little too influenced by the spiritualist movements of the nineteenth century, perhaps, as she had spoken of "God's healing energies in the very air" and the "spiritual flux of nature, which is just His disguise. . . ."

The days spent felicitously, by evening the guests would gather in the inn's bar, whose oldest patron, from the nearby town, was nearly one hundred and seemed to be constantly smiling, swigging down his whiskey—"a frisky fellow," as Ives described him to Ramirez, *"Sabes que quiero decir con* 'frisky'?" Ives came in to find Annie, in a floral-patterned dress, her hair tied back, a rosiness to her cheeks, sipping a "wee" dram of scotch. Later, by the fire, they each drank brandy, and waited, with the others, for the evening's entertainment.

In the way that the inn, set up on a slight incline, was surrounded by woods, so were Mrs. Parsons' guests, gathered in the sitting room, surrounded by a fine and very old library of books. Because there was not much else to do in the evenings, except to sip brandies and watch the fire, Mrs. Parsons, in the tradition in which she had been raised, would hobble over to a stately chair and, in a voice that was remarkably strong and in a manner that was theatrical, read aloud selections from certain volumes.

It happened that Mrs. Parsons had noticed the way Mr. Ives would studiously examine her books, and how he had seemed particularly enthralled with her 1867 edition of *The Pickwick Papers—The Charles Dickens Family Edition*, identical to that signed edition that his adoptive father had come by years before, and that had been stolen from their Claremont Avenue apartment. Hers also bore an inscription, not by Dickens, which had made his much more valuable, but from a husband to his wife: "To my darling, Mary—May God bless you, this Christmas and for all the Christmases to come. Edward, Hampstead Heath, 24 Dec. 1867."

She had seen him looking through it a number of times, and because she liked them both and appreciated the drawing that he had given her earlier in the day—a rough but charming pen-and-ink rendering of Annie and Mrs. Parsons in matching sun hats walking along a garden path, picking flowers—she insisted that they accept her edition of *Pickwick* as a gift, even if it was worth "something"—twenty-five pounds perhaps in an antiquarian bookshop near the British Museum. From that same volume, for an hour, she had read the chapter in which Mr. Pickwick goes to Bath.

Afterward, Ives and Annie were in bed and Ives, in his usual manner, had difficulty sleeping. The darkness always inspired in him sad thoughts, memories once again pouring through him, and yet, being so far from home, and truthfully more relaxed and happy because he had finally forced himself to move away from a state approaching mummification, he could not understand why he still suffered. This trip, which he had almost dreaded, was making them both feel younger. They had so enjoyed themselves they were already making plans for the next year. Someplace far away like Tahiti, perhaps.

Even after he'd experienced a moment of pure earthly happiness in Scotland, he later trembled and suffered terribly when, coming out of a roundabout in a Scottish village, his rented car ran over a cat in the road.

He'd felt like a murderer.

But for all that, there hummed through his body a sorrow and loneliness that took him back to his son's death. The very thought made him dig into his own skin, deep scratches further enflaming his condition of old: cutting himself and bloody and restlessly turning all night, an impossible itchiness—*"un picazón"* he told Ramirez—hives ravaging his knee and arm joints, bumps formed under his arms. He knew it was really bad when welts rose on his back and blotches appeared floating like large measle dots on his face, a depressing state, because he felt like a leper, not wanting to touch or be touched, and he would twist and turn and ask, "Why me?" and "Why is it going on and on?"

It was so bad at times that he had gotten into the habit of keeping his fingernails clipped, and upon occasion had been forced to go to bed wearing a mitten over his right hand. Even in good spirits, he was thus afflicted, and it made him feel that it was the price he had paid. But on that night, the brandy had agitated him—an allergist had told him not to drink, but that would make his life impossible—and he particularly suffered. Suddenly he had to sit up, the weight of the sheets and the heat of his wife's body irritating him. Why? Then he started to sweat, and it was as if he'd poured vinegar over his cuts. Maybe he needed some air: he opened a window out to the fields, over which a half-moon sadly floated, heather glowing in its light. And a wind blew, shadows shifting in the trees, and he started to think of several things at once: of Lazarus rising and his skin stinking so much that people turned away in disgust; of his son in the ground; of his father, and, for that matter, of everybody and every living thing who had ever died in the world, which struck him in those moments as a graveyard.

Such dark thoughts provoked him; he scratched his arms until he was bleeding again, and he went back to bed, truly wearied by the endlessness of his plight. In the morning, he'd have to deal with a day of travel, after a sleepless night, and with a body that felt raw, like his heart. . . .

And although he told Ramirez that he had then prayed, he had lain in bed drifting, even in his discomfort, into a kind of half-sleep, imagining, nearly inch by inch, the Lord's body and His skin. He imagined Christ as an Aramaic Jew with dark Arab's skin. He imagined thick, bristling black hairs all over his body, slender limbs of a smooth texture, long-fingered artistic hands, covered with calluses and bruises. He imagined passing his hand across His brow and feeling healing scabs and blood-damp hair. But thinking those wounds as necessary to the resurrection, when Ives came to where the nails had pierced, he dug deeper into himself, and only stopped himself when Annie, asleep but hearing him, reached over and grabbed his arm by the wrist.

Then Ives had the dream. He was walking in a field in Riverside Park, not unlike the field outside the inn, and at its edge, near the woods, he saw a stream. This he followed around a bend into the woods, and there, at the turn, he saw his son, Robert, as he might have been at forty-three years of age: a grown man in choristers' white-and-black robes, handsome, serenely wise, wading waist high in the water. The sight of him made Ives both happy and frightened.

A benevolent smiling presence, his soft eyes upon Ives, he beckoned his father to come forward.

Meekly, head lowered and barely able to look at him, Ives approached his son, and felt Robert's hand taking hold of his own as he helped him to step down over some stones. For a moment he had felt mesmerized by the glowing pebbles that lay on the waterbed, ever so slightly moving in the current, and he had wanted to reach in and touch them. But his son touched his shoulder and said, "Pop, why do you keep doing this to yourself?" Then, bending, his hands cupped, his son scooped out a handful of water, and this he poured over his father's head, and then he brought up some more and washed his limbs with that water; and then he was gone.

"And what happened, Luis, is that when I got up in the morning, and went to take a shower, I looked in the mirror and could not find a single mark on my body, not on my arms, or legs, not on my back. Not anywhere."

Ramirez looked at Ives strangely, and then thinking of his own experience, revised his opinion and nodded. One of the dogs, tugging the leash, pulled Ives toward a favorite glen.

THE TELEPHONE CALL

Perhaps it was the fact that just the night before Paul and Caroline and their children had come over to have dinner and help Ives pick a Christmas tree for his living room. Perhaps it was that his daughter had been especially affectionate toward him, and a kind of mutual nostalgia affected them both, as they wandered about a large lot on Columbus Avenue, one of those places so lit by overhead floods that it seemed as bright as day. Even now, Caroline still expressed a strong aesthetic opinion, as she used to when they all walked over to Amsterdam to buy a tree, while his two granddaughters, Carmencita and Mary-Ellen (after Annie's mother), ran from tree to tree, like excited winter sprites, tugging at their grandfather's hand and dragging him around. Perhaps it had been the way they conned him into drawing silly cartoons, so that, reciprocating with some measure of pride, the older one, sucking on her lower lip, could climb up onto his drafting chair and, kneeling there, lean forward onto his drawing board, showing him how she could draw a popular modern cartoon character, of whom Ives was vaguely aware, called Bart Simpson. Perhaps it was the fact that Paul walked in feeling on top of the world, because he had finished a draft of a new book, about a trip he made to Cuba a few years before, and now had it with an interested publisher. Perhaps it was going through the ornaments for the children, and just sitting back, with a drink in hand and watching them speculate over the arrangement of certain lights and bulbs and such, the enjoyment of watching them set up the crèche beneath the fir. Perhaps it was the Bach chorale over the stereo or the good smells that came out of the kitchen, but when the telephone rang about eight-thirty in the evening and Annie came down the hall to say, "It's that priest, Father Jimenez," he took the call.

The priest was calling from the city of Troy, in Upstate New York, from the home of Mr. Gomez.

"Yes?"

"Mr. Ives, I don't want to take your time, and I know it's probably a bother, but it's been over a year since we last spoke, and I've got to ask you once again: Would you consider a meeting with Danny? Really, he's a changed man, and as I've said before a little forgiveness and goodwill would go a long way." Then: "Please, it's Christmas: you don't know how dark his holidays have been: he has been sick about all these things for years."

And because he had started to lighten up over the past several months, Ives, still cautious, let slip out: "When?"

"You set the day, the time. Anytime you want. Anything would be good. You name it, sir."

And then he heard the priest saying rapidly in Spanish to someone, *"El señor está interesado."*

He thought about it and said: "How's Wednesday?"

"That would be fine."

And they worked out an hour and the best route to travel. And the priest, pleased with the outcome, said, "Would you care to speak to him? Mr. Gomez is right here."

"Sure."

Momentarily, Daniel took the telephone, and when he started to speak he surprised Mr. Ives by the youthful pitch of his voice and its quality of weary tenderness. He had expected a blunter, deeper voice, crude in its intonations, the kind of voice, scarred and wicked, that one would expect from a felon convicted for second-degree manslaughter. They spoke briefly, mutual greetings and the expression that it would be a good thing.

"Then we'll see each other on Wednesday, at one o'clock?"

"Yes. I'll see you then."

IN TROY

Annie still did not want anything to do with it, and so Ives, his heart in his throat, had asked Ramirez to accompany him, and the Cuban had a fit. But because he was Ives' friend, he agreed to drive him up to the house in Hudson on Tuesday night, there being some things Ives wanted to bring back to New York. During that cold evening, the property covered in snow, the stars clear, Ramirez cooked up a late dinner while Ives shuffled about in his attic study, looking around for some of the earlier versions of the drawings he had made for the book that Annie was writing for children about Dickens. He had Dickens down well enough, drew him as a kindly, energetic man with a compassionate and intelligent face—in short, he recalled the qualities of his adoptive father, whose face, feature for feature, he brought back neatly in the form of an eighteenth-century gentleman. And he went through boxes of photographs, setting some aside and putting them into an envelope, and found some books to bring back down to the city, mostly history books, of which he had become rather fond: later they sat around and fell asleep, snoring loudly by the fire.

Gomez's house was not like some of the splendid houses one would see driving around Troy; it was close to the train station, and although it was set on a lot between two higher buildings, in which mainly working-class families lived, the street itself was rundown, the very steps to his front door in need of repair. Ives and Ramirez parked, and upon approaching the entranceway saw Father Jimenez, an old man now in wire-rim glasses peering out from behind the screen. Ives was nervous. Something was strangling inside, and he worried that it might be some kind of coronary. He carried in one hand a box of bakery cookies, which he had bought because he remembered that the couple had two kids, and an envelope. Ramirez followed him and was carrying a small night bag, which he kept on his lap during the hour or so that they were there, fidgeting restlessly during the "meeting."

Ives wore a tie and jacket, and when he was led in, he thought that whether they owned a restaurant or not these people were poor. Ives was startled. It was almost a repetition of the apartment he remembered visiting on 137th Street years before: the furniture was either worn or cheaply new and covered with plastic. The color television was the biggest and newest piece of furniture. There was shelving with little bric-a-brac here and there, cheap throw rugs, family photographs in Woolworth's frames, and a crucifix and plaster Virgin Mary with Child on a table; the kitchen was small and narrow, with a backdoor that led out to a porch where garbage cans and bicycles were piled.

Her two sons, twelve and fourteen, were out working, but there was evidence that they had just been there. There were plates on a card table covered with leftover food and a half-empty bottle of soda. In the corner of the living room stood an artificial blue-green tree.

Gomez himself had been putting on a jacket in the bathroom, when his wife called up the stairs, shouting, "Dan, they're here."

He had been so nervous about finally meeting with Ives that he had spent half the morning throwing up and trying to relieve himself on the toilet. No sooner had he looked out the window, seeing Ives and Ramirez pulling up, than his attacks started all over again. Pushing open the door, he shouted, "Be down in a minute," then spent another few minutes trying to collect himself. He was tremendously heavy, about three hundred pounds now, his head sweaty, his walk lumbering: although he had to live with the two tear-shaped tattoos on his face and still retained an air of severity, his expression, as he came down the stairs, was that of a penitent. He had put on a blue suit, a tie. His scuffed black shoes had been brightened with some enamel paint.

But when he stood on the landing and first saw Mr. Ives, he was somehow relieved: he had expected a face of torment or wrath or unending sorrow and had found an older white-haired man in a tie and jacket, almost demurely standing with his hat in hand, head lowered, his face filled with compassion. And for his part Ives, who had spent the morning replaying his son's death over and over in his head, had expected the hardened convict of an earlier photograph. Now there he was: Ives found himself trembling—with rage, joy, forgiveness? And was his stomach in knots because he felt like leaping forward and strangling the man?

But he controlled himself and, like a fine gentleman, his smile restrained, he strode forward and put his arms around Gomez, who had started to cry, over the very goodness he had glimpsed so briefly just then in Ives' gaze. Gomez awkwardly reciprocated, and he was touched by the scent of cologne about the face of a man who had quite carefully shaved that morning, his skin, in those moments, releasing so much pent-up grief and forgiveness, sweet as church incense. And Gomez found himself repeating, "Thank you for coming here, sir. Thank you, and God bless you."

In those moments, Ives knew, his son was somewhere in that room, and approving of what he beheld.

Nothing monumental transpired. Niceties were exchanged. Polite conversation. What could be said? Gomez' continuing struggles were evident in his expression and manner, in the very setting. He did show Ives the shelf filled with the books that Ives had sent him years ago and spoke appreciatively of what he had done. He was proud of his education and hard work, but what with times being difficult, money was hard to come by. He sometimes looked down at the floor. As for Ives, he left a parting gift for Daniel Gomez to open later, a photograph of his son, Robert, at seventeen.

When they left, the priest heartily shook Ives' hand and thanked him again: "Only God knows how much good you have done." And *"Feliz Navidad."*

They were sitting waiting for traffic to move on a turnoff to 87 South, when Ives summarized his attitude about the meeting: "You know, I'm glad I did it. It's not anything I would want to do every year. And you know what, Luis? I think that, for all his trouble, he's turned out all right. Don't you think so?"

And Luis, behind the wheel, said, "Good for him that he did change, Eduardo, because if he had turned out to be a son of a bitch with you, I would have shot him dead."

Then, just before shifting into gear and heading back toward the city, Ramirez told Ives to open his night bag; sitting snugly between a traveler's bottle of an evergreen aftershave and his wallet was a small snub-nosed revolver with an ivory-plated handle.

IN CHURCH ON ANOTHER CHRISTMAS DAY

Ives was sitting beside Annie in his old neighborhood church on another Christmas Day looking up at the altar. There were vases with dozens of orchids on either side of the chalice and pots of blossoms set out on the marble floors and against the columns, garlands of ivy strung along the gallery above. In the choir stall they had installed the crèche with its figures of the shepherds and kings and angels on high and the Holy Family inside the stable, the baby Jesus, the light of this world, at its center. And they had covered the roof of the stable with evergreen boughs and someone had burned fragrant incense. That morning as Ives first walked into the sanctuary again, hat in hand and with his wife by his side, he remembered that beautiful and familiar glory.

Here and there were some of his friends from the neighborhood. Ramirez had come in with Juanito the barber and his wife, and they had said hello and chatted for a moment with Ives and Annie, and Ives had run into Mr. Garcia and Mr. Farley, friends from Claremont, and others they had known for years, a kind of reunion taking place. He usually went to a different church, closer to home, on Ninety-sixth Street, but during the holiday he could not avoid the church in which his children had been raised, and where his son had first sung in a choir and assisted in the service as an altar boy. And where they held his funeral.

With some difficulty, he waited for the services to begin. He did not know if it was the candles or the crowd or the heating, or the heavy perfumes in the air, or his age—he was nearly seventy-five—but that morning he found himself frequently yawning. Lately, Ives had been dozing off during Mass, his eyes heavier with each visit. A kind of sweet drowsiness came over him, and the sensation that someone was about to whisper, ever so gently, "Come along now."

It was in fact a blessing. An ability to sleep more easily and deeply had come to him during the past few years. Where he used to toss and turn and drive his wife crazy at night, no sooner would he now lay his head upon the pillow than he would fall asleep. But not into that sleep of old age, but into the sleep of a child, an infinitude of possibilities swaddling him.

After so many years of indifference, even trepidation, about sleeping, Ives closed his eyes and would enter his slumbers peacefully; it amazed him how much he had started to dream at night. He once mentioned this to an old Cuban woman whom he knew from his other church, and she laughed, telling him: "Oh, that, my friend, is just preparation for the other life. That happens when you get closer to the time, you know."

THE DREAM ABOUT THE TOY SOLDIERS

The night before, on Christmas Eve, after spending the evening with Luis and the family in his living room; after a lamb dinner and after making toasts to friendship and love; after Luis had left (around midnight) and Ives had finished talking to his daughter and his sister, Katherine, about the next day's plans (dinner at his daughter's and son-in-law's apartment at three), he got into bed beside his wife; after carrying on to Annie about the cruel and selfish changes in the political climate of the country in regard to the poor and disadvantaged (unfairly condemned in Ives' words to "a hopeless future") and after kissing his wife, Ives slept through the night serenely. That morning he awoke in his bedroom to find his son, Robert, about six years old, in red pajamas and thick black stockings, alive again and playing quietly in the corner of the room with his toy soldiers, jousting horsemen, black knights versus white, moving them across the floor. And even though Ives knew that his son had been dead for nearly thirty years, he now saw the boy looking out the bedroom window of their old apartment on Claremont into the courtyard, which was glaring white with falling snow. And once again, as he used to, Robert came to his bedside and began to tug on his pajama sleeve, and just like that, Ives found himself climbing a hill on 120th Street in Riverside Park and pulling his son along on his sled, Grant's Tomb and Riverside Church looming above them and the Hudson covered with ice floes, stretching into the distance, the city ever quiet. In one moment his son was speeding on his sled down the long and steep slope, and the next he was carrying his son up the street, and dragging the sled behind him, the boy exhausted, feet frozen, cheeks red, the inside of his hooded snowsuit sweaty, and barely able to keep his eyes open. . . .

In the same dream he found himself standing before a display case of lead soldiers on the second floor of the old F A O Schwarz toy store, with his hand on his son's shoulder, the two of them enacting their annual Christmas expedition to choose just which sets of Britains or Mignots or Imperials that "Santa Claus" would leave for Robert under the lowest branches of their tree. How was it that Ives' face was almost touching his son's, as he also bent low to peer into the case, his nose not an inch away from the glass? How was it that his son seemed quite real to him?

Arranged in rows were the soldiers, for the benefit of the dead: a batallion of Royal Guards in bright blue-and-white uniforms with high, stiff, cord-faced, black-brimmed shako hats with short plumes, like nutcrackers in candy-shop windows; a cohort of Swiss cavalrymen, sabers and flags-of-the-cross raised, and a contingent of outlandishly handsome French *cuirassiers*, in dazzling breastplates and tasseled Periclean helmets, on high black stallions, charging. . . .

There were North African Tuaregs and columns of mounted *spahis*. There were fierce Dahomean warriors and turbaned French Zouaves, and Siamese Royal Guardsmen, Sikhs from India. . . .

His son examined the dandyish French *chasseurs à cheval*, and then Crusaders fighting the Saracens. He lingered before the figures of Richard the Lion-Hearted and Suleiman the Magnificent, Ives not once leaving his side. How beautiful were the Prussian *garde de corps*, splendid in red-and-white-striped uniforms, hats like golden hawks upon their heads; how beautiful was his son's soft, measured breathing. . . . He asked his son, "Have you decided which sets you like best?"

What about the Templars or the Maltese Knights? Or that set of Coldstream Guards? Or Somerset Light Infantry? Or the Royal Welch Fusiliers? Can you tell me, son, which of those you want for Christmas?

IN CHURCH AGAIN

And in church he recalled certain recent fantastic dreams. There had been a dream about ancient Egypt recently. Of it he could remember this: of riding across a desert in a chariot to attend a dinner party at a nobleman's house. His driver was a Nubian slave. In that incarnation Ives was a minor architect of some kind. He wore a silken cape and a soft gold skullcap and gold bracelets around his arms. He carried vials of perfume as a gift for his friends. On another occasion he dreamed that he was a monk in twelfth-century France and that he spent most of his life carving stone sculptures for a cathedral that was being constructed in a nearby town. As this monk he witnessed a miracle: God lifting cut stones from a quarry and sending them flying through the sky to the cathedral square. He dreamed that he lived in Arabia during the time of Christ, as a Parthian, and that he had journeyed into Syria and then into Judea on business, and that as he wandered through a market he saw Jesus preaching from the steps of a temple. He remembered moving closer, to hear His voice.

He prayed, his eyes upon the painting of the Mother and Child near the altar. He prayed for his dead adoptive father, and for his mother and father whom he had never known. For all the things he never knew.

Ives kneeling, the choir started to sing "Jesu, Joy of Man's Desiring," and his head tipped back.

He thought about that crisp afternoon, years before, when the sky had opened and the world had seemed full of goodness, its meaning still baffling him. . . . He remembered how, in the foundling home, the nuns gathered the children around a Christmas tree, and that one of the nuns had read aloud from a book: "And behold there was a star, a beacon in the night. And from the east there came angels and kings to worship the newborn son of God."

He remembered what it was like to go to Midnight Mass at his local church in Brooklyn, when he was a boy, how on the street corners there were bonfires glowing in the early morning of Christmas Eve, pine branches sending up flares from burning resin, how he and his brothers walked over to Flatbush to watch them. . . .

There he sat, and as was his habit of old, he began his quiet meditations. Above the altar in that church, was a statue of Christ, set back in a kind of nook, and on either side of Him, representations of the Holy Mother and Saint John the Baptist, with their expressions of divine knowledge. Looking at the altar he remembered another of his childhood thoughts: in the same way that the baby Jesus, the promise of the world, lay resting in His crib, adored by the magi and the shepherds and basking in the warmth of angelic and familial love, so did the man Jesus, down from the Cross and awaiting His final resurrection, lay resting *inside* the altar, beneath the chrismoned cloth. He laughed, remembering how the slightest breeze from the church's opened doors, rustling the altar's cloth, had made Ives' little heart jump: at any moment, Jesus would be coming out of His resting place and the world would be filled with miracles. He would be dressed in great flowing white robes, a beautiful light filling the church.

With pained but transcendent eyes, bearded and regal, He would come down the central aisle toward Ives, and placing His wounded hands upon Ives' brow, give His blessing before taking him away, and all others who were good in this world, off into His heaven, with its four mysterious winds, where they would be joined unto Him and all that is good forever and ever, without end.